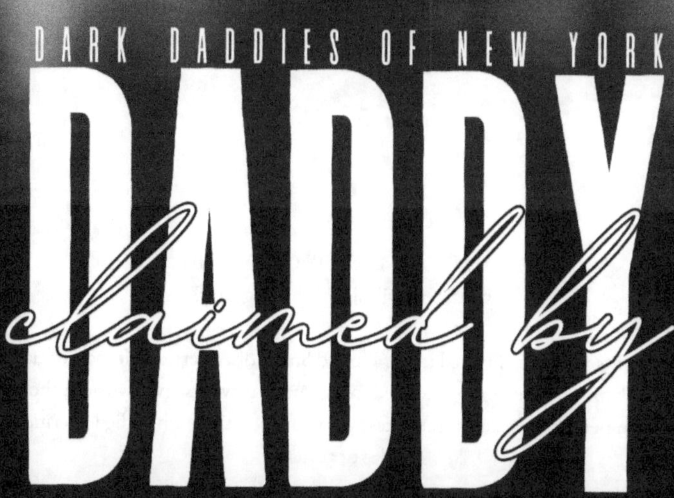

DARK DADDIES OF NEW YORK
claimed by
DADDY
J.L. QUICK

This novel is recommended for adult (18+) readers.

As a contemporary, dark romance work of fiction, this novel is not intended to be a portrayal of a healthy relationship or a 'how to guide' for the kink and lifestyle elements depicted within. For those interested in exploring aspects of kink and/or dominant-submissive relationships explored in the following chapters, please do so responsibly and with appropriate reference materials.

This novel may contain scenes and descriptive adult content that might be triggering for some readers. To see what you can expect, please use the QR code below.

To the brats who talk back with a smile and misbehave just enough to make Daddy put you in your place...

Keep earning those handprints, princess.

"Where the fuck have you been?" I shout when the front door clicks open. After shoving from my stool at the kitchen island, the leather soles of my Ferragamo Oxfords slap against the hardwood floor as I storm toward the foyer. "The meeting is in twenty fucking minutes. We were supposed to leave five minutes ag—"

A shrill scream—definitely not belonging to the extremely tardy Cillian who I'm berating—interrupts me. "Put me down, Cian!" As soon as I step around the corner and into the front hall, my eyes are immediately drawn to the perfectly round ass slung over his shoulder. Her fists pound his back and every flailing kick of her feet causes the tiny little black dress she's wearing to inch further up her thick thighs.

Gritting his teeth and his knees buckling—likely a result of her foot connecting with his groin—he snarls, "For fuck's sake! Would you fucking stop? I'm not going to hurt you." He pushes past me carrying the still-screaming woman, and I follow behind him as he carries her deeper into the apartment. She continues to fight him with every step, her long copper hair swaying against the back of his pants and shrouding her face.

"What the actual fuck?" Nikolai huffs. "We're bringing women here now? Or *anyone,* for that fucking matter?"

We don't bring people here. *Ever.* It's an unspoken rule between the three of us. Most men of our kind who keep a secret apartment in the city hide their mistresses in it. We keep this one to hide an even more forbidden indiscretion—our friendship. Outside these walls, Cillian O'Brien and Nikolai Romanov are the sons of rival families that I've been taught to hate my entire life. But in here, those same men are my brothers. Soon enough, they'll be my family.

"If she's for later, Cian, I'm gonna pass." Nikolai disapprovingly shakes his head as Cillian walks past him. "I like my women feisty as fuck, but I also like them willing."

With the girl still slung over his shoulder, Cillian abruptly turns on his heel. The heated flush creeping up his neck and over his cheeks burns a deep shade of crimson by the time he fists the front of Nikolai's crisp, white shirt. His angry, narrowed eyes dart between me and Nikolai as he spits, "Even if she were fucking willing, I'd fucking end you for trying to put your *manky* cocks anywhere near her. Either of you." He lets out a heavy exhale and shoves Nikolai away from him, muttering, "She's my little sister."

"I'm sorry? Your fucking what?" I exclaim, storming behind him—unable to withhold my anger—as he crosses the open space to the adjoining living room. "We are about to... And you brought your fucking sister here?"

"We're late. We can talk about this later," he gruffs, dropping the fiery redhead to the couch. With hair tousled over her face, she quickly clambers to her feet, and he lightly shoves her back into the cushions. "Stay," Cillian demands like she's a dog. "We'll be back in a few hours."

The three of us briskly walk from the apartment to the elevator, leaving the grumbling and unwelcome house guest behind. Waiting for the cab to arrive, I listen to her muffled screams and fists hammering against the front door as I anxiously tap my foot and glance down at my watch. *7:22 p.m. There is no way we'll make this meeting on time.* We step into the cab when it arrives, and Nikolai slaps at the button for the parking garage. Staring at the rattling front door as the elevator closes, he grouses, "Really? Your fucking sister?"

"Later," I huff with angered annoyance. I'm as pissed about this change in our meticulous plan as he is, but this isn't the time. "We don't need the fucking distraction. Not tonight." *Definitely not tonight...*

Our heavy footsteps clap against the concrete and echo through the parking garage as we make our way toward my G-

Class. I turn over the engine and slip the gear into reverse, glaring at Cillian in the rearview mirror. Meeting my stare, he grumbles, "I know I fucked up. I had no cho—"

"Fucking later!" I shout, pulling into traffic. "We have twenty minutes until the biggest meeting of our family's lives. Your sister isn't what any of us need to be thinking about." *Not what I need to be thinking about.* Tabling the dissension between us, we verify our strategy for tonight. While it might not be complicated—*at least not from an execution standpoint*—there is zero room for failure. If even one of us falters, we're all fucked.

The SUV falls silent by the time we reach the meatpacking district of Chelsea. When I make a left toward our destination, I note four very out-of-place cars parked in front of the abandoned warehouse the moment I spot the building. My father's prized Rolls Royce Ghost, a black Tahoe, a Bentayga, and a BMW Z4—the latter three I assume belong to Cillian's and Nikolai's fathers and their guest.

"They're all here," I mutter, more to myself than my brothers as I park in the alleyway. Being honest with myself, I didn't expect all of them to show. A meeting between our three families is unheard of. One to discuss a joint business venture —like they're doing tonight—is even more ludicrous. Apparently, the opportunity to make billions trumps decades of disdain.

For years, Cillian, Nikolai, and I have talked about how great it would be to merge our families. How strong and powerful we could be if we were working together instead of fighting each other at every turn. The three of us should be pleased with this turn of events. But not one of us supports this, at least not the venture our fathers are planning to enter into. By combining our family's attributes—importing and exporting illegal goods, strip clubs, and massive networks of powerful people—all they're seeing are the dollar signs that come from human trafficking. Not one of them is giving pause to think about the innocent lives that will be ruined.

We've individually shared our hesitations and objections with our fathers—only for them to fall on deaf ears and find ourselves reminded of our place. *Not at the head and not yet our turn to make decisions.*

My reminder came in the form of the back of my father's hand crashing across my cheekbone as he spat, "You might have been groomed to take control, son, but this is still my fucking empire. You *will* come to this fucking meeting. You *will* shake fucking hands with our enemies. And you'll keep your fucking mouth shut while I make you more fucking money than you can ever spend." He made it very clear that as long as he is in charge, I would be crossing a line that pushed my morality, whether I wanted to or not.

The three of us pause at the door to the warehouse, my gaze meeting Nikolai's and then Cillian's. Both their faces are stoic, but I know there's faint hesitation hiding behind their eyes. I'm sure they can see the same tinge of it in mine. "My brothers," Cillian exhales with a slight nod. Nikolai and I both echo his sentiment. With a deep breath, I pull open the door.

This is it...

It creaks loudly on the hinges, alerting our fathers to our arrival. The three of them—Tazio Roseti, Rian O'Brien, and Rurik Romanov—are seated around a dimly lit table with the fourth man in their business plan, an Armenian who is going to supply the women from overseas. Their eyes lift to watch us as we file into the dark space. All four of them rise from their seats almost in unison to greet us as we approach, and I vaguely hear the Armenian grumble, "I thought you were bringing your daughter."

But I'm unable to pull my eyes from my father, his narrow gaze and clenched jaw letting me know my tardiness clearly angers him. He claps his hand around the back of my head, pulling me into an embrace of sorts when I reach him. His fingers dig into my flesh as he tightly grips my neck while harshly whispering into my ear, "You're fucking late."

"I know," I return, grabbing my gun from the back of my waistband. Before I have a moment to second-guess myself, I shove it into his gut and squeeze the trigger. He gasps loudly against my ear, and I pull back to find a pained look of horror on his face as a deafening bang reverberates off the metal walls and through the massive space. I hold his conflicted gaze for a moment before hauling him back into me and squeezing the trigger again. "I wish I could say I was sorry, Papa."

He pushes from my embrace and stumbles backward a few steps before slumping to the floor at Cillian's feet. My father presses a hand to his bleeding gut. The thick claret liquid soaks through his otherwise pristine, pale blue shirt and oozes between his fingers as he clambers for the gun tucked into the waistband of his suit pants. Without hesitation, Cillian steps away from his father and raises his gun toward mine. I close my eyes as he fires a shot into my father's chest. The room is in complete chaos—our fathers and the Armenian fighting for their lives from the floor—but all I hear are the sounds of heavy breathing, the sploosh of blood pumping from bullet wounds, and the thumping of my racing heartbeat.

Adhering to the plan, I round the table and step over Rian O'Brien. With my feet straddling his waist, I stare down at the near lifeless man. He glares up at me, pleading, silently asking to be spared. An ask I will not heed. I lift my gun and he parts his lips, blood spilling from them instead of words as I add another bullet to his chest.

Still standing over Rian's body, I pump two rounds into Rurik. They aren't needed. He's already dead. But this was the plan—a bullet from each of us into our fathers. Each of us as guilty as the next in their murders. Cillian empties the rest of his clip into the Armenian. *He deserved death as much as they did, but that many bullets into a dead man is fucking personal.*

From my position beside the table, I stare down at the dead men splayed across the blood-soaked floor—the men who have ruled this city for decades. Their reign is now over.

"To my brothers," Nikolai's toast cuts through the silence that has filled the room. I turn to find him raising a bottle of vodka from the table into the air. He takes a swig and wipes his chin with the back of his hand as he passes it to Cillian.

Cillian takes the bottle from him and swallows back a couple of gulps. When he pulls the bottle from his mouth, vodka spittle sprays from his lips when he speaks. "Ugh... fucking vodka... To my brothers."

"To my brothers..." I echo, taking the extended bottle from Cillian. I throw back a shot, and the warm liquor burns down my throat and into my chest. "The Kings of New York City."

Our father's reign is over... But ours is just beginning.

"Stay?" I grumble, frantically brushing my hair from my face to find my brother leaving the room with two other men. After pushing myself from the deep cushions of the dark gray couch and to my feet, I quickly pad barefoot across the cool hardwood floor after them. "What am I? A fucking dog."

As I round the corner and step into the front hallway, the door clicks shut. I grip the knob and pull, but they've locked it. I reach for the deadbolt, only to find there isn't one. My hand slides along the cold steel loft-style door for a moment —not finding a single way to unlock it—and I anxiously pull the knob again, to no avail. My heart races and I panic.

terrified that my brother is going to lock me away worse than my father did.

"Cian?" I slam my hand against the door so hard that pain radiates across my palm. On the other side of the steel, I hear the distinct ding of an elevator. The elevator door slides shut in the hallway and deep, muffled voices echo in my ears as everything falls silent and I stare blankly at the door. *He wouldn't do this to me...* I pound on hard metal. "Cillian! Please! Don't lock me in here!"

My screams go unanswered, and I stand frozen, staring at the door. Breathing out slowly, I try to wrap my head around what the hell just happened. *Why would he leave me here instead of taking me to the meeting with Father?* This late dinner was so important to our father, and there is no way Cillian would want to endure the wrath that is going to come from not delivering me to it as planned. It just doesn't make sense.

But locking me in his apartment? That takes the cake. Cillian has watched me survive in my father's prison—a figurative one, at least since *Mam* died—nearly my entire life. Cameras watching my every move, bodyguards at every turn, and never having a moment of privacy—ensuring I stayed my father's perfect, innocent little girl. Cillian was the only person who hated it as much as I did. Of all people, he's the last one I ever expected to lock me away. *Apparently, I thought wrong...* As I lean my forehead against the cool steel, I angrily exhale, "Fuck you, Cillian."

My hand lingers on the door when I push back from it, my fingertips dusting along the smooth metal as I turn to face the apartment. So caught up in trying to escape that I didn't realize it at first, but this isn't the same apartment I've visited Cillian at before.

Where the hell am I?

Tentatively walking back in the direction I came from, my eyes scour over the wide-open living space. This place is massive. Far too big—*and probably expensive*—for just Cillian.

The rich, dark navy cabinets and matching subway tile in the kitchen gleam under the soft light, blending seamlessly into white granite countertops. *This is not the kitchen of a man who hasn't cooked a meal in his life.* It's immaculate—pristine and sterile. It feels like a show apartment—meant to be impressive—not a place to be lived in. I run my fingers over the countertop, tracing the veins in the stone, as my gaze wanders to the living room.

Floor-to-ceiling windows stretch across the far wall, giving a breathtaking view of Manhattan's skyline. With my hand dragging along the cool sheet of glass, I peer through it into the night on the other side. The lights on the other side of the window shimmer just enough to illuminate the terrace. The grand patio looks like it wraps around the entire floor.

This place might be bright and airy when the sun is shining into it, but under the cloak of darkness, the room is practically cavernous. Dark gray walls. Coordinating charcoal couches. Even the pool table is a black frame covered with a slate felt. The only warmth in the vast space comes from the rich wood of the tables and the bronze light fixtures hanging from the high ceiling.

What is this place? A fucking villain's lair? Have we not heard of color?

A wrought iron spiral staircase twists up toward the second floor. Unable to stop myself, I walk toward it. *If Cillian didn't want me to wander, he would've tied me to the couch... right?* My hand runs along the smooth railing, and the soft thud of my footsteps is barely audible as I climb the staircase. A hallway stretches before me when I reach the top—one door directly in front of me and two more at either end.

I feel like an intruder and contemplate going back downstairs to wait for Cillian, but curiosity has taken hold. *I want to know where the hell I am.* Turning to my right, I walk down the hallway, the wood floor creaks beneath my feet as I reach the room at the end of the hall.

After pushing open the door, I hesitate for a moment before stepping into a massive bedroom. The large, dark bed frame faces the massive windows, matching those on the main floor. The white bedding is meticulous—the pillows arranged so neatly it's as if no one actually sleeps here.

I take a few more steps, finding myself in the attached closet. It's massive, almost the size of the bedroom itself. Row upon row of athletic sneakers—*more shoes than I own*—and crisp, polished suits hang neatly in place. These definitely aren't Cillian's belongings. The shoes are too flashy, the suits too luxurious. *Not his modest style.* These belong to someone else —someone with a taste for excess, someone who's concerned with vanity. *Someone vastly different from anyone I've ever seen my brother spend time with.*

Being polite, I flip off the lights and step out of the room, making my way back to the one at the top of the staircase. The difference between the two is stark. The walls are lighter —a silvery gray instead of the deep charcoal that coats most of this apartment. Curtains cover most of the windows, shielding the space from the unwanted eyes in the adjacent buildings.

The bed is covered in a dark duvet, and the bedside lamp gives off a soft, warm glow, casting faint shadows along the walls. Beneath it, a small stack of books sits on the nightstand— most of them read a handful of times, the covers creased and worn. I lift a soft, leather-bound copy of Immanuel Kant's *Critique of Pure Reason* and immediately recognize Cillian's taste in literature. *His boring taste.* Bookshelves line the wall, likely full of more philosophical and non-fiction books.

Curiosity piqued, I move to the last door at the other end of the hall. It creaks open, and I'm greeted with the first room in this apartment that actually feels lived in. The windows stretch from floor to ceiling in this room, too. A platform bed has been shoved into the corner of the room, the gorgeous panoramic view of the city shimmering below. The dark covers of the bed are thrown back, revealing twisted black satin sheets beneath them. *Satin? Really? Who actually sleeps on those?*

The room opens to a massive closet full of custom Italian suits, shirts, and dark shelves lined with expensive men's dress shoes—Ferragamo, Gucci, Louboutin. When I pull open drawers, I find ties—silk, of course—rolled so perfectly they could be on display in an upscale custom men's clothing store.

The valet holds more rings, watches, and cufflinks than any man could ever need. Tucked into the corner is a small, mangled piece of metal, bent almost beyond recognition. Picking it up, I turn it over in my hand before realizing it's a bullet. I put it back as I found it quickly, flip off the lights, and leave the room.

What kind of secret friends are you living with, Cillian?

My curiosity—and exploration—has only left me with more questions. Questions that I can't answer on my own. Ones I really need my brother to come back for. After grabbing some dry treatise on the meaning of life—something he probably finds fascinating—from Cillian's room, I head back downstairs.

I help myself to a bottle of wine from the small fridge under the counter in the kitchen and curl up on the couch. Sipping at the bitter Pinot Noir, I thumb through the pages of the book resting in my lap. But with everything else on my mind —and how boring I find the words sprawled on the pages—it does little to hold my attention.

Hours tick by as I wait for my brother and his friends to return, and the buzz of the city below the apartment fades to a soft hum. With the warmth of the wine lulling me to sleep, I find myself struggling to stay awake. A struggle I'm not going to win.

I've washed the last of the physical blood from my hands, but the metaphorical claret still stains my skin. Following Cillian and Nikolai through the dimly lit warehouse, I step over our fathers' bodies as we collect every last shred of evidence that could link us to their murders. We rid the scene of bullet shells and fingerprints—erasing every trace of us ever being in this room.

The reality of what we've just done starts to settle in as I flick off my gloves and shove them into my pocket. *We've made our mark.* We've been preparing for this for weeks, moving pieces like a game of chess—a discreet location, a secret meeting, and a mafia execution that will go down in history.

"All right," Cillian mutters, slipping the last of the shells into a bag, his face emotionless. "Let's get the fuck out of here."

Nikolai doesn't need to be told twice. He grabs the bottle of vodka we toasted with off the table and takes another swig. "It already has our DNA on it. Might as well bring it with us." He smirks, wiping his mouth with the back of his hand.

I push open the warehouse door, and the three of us step into the unseasonably brisk evening air. We head down the alleyway toward my G-Class. It's dark—the only light coming from an occasionally flickering streetlamp—and the city is eerily quiet. We add to the silence, not saying anything as we climb into my SUV.

The drive from West 15th Street to Gansevoort Beach is fast this late at night. I park in a nearby lot, and we walk toward the river. The dark expanse of water stretches out in front of us like an endless abyss, swallowing everything in its path. *Exactly what we need.* This location might be far too public to dispose of a body—or four—but it's perfect for a few shell casings and guns.

It's vacant tonight—likely due to the chill in the air and the late midnight hour—but most nights, the benches are full of couples or friends. The three of us sharing a bottle of vodka on the riverfront wouldn't draw anyone's suspicion.

Nik and I toss the evidence of our crimes into the Hudson while Cillian paces between the water's edge and the nearby park bench. When he sits on it, he hunches over, resting his forearms on his thighs. His eyes narrow slightly, and he clenches his jaw as he stares at me and Nik. From the look on his face, I half expect him to lose his shit over what we just did. His voice low, he mutters, "I fucked up…"

It isn't like him—or any of us—to apologize, and those three words are about as close as we're going to get. Glancing at him, I find his eyes as apologetic as his words. "You fucking think?" I huff, my hands rising with my brows.

"I shouldn't have brought her to the apartment. She's going to fucking hate me. But, I just…" His jaw is tight, and he almost sounds like he's trying to rationalize his decision with himself. "I couldn't leave her to fend for herself. She's my fucking sister, Enzo. The only family I have left."

Nikolai doesn't look at him. He stares over the Hudson to Jersey as he takes another swig from the bottle. "We're your family, Cian. Tonight, sworn over spilled blood, we became brothers."

"I know." Cillian drops his head. "She's the only person in this world I care about other than the two of you."

I take a deep breath, trying to empathize with Cillian. Neither Nikolai nor I can put ourselves in his shoes—we don't have siblings. The only people we have to think about are each other. "I know she's your family. With us or without us, she's going to be in danger. Bringing her to our place puts us all at risk."

"She's safer with us than anywhere else," he rebuts, standing from his wooden bench. "I should've said something before I did it, but it was impulsive. I couldn't live with myself if anything happened to her because of what we did tonight."

We don't respond. For Mr. Rational to do something impulsive, I know beyond a shadow of a doubt how important she is to him. Still, thrusting his little sister into this mess we've made doesn't sit right with me. Our lives are about to be complete and utter turmoil, and taking care of his little sister wasn't on the agenda for any of us. The whole city is about to go to shit with the members of our families being forced to choose a side—with us or against us. The last thing we need is someone using her as leverage against Cillian. Someone will know that she's his weakness. For her safety—and ours—he couldn't leave her out there on her own.

"She's going to be fucking pissed," Nik imparts, passing the bottle of vodka to Cillian.

"I know." Cillian sighs, accepting the olive branch.

"You don't." I shake my head. "We've been your friends for years. But she's spent all those years learning and thinking that we're the enemy. She's going to be fucking livid."

Cillian takes a generous gulp from the bottle and passes it back to Nikolai, who doesn't hesitate to take another drink himself. "It'll be all right." They both fall quiet, and I take the bottle when Nikolai pushes it toward me. My hand steady, I bring it to my lips. The burn tingles over my tongue and down my throat as he promises, "She won't be a problem."

In my experience, women are always a problem...

"It's settled then?" Cillian asks, not expecting an answer. "Eavan stays."

"The girl stays," Nikolai agrees, and I nod in acknowledgment.

His tone turning more serious, Cillian asks, "So, what's next?" His eyes dart between me and Nikolai as we pass the bottle of vodka between us.

"Next?" I exhale slowly, glancing at the water, the lights of the city flickering on the surface. Turning to face him, my eyes span our sprawling empire. "We keep pushing. We take what our fathers built for us to inherit. Without the fucking trafficking."

"Fucking right we do!" Nikolai raises the near-empty bottle of vodka into the air before taking another swig.

"We build our fucking empire!" My gaze flicks between my brothers before me and the skyline behind them. It's far too soon to think about what we can build—the kingdom we plan to forge together. Right now, we shouldn't be thinking about anything more than surviving and making sure that no one gets in our way or comes for what is rightfully ours. But I can't help myself when I vow, "And then we burn everything else to the ground."

Gone are the days of the Rosetis, O'Briens, and Romanovs. There will be no more families grappling for control. Together, we're going to build something new. Something bigger than any of us individually.

Cillian looks like he's ready to speak again, but he doesn't. Instead, he takes another long gulp from the bottle, and I can see the resolve setting into his features. "Burn it," he echoes.

"Burn it until we're all that's left. Until there's nothing but... The Kings."

The Kings.

It's fitting. It encompasses everything we are and what we plan to build. A smile pulls at my lips, and I nod as I firmly squeeze Cillian's shoulder. "The Kings."

Swiping the empty bottle from Cillian's hand, Nikolai tosses it into the river with a roar, "The fucking Kings." The splash of it hitting the water is swallowed by the night as the three of us fall silent.

"We should probably go." Cillian breaks the silence, looking at his watch. "It's probably too late tonight, but I still have to find some way to break this news to Eavan."

While walking back to my G-Class, we go over the next phase of our plan—solidifying each of our parts and making arrangements to tidy up any potential loose ends. All of us are ignoring the biggest one—the fiery redhead locked in our apartment.

CHAPTER 4
eavan

Sunlight seeps through the slit of slightly parted curtains, the rays shining directly onto the pillows and in my face, stirring me from my slumber. As I sluggishly sit up, I wipe the remnants of sleep from my eyes as I try to wake up. The smooth, dark gray sheets pool around my waist, and I quickly realize that I'm not in my bed. *Not my room... Or even my father's penthouse.* My heart races for a second, and my eyes dart anxiously around, before I remember... *This is Cillian's room.*

Tossing back the covers, I slide my legs off the side of the bed and hiss when my bare feet hit the icy hardwood floors. Groaning, I groggily push from the mattress, stretching my arms, and trying to piece together my thoughts despite the dull throbbing ache in my head. *Wine... Way too much wine.* So much of it that I apparently fell asleep on the couch waiting for Cillian to come back. All I really remember is the vague, dizzying feeling of being led upstairs in the dark and the faint promise of him explaining everything to me in the morning.

It's the morning now. And I want some answers.

I glance down at the oversized Fall Out Boy concert T-shirt I'm swimming in. Cillian must have given it to me before I passed out again once he brought me upstairs. *It's his. I think.* Yanking it down my legs to cover myself, I pull open the bedroom door and tentatively glance into the hallway to find it empty and quiet. *Too quiet.*

My nostrils flood with the nutty aroma of coffee as I walk down the spiral staircase, the soft thump of my feet against the wood the only sound accompanying me. The delectable scent grows stronger with every step I take toward the kitchen, and my mouth waters in anticipation. After last night, I need it. *And a half-dozen ibuprofen. Maybe even a Liquid IV.*

Pulling open the cabinet above the coffeemaker, I am pleased to find it full of glasses and mugs. I stretch to grab one of the mugs on a shelf just out of my reach. My fingers brush against the ceramic handle, and I press onto my tippy toes, trying to reach it. The loose hem of my shirt lifts with my stretch, and the fabric dusts against my upper thigh. Being forced to choose between modesty and coffee, I lean onto the counter, attempting to reach a little higher. Coffee will always win.

"For fuck's sake, Eavan," Cillian's disgusted voice cuts through the silence, startling me. "Put on some fucking pants, I can practically see your—"

"I don't have any *fucking* pants, Cillian," I snip, cutting him off—annoyed at both his remark and my inability to grab the damn coffee cup. *Who puts cups this high?* A rich, woodsy scent laced with spice slowly overpowers the strong aroma of coffee, and I'm about to thank Cillian for reaching over me to get the cup when he presses against me—a little too close. *Way too close.* My body tenses instinctively as his firm chest brushes against my back, and my breath hitches.

"Or don't," a deep voice murmurs against my ear, low and flirtatious. *Definitely not my brother.* His warm, coffee-scented breath blows over my cheek, sending a shiver down my spine and a flush over my cheeks. "You look fucking good without them."

Jerking my head to the side, my heart slams against my chest as I whip around to see who's behind me. And I'm suddenly glad his comment left me holding my breath, because I think I would've forgotten how to breathe. He's tall—probably a foot taller than me—and his presence is... overwhelming. Gorgeous as sin, with a face I know I've seen before.

With the cup handle dangling on a hooked finger, he playfully outstretches his hand to me as he rubs the other over the scruff on his jaw. A devilish smirk pulls at his lips, and a dark glimmer sparkles in his smoldering chestnut eyes when I reach for the cup. He arches the scarred brow above his left eye and takes a step back, teasingly keeping the cup just out of my reach, running his fingers through his onyx hair.

"You... You're..." I gasp, my voice catching in my throat, and my eyes blowing wide when I recognize his familiar face. My pulse skyrockets—for a much different reason than only a moment ago—the name racing through my thoughts, causing my blood to run cold. This can't be real. I must still be dreaming in bed. *All of this is just some weird nightmare.* I choke out his name. "Enzo Roseti?"

My eyes dart between him and my brother, who appears completely unfazed by Enzo's presence, seeking some sort of explanation. Some reassurance from Cillian. But he doesn't give me any. My breathing grows rapid, the room closes in, and Enzo suddenly feels far too close.

"What the fuck, Cillian?" I shout, my voice rising an octave in panic. Pulling a knife from the butcher block on the counter beside me, my hand trembles as I lift it toward Enzo—my instincts screaming that I need to protect myself from him. From my enemy. "Why is he *here?* Why the hell is Enzo Roseti in your kitchen?"

With the smug smirk not falling from his face, Enzo takes a step toward me. My hand shaking, I hold the knife in front of me to keep the distance between us, but it doesn't deter him. He leans forward, and the sharp tip of the chef's knife presses against his bare chest. It dimples his firm pec—a hair's breadth from piercing the skin—as he reaches around me to set the mug he pulled from the cabinet on the counter. "*Our* kitchen, princess."

"What the hell is he talking about?"

"He lives here. We're friends," Cillian answers flatly. I shake my head, not understanding. A friend? From the Roseti family? The same family that our father has been fighting with for years? How the hell can Cillian sit there and say that Enzo Roseti is a friend with a straight face? I can barely comprehend what he's saying. "He's like a brother to me. He isn't going to hurt you."

"A friend? A *brother*?!" I exclaim. "He's a Roseti, Cillian! They're—"

"Getting real tired of having a knife shoved in their chest," Enzo interrupts, wrapping his hand over mine and squeezing until the pinch forces me to let go. He pulls it from my grip before it can clatter to the floor. Not releasing his hold on me, he tenderly massages his thumb over my now-sensitive skin as he drops the knife into the sink.

"*This* is what we needed to talk about," Cillian insists, with a seriousness I've never heard from him before. He pushes from his seat and quickly strips from his baggy gray sweatpants, tossing them at me without hesitation. "Put these on," he barks, his tone clear that this is not up for argument.

I blink—confused—until I notice Cillian's narrowed eyes are moving from me to Enzo, whose gaze is roving up and down my bare legs. My skin prickles with heat, and I slip into the oversized sweats quickly. Even covered, he doesn't stop staring —his gaze dark and predatory.

Cillian scowls at Enzo as he shakes his head, his features softening as he turns toward me. "I'll explain everything. *We'll* explain everything. Trust me."

I don't know what to say. Absolutely nothing makes sense. My brother has me standing in the lion's den, and the pride's alpha male is eyeing me up like I'm his dinner. Against my better judgment, I let out a heavy exhale and nod. "I trust you. *Just* you."

"Fuck, Cillian," a tall, muscular man with short dirty-blond hair gruffs from the living room. Staring at Cillian in nothing but his boxers, the blond scoffs, "Put on some fucking pants."

"The other O'Brien looks much better without them." Enzo obnoxiously winks at me, a grin tugging at his lips as his gaze runs up and down my body once more. "Trust me."

Ignoring his comment and fighting the urge to roll my eyes, I stare at my brother in disbelief. "Really?" I shoot my arms toward the blond man walking into the kitchen. "A fucking Romanov too? What in the hell is going on, Cillian?"

Sipping my black coffee, I take a seat on a lounger near the railing of the terrace. Cool spring air brushes against my face and nips at my bare chest as I pull on a much-needed T-shirt. Nikolai leans against the glass railing, cigarette in hand, staring out at the sprawling concrete of the city as we both wait for Cillian to join us for the private conversation he demanded.

Cillian storms onto the terrace, pulling on a white T-shirt and having replaced the pants he threw at his sister. He silently paces back and forth like a caged animal—clearly on edge. Cillian's gaze flicks between us and Favan inside the apartment until he calms enough to sit on the lounge chair beside me.

Watching him settle, my gaze is drawn over his shoulder to Eavan. She's standing in the kitchen, swimming in her brother's clothes. Leaning against the counter and slowly sipping her coffee, her eyes never stray from the three of us— like she's trying to read lips and follow our conversation through the glass. *Clever girl...*

"She may act tough, but she's scared," Cillian mutters, dragging a hand through his hair. "She doesn't understand why she's here. Why we're here with *you two* of all people."

"Why would she?" Nikolai asks rhetorically, without turning from his view of the city. "We're the enemy. She'll never understand."

"Don't say it like that." My face scrunches as I shake my head. "It makes us sound like we're *together*."

"I have to tell her," Cillian insists, ignoring my comment. "I told her I would explain... but the only way is to tell her everything."

"Everything?" Nikolai turns to face us before leaning against the rail and taking a long, deep drag on his cigarette. "You can't be serious."

Cillian glances through the windows at his sister, and we follow suit. Her fiery red hair catches the sunlight, setting it ablaze. She looks softer than I expected—outwardly calm for someone ready to stab me only minutes ago. But I saw the panic in her emerald-green eyes. The confusion. The fear. The way she stared at me like I was some kind of monster. *Because I am.* It's a look that I should be used to, but I'm not.

"She deserves the truth." Cillian sighs.

My gaze lingers on her, watching her round cheeks flush pink when I don't look away. "She deserves to be protected from it," I counter. "Telling her puts us all—all four of us—at risk. You know that."

"She's my sister, Enzo. I was honest with both of you from the beginning. I did this for *her*. Every drop of blood I spilled... Every lie I told... Every goddamn betrayal I committed. It's building our empire, but you both know that for me, it started because of Eavan." Cillian's voice cracks. "You know what my father was going to do. You know the kind of man he'd promised her to."

"We know," I softly respond, holding Cillian's stare. I don't have a sister of my own, but I've spent my entire life in this world, and I know how dark it can be. How men can somehow treat their wives, daughters, and sisters like property, trading them away like cigars and wine to make a deal.

"She needs to know what we did," Cillian insists again. "That I put two bullets in our father's chest to keep him from signing her over to that woman-selling bastard. How we killed your fathers, too, so they couldn't uphold their end of the deal."

Flicking his cigarette butt over the terrace rail, Nikolai mutters, "We take this to the grave or risk being put in one."

"Who the fuck is she going to tell?" Cillian spits. "I have her locked in here with the three of us to keep her safe. You think she's going to break out and run to the cops? The feds? She'd never... and you both know it."

"*We* don't know what she'll do," Nikolai snaps, his tone sharp as he gestures between the two of us. "*We* don't know anything about her, except she's not like us, and she clearly doesn't trust us."

"She's *better* than us," Cillian proclaims, his fists balling at his sides. "That's the whole fucking point."

Silence falls over the terrace as we weigh up his argument. I look through the glass again, finding Eavan leaning with her forearms resting on the counter, the pristine white cup cradled in her hands. Her lips are pressed together, and her brows are slightly drawn as she watches us intently.

"Tell her." The words fall from my mouth as I continue to watch her. She shifts her weight, and the sun catches on the soft curve of her round cheeks and the delicate slope of her neck. She is undeniably beautiful. Untouchable and forbidden—Cillian would end me for trying. Yet, I can't stop looking.

"This is fucking stupid," Nikolai exhales. "Fucking tell her, I guess."

"Then *we* tell her." Cillian pushes himself from the lounger and to his feet. "I know my sister. She'll understand." Nikolai and I follow him to the door, nearly bumping into him when he stops abruptly before opening it. "One more thing... Stop fucking looking at my sister like that," Cillian demands, glaring at me.

I'm guilty as sin, and he's clearly seen it. A lazy smirk tugging at the corner of my mouth, I ask, "Like what?"

"Like *that*," Cillian snarls, his jaw tightening when my eyes flick through the glass to her. Roaming down her body and over the roundness of her hips—curves that I haven't been able to pull from my thoughts since seeing her draped over his shoulder.

"Noted," I murmur.

"I mean it, Enz." Cillian pushes harder, his body growing as rigid as his words at my insincerity.

"I know you do."

"Then knock it off," he insists. "She's not like the girls that rotate through your bed."

I don't respond. I don't need to. The more he forbids it, the more I enjoy stealing glances. She's beautiful and unbelievably tempting to look at—nothing more. *A little playful admiration.* Stepping inside, my gaze drifts straight to the kitchen. To her. *I'm only looking.*

Eavan doesn't flinch as we all step back inside and walk toward her, nor does she hide the fact that she was watching us the whole time. Her expression is neutral, but it's the kind of even-handed look that takes effort—like she's holding back any emotions bubbling under her surface.

Reaching the counter, Cillian leans on it with his forearms. "We need to talk."

She raises a brow and snarks, "No fucking shit."

"Sit." Cillian gestures to the bar stool beside her at the island.

"I'll stand," she brattily refutes. He hesitates but doesn't argue. Meanwhile, I bite my tongue and stare across the counter at her, wanting to pick her up and forcibly plop her perfectly round ass in the seat.

"This isn't easy," Cillian starts, rubbing a hand over his jaw.

Eavan snorts into her coffee. "Let me guess. It has something to do with why I woke up in a strange bed and you just had some secret boys' club meeting with our family's enemies—about me."

Her snarky attitude quickly confirms that those pouty, pink lips come with a complementary sharp tongue. Her bratty disrespect hits a nerve, and I over-aggressively pull out the stool Cillian offered her. When she hears what we have to say, she's going to need it. She lets out an exasperated sigh and instead of kindly insisting—as intended—I snarl, "Take the seat, princess."

She says nothing, her eyes darting to Cillian, waiting for him to come to her defense. "Sit," he demands, significantly softer than I did. Glaring at me, she begrudgingly climbs onto the barstool with a slight roll of her eyes. It's subtle, but enough to cause my jaw to tick in response.

Nikolai rounds the counter and leans against the refrigerator, arms folded, saying nothing. The one corner of his mouth curling the slightest bit when he looks at me, obviously entertained by my annoyance at our new houseguest's defiance.

"I killed our father," Cillian bluntly confesses, and the rosy blush washes from Eavan's round cheeks as her face grows pale. Her lips part slightly, but she doesn't say a word or make a sound. "He was going to arrange your marriage to Andranik Sargsyan."

Her eyes snap up from her lap. "No... He wouldn't—"

"He would've." Cillian reaches for one of her hands resting in her lap. "He *was*. Everything was done. The agreement had been made. Our fathers"—I glance from her to my brothers—"were going to use you as a pawn to buy into his family business. That's the *meeting* I was supposed to take you to last night. The one you weren't coming home from."

Her hands grip the armrests of the stool so tightly that her knuckles grow white, and I can't tell if her clenched fists are in anger or fear.

"They were going to sell you to that horrific bastard like cattle." Cillian shakes his head and bitterness creeps into his voice. "He would've destroyed you, and I couldn't let that happen. So, I stopped it... I ended it... I ended *him*."

Her lower lip trembles as her eyes dart between the three of us. With her voice barely above a whisper, she asks, "And the others?"

She's a smart girl—knowing that both my father and Nikolai's would've taken her to forge the deal after her father's untimely demise. When Cillian doesn't answer right away, I step forward. "They're gone. All of them. Including Sargsyan."

Her eyes flick to me, wide and full of disbelief. "You're not just *working* together," she speculates slowly, pushing from her barstool. "You *are* together... the new heads of your families."

"We are." Nikolai nods once, and the realization hits her. Her knees give out slightly as she stands and grips the granite countertop to keep her balance. Stepping back, she wraps her arms around herself so tightly it looks like she's holding herself together.

"You brought me into this?" she huffs at Cillian. "You dragged me into the middle of what's going to be a blood war and expected me to what? Say thank you?"

"I *saved* you."

"No. I mean, maybe, but that's not all you did." She vehemently shakes her head. "The three of you have turned this city into a war zone."

"I *chose* you," Cillian snaps. "Over him. Over *them*. Over *everything*. You were the only one who mattered."

"Don't lie to yourself, Cillian. Saving me got the three of you a fucking empire."

Unable to stop myself, I step toward Eavan—so close that her heaving chest brushes against mine with every angered exhale. "Think whatever you want of me and Nik, princess, but know that none of us went into last night lightly. Regardless of our reasons for doing it, all of us saved your ungrateful little ass. But Cillian... he did what he did to protect *you*," I grumble in a gravelly whisper, looming over her. She stares up at me, her defiance not wavering, and it takes every bit of restraint to maintain my dwindling composure. "Now, don't be a fucking brat and thank your brother."

"I'll come with you," I blurt, shooting up from the couch at the possibility of joining Cillian to collect some of my things from our father's penthouse. I've only been locked in this apartment for a day, but even in this vast space, I'm already claustrophobic. *At least with my father, I had bodyguards and could leave to shop or grab a coffee. A tiny falsehood of freedom.* "I can grab my stuff quicker than you can. I know what I need and where to find it."

From where he's sitting on the bottom steps of the staircase, Cillian doesn't so much as look up from lacing his boots. "No."

"What do you mean, no?" I sass, annoyed that he isn't even considering my request. "You just said you're going to *my* apartment to get *my* things."

Ignoring me until he finishes tying his boot, he stands and finally meets my gaze. "I mean no, Eav. No one can know you're with me. Not until it's safe. You need to stay here."

I stare at him, blinking slowly and trying to process his words. "You mean... with *them*?" I ask, my voice a lot louder than the whisper I was intending. My eyes dart to Enzo and Nikolai, playing pool at the far side of the room, and from their narrowed eyes and disapproving scowls, I'm quite certain they both heard me.

Cillian blows out a heavy exhale, expelling his frustration. "I can't exactly take them with me. I'm pretty sure it would raise some suspicions if I brought Enzo Roseti *and* Nikolai Romanov to Father's place to pack a suitcase." I roll my eyes at his unnecessarily sarcastic tone. "And we aren't at the point where we plan to let everyone know about the three of us yet."

"Relax, princess. I don't bite," Enzo quips, bending over the table to line up his shot. He stares down the pool stick—his eyes focused on me instead of the cue ball at the end—as he takes his shot. "Unless you want me to."

Shaking my head, I stare at him in disbelief. *He's absolutely incorrigible.* "For fuck's sake." Cillian pinches the bridge of his nose and groans like he's aged a decade in the past few hours. "Enough already."

"I want my things, Cillian," I push again, ignoring Enzo's overt flirting. *Again.* "I want my clothes. My stuff. My *life.*" *As shitty as it was, at least I could leave occasionally. At least, after I got permission with several bodyguards tailing me.* "I didn't ask to be dumped in this damn apartment under house arrest."

"I know," he mutters. "In time, you'll get your life back. A better one than Father ever would've let you have. But we need time, and I have to know it's safe out there for you."

Cillian pulls on his jacket and walks toward the front door. My stomach twisting in knots, I follow him. As he swipes his phone to unlock the door, I grab his wrist and whisper, "You really trust them enough to leave me here alone?"

"Yes," he answers without a second of hesitation. "I wouldn't leave if I had even a sliver of doubt about them. I trust them with my life. And I know that they would give theirs to protect you. You have absolutely nothing to fear with either of them."

I don't know if that makes me feel better or worse. I've never thought about anyone—even my bodyguards—being willing to die for me... Or that anything could happen where that scenario would be a reality.

"I'll be back soon," Cillian promises. The door clicks shut behind him, and then it's just me. And *them.* Stepping back from the door, I tentatively walk back into the living room. I glance toward Enzo and catch him watching me. His head is tilted slightly, like he's trying to figure out what I'm thinking. I quickly look away and settle into the corner of the couch.

"That's game," Enzo boasts and racks his pool cue before stretching, which pulls his shirt tight over his chest. "I'm gonna head upstairs and take a shower," he announces, walking past me. "Try to behave for Nikolai." I try not to look too relieved—or maybe it's disappointed. I actually can't figure out what I feel around him, and I fucking hate it.

Enzo heads up the spiral staircase two steps at a time, disappearing from view. And I'm left with Nikolai. He's leaning against the kitchen island now, so stoic that he's practically part of the furniture—sharp, cold, and completely unreadable. Without moving, he asks, "You plan to be this sassy the whole time you're here?"

I blink, his question catching me off-guard. "Excuse me?"

"You heard me." He pushes from the counter with a smirk— the first actual emotion I've seen from him since I got here. "It hasn't been a day, and I'm pretty sure Enzo is ready to throttle you."

My eyebrows shoot up. "I'm sorry. Am I supposed to be grateful to be locked in a penthouse with two mafia killers I've known for a collective five minutes? Forgive me for not parading around the apartment singing Kumbaya."

Nikolai snorts—*actually snorts*—the smirk at the corner of his mouth spreading into a full smile. "Got it. Sassy as fuck the whole time."

If I'm going to be stuck here, I might as well enjoy myself. "Probably," I brat, leaving him in the kitchen and heading upstairs. My hand on the knob for Cillian's room, something catches my eye, and I glance down the hall. *Oh...* The door to

Enzo's room is open, and he's standing in view with his back turned to me.

Still wet from his shower, water trickles from his hair and runs down his spine. His back is all muscle—every inch of him taut and carved like a Roman statue. A white towel hangs low on his hips—*really low*—and as he turns slightly, my mouth gapes open at the sight before me. My eyes follow the deep V running along his hips and beneath his towel—a gasp escaping my lips before I can stop it.

He turns—ungodly slowly—to face me. *Shit! Did he hear me?* Our eyes meet, and I freeze, the burn of being caught gawking slowly creeping over my neck and face. He stares at me with that damn smirk pulling at the corner of his mouth. "See something you like, princess?"

Yes.

My mouth opens, and I struggle to say something. *Anything.* "Uh... I... Um..." Nope. No words. Just complete mortifying embarrassment.

Turning the knob still in my hand, I dart into Cillian's room and slam the door behind me. My heart pounds against my ribcage as I press my back against the door. "Shit," I mutter to myself, covering my burning face with both hands.

Why is he so... infuriating? So smug. So... unbelievably hot.

Shoving myself from the door and flopping onto Cillian's bed, I bury my face in the sheets. I try to shake the image of him from my mind, but the harder I push it away, the tighter it clings. That smirk. His perfect body. The way he *looked* at me, like he knew exactly what I was thinking. He probably did. *Hell, he probably enjoyed it.*

I hate how his constant flirting makes me feel—like a giddy schoolgirl again. Nearly as much as I hate how my body reacts to seeing him—the heated flush on my face he can see and the flutters in my stomach he can't. And how I can't stop myself from enjoying either. If this is an act to get a rise out of me, it's fucking working. *Better than he could've planned...* Pulling the pillow tight to my face, I scream my frustrations into it.

"Enzo Roseti," I mutter to myself, pulling my face off the pillow. "Why the hell are you even thinking about this, Eavan?" *About him...*

When I finally gather enough mental strength to get off the bed, I slip into the bathroom to shower. The water is hot, but not hot enough to cleanse me of the inappropriate thoughts running through my mind. I wash my hair, not twice but three times, trying to scrub Enzo from my brain. Yet, when I step under the steamy spray and close my eyes, all I can see is that smug fucking grin and his chocolate-brown eyes staring back at me.

God help me. Living here—*with him*—is going to be a challenge.

CHAPTER 7
enzo

The alert flashes across my phone, and I quickly lift it from the island. After swiping it open, I read the headline again and skim through the article before saying anything.

It's out. It barely took two days for the world to learn our fathers and that bastard Armenian are dead. My heart thumps, a deep thud behind my ribs. Not from fear—that weak shit left me a long time ago—but from the finality of this part of our plan. We did it. We actually fucking did it. Our new empire starts now.

"It's out," I announce, lifting my phone to alert the others. Cillian and Nikolai stop whatever ridiculous argument they're having about the Knicks, and Eavan glances up from the couch, where she's been doing her best to keep her face buried in a book, pretending to ignore me since her Peeping Tom moment earlier.

All of them are talking as they walk into the kitchen, so much chatter that I can't make out what any of them are saying. "Everyone shut up," I bark, laying my phone on the island. My thumb hovers over the play button as I wait for them to gather around it. "We all need to see this."

The newscaster's voice spills from the speaker and fills the kitchen the moment I press play. *"In what authorities are calling the hit of the century, four high-profile organized crime figureheads were found dead last night in an abandoned warehouse in Chelsea."* Images flash across the screen—out-of-focus shots of the crime scene from outside the police caution tape, the red and blue flashing lights of police cars, and then photos of the dead. Tazio Roseti. Rurik Romanov. Rian O'Brien. Andranik Sargsyan. Our fathers and the abhorrent excuse of a man who would've ruined Cian's sister. *"Police are asking anyone with information regarding this crime to contact the NYPD Organized Crime Division."*

I glance at the others. Nik is virtually unmoved, his face its usual unreadable mask. Cillian's jaw is tight, and the muscle in his cheek ticks as he continues to watch the broadcast on my phone. But it's Eavan's gaze that has my attention. Her wide green eyes—laced with panic—are flicking from the screen to each of us. She's gripping Cillian's arm as though it's a life preserver keeping her afloat. Her hold on him tightens, and she stares up at him. "Cian... Does this mean you're all in danger now? Am *I* in danger?"

"You're safe in here," he promises. "Nothing will happen to you inside these walls." She knew this moment was coming— we all told her. For a moment, even *I* want to comfort her. But right now, we have to stick to the plan.

"Call him." I lift my phone from the granite countertop and shove it into Cillian's hand. "Call him before he sees the news or hears it from anyone else."

His fingers move quickly, dialing the number from memory. He paces at the other end of the kitchen, waiting for the call to be answered. "Davit Sargsyan? It's Cillian O'Brien. Rian's son." There's a pause—all of us listening in silence—and Cillian's voice softens. "I'm sorry for the late call... And to be the one to tell you... I just saw the news. My father had mentioned him a few times, and I wanted to offer my condolences for Andranik."

Lying through his teeth like a pro, he walks to the far window of the living room and stands with his back to us. All we can hear are his clipped responses to the new head of the Armenian mob on the other end.

"Yes, sir."

"Eavan... My sister..."

"...Of course."

"...Understood."

"Tomorrow."

He ends the call and holds the phone at his side as he stares at the city beyond the terrace. "Well?" I ask, too impatient to wait for him to divulge the details of his call.

Cillian turns slowly, running his fingers through his hair to smooth it back as he faces us. His eyes light up just a glimmer, and he smiles. "According to plan... Everything is going according to plan."

"I'll book our jet." Nikolai gives a short nod.

"Maybe not *entirely* according to plan," Cillian murmurs, his eyes falling on Eavan. "We can't all go like we originally intended. Someone has to stay here with Eavan."

"Yeah. *You*," she chimes quickly, overtly eyeing her brother.

Cillian tenses—knowing he has to deny her—but stands his ground. "It was our father's deal. He was marrying you off. Out of the three of us, I *have* to go. I'm the only one Sargsyan will be expecting. And Nik... He's the closest thing I have to a translator. So he has to go."

That leaves... Cillian's apologetic eyes meet mine, and I already know what he's going to say before the words leave his mouth. "Enz, you have to stay behind. To keep an eye on Eavan. *Just* an eye."

My jaw tightens as I look between them. *Of course it would be me.* I nod slowly and swallow hard, forcing down the *hell no* bobbing in my throat and struggling to come out.

Me. Alone. Stuck in this penthouse with the bratty, redheaded princess I can't stop thinking about—who'd probably stab me in my sleep if she thought she could get away with it. *Perfect.*

I don't even bother hiding the sigh that escapes my lungs. "Babysitting isn't exactly what I signed up for, Cian."

Across the room, Eavan makes a disgusted noise in her throat. "*Him?*" she hisses, gesturing at me like I'm some bum off the street. "You can't be serious."

"Oh, relax, princess," I shoot back, unable to hide my smile. "I'm not thrilled about it either. But at least now we can finally get some *quality* alone time."

Her eyes narrow, and she purses her lips, looking like she would throw something at me if there were anything within arm's reach. "You mean the kind of alone time where you ogle my ass and make more comments about biting me?"

Yes...

"I only bite when asked nicely."

"Ugh, gross." She rolls her eyes, and I swear it's because she knows the reaction it causes in me. The bratty princess enjoys watching me rub my hand over the beard of my clenched jaw, fighting the urge to use it to correct that little attitude problem of hers. *A few handprints on that perfect ass... And she'll learn to behave for me.*

Cillian runs both hands over his face. "For fuck's sake, can you two... just... *not?*"

"I'm not the one ogling her when she gets out of the shower," I mutter, just loud enough to be heard. Her face flushes immediately, and I swear her nostrils flare.

"I didn't... That was... an *accident!*" she stammers. "You left the door wide open."

"And yet, you stood there in the hallway and watched. You can admit you liked it," I taunt her. "I won't tell." My grin spreads into a full smile as I wink at her.

"Cillian," she growls, turning on her brother. "I swear to God, if you leave me with him—"

"I'm sorry, but it's the only way," he apologizes, and I can tell he means it. And from the disapproving glare I'm currently on the receiving end of, I can almost hear the lecture I'm going to get about leaving his sister alone before he leaves.

Eavan doesn't argue again. At least, not in front of the rest of us. But the look she throws at me as Nik and Cian leave the room, to make their travel plans, could set ice on fire.

I grab a bottle of water from the fridge and sprawl across the couch. As I settle into the throw pillow behind my head, Eavan paces between the kitchen and the living room. She chews on her thumbnail with every step, her whole body radiating annoyance. She doesn't say anything, and she tries to be discreet, but I can feel her eyes on me. Glancing. Watching. Assessing. *Probably wondering if she could sneak up on me to slit my throat before I caught her.*

I take a sip of my water and place the bottle on the coffee table. Sitting up, I rest my forearms across my thighs and tilt my head toward her. "Are you going to be this much fun the whole time they're gone?"

She stops stomping and glares at me with angered, emerald eyes and pouty pursed lips. "You know what?"

"No, princess. What?"

"You are not nearly as charming as you think you are."

Yes. I am.

"Are you sure?" I tease. "Because you sure fucking blush when I talk to you. And you definitely keep staring at me."

"It was an *accident.*"

Yeah... an accident. Just like I accidentally thought of her when I had my hand wrapped around my cock in the shower this morning. That was also *totally* an accident.

She crosses her arms and huffs, "I don't trust you."

"Good," I exhale. My comment throws her for a second, and she blinks in confusion. Watching her carefully, I lean back onto the couch. "Because you shouldn't, even if your brother does." *Even if he shouldn't.* Because, fuck, right now even I don't trust myself. And her brother is only a few rooms away. Following his one rule is going to be a grave undertaking when he's halfway around the world. *And I've always been shit at following rules.* "Good," I exhale.

"And I *don't* like you," she snarks, ever so slightly biting her lower lip. *She's cute when she lies.*

"Funny thing about that…" I rise from the couch and quickly cross the room to where she's standing. Her eyes roam up my chest and to my face as I tower over her. "*I* never said you liked me, princess."

The sky is still a soft, hazy indigo when I wake, the sunrise resting just below the horizon. It's so early that even the city that never sleeps is still quiet. Not the apartment, though— my brother, Enzo, and Nikolai are making more than enough noise downstairs to rouse me.

I make my way toward the quieting commotion and pad barefoot into the living room with my arms wrapped around my chest, regretting not putting on more clothes before coming down here. Cillian is in the kitchen, struggling with the telescopic handle on a small carry-on suitcase. His dark red hair is wet, and his tight jaw and furrowed brows make him appear years older than twenty-nine.

"Are you sure you have to go?" I ask, my voice still rough and scratchy with sleep.

He glances up at me as he fidgets with the handle, and his sincere expression softens. "We've talked about this, Eav."

"I know. Just…" My words trail off as I try to find the right ones. *I can't exactly tell him I don't want to be left here with Enzo.* "Just asking again, on the off chance you're going to change your mind."

He sighs as he stands, leaving him suddenly towering over me. "I need to go make nice with Sargsyan. Explain that we're pulling out of the deal our fathers made. We need him to believe we had nothing to do with what happened to his brother and that we want peace. Trying to bring our three families together will be a tough enough feat. We don't need a fourth trying to tip the scales. And we definitely don't need him coming after us. After *you*."

I gulp at his final words. *After me.* Our family. The Roseti and Romanov families are the ones I expected that I would need to be kept safe from. I somehow thought that with Sargsyan dead, the Armenians wouldn't be an issue anymore. The last reason I want Cillian to fly halfway around the world is for me, but the three of them made it very clear last night that this was part of the plan well before I was carried into it kicking and screaming.

Stepping toward him, I hug him tightly. He hugs me back and groans as I squeeze him, shifting his weight. "You okay?" I ask, pulling back from our embrace to look up at his face.

"The couch," he mutters. "When I get back, we're figuring out some new sleeping arrangements. I want my bed back."

"She can sleep in mine." Enzo's smooth and flirtatious voice cuts through the room like a knife. When I step away from Cillian, I expect to find Enzo with that smug smirk behind me. *And like clockwork, there it is.* Leaning casually against the kitchen island, his dark hair is tousled from sleep, and he somehow still looks like he just stepped out of a GQ photo shoot. Barefoot. Gray cotton pants resting low on his hips. A soft black Henley that clings just right—enough that I'm remembering *exactly* what he looks underneath it.

Near certain he's baiting me, I stare at him silently for a moment. "You'd give up your room for me?" I ask warily.

"I never said I wouldn't be in it, princess." His smirk widens to a full-on grin.

Turning away fast enough that my hair swings behind me, I snip, "In your dreams." *And mine.* Because if my dreams are going to continue anything like last night, they are far too detailed—with an unwelcome co-star's deep brown eyes staring at me as his warm hands roam over my skin with finesse, knowing *exactly* what they're doing. *My sex life in my dreams is a thousand times better than my nonexistent real one. It's infuriating.*

His eyes glancing between the two of us, Cillian lets out a deep sigh, but he doesn't say a word about Enzo's offer. He gives me one last look, then nods to Enzo. "Take care of her."

Enzo returns the movement, and his tone is sincere when he vows, "Always." *I'll try not to read into that.*

"You ready?" Nikolai calls from the front door. "Our car to Teterboro is waiting out front."

"Yeah," Cillian mutters, not turning his attention from me. "You'll be safe here. Please, do as Enzo says."

The two of them leave, and the front door clicks shut before I'm given a chance to protest. The tension that suddenly fills the apartment is so thick I can barely breathe. I'm alone... *with him.*

I spend the entire day trying to keep myself occupied. Drifting from room to room, I don't really settle anywhere for long. Cleaning the pantry to feel useful. Reading a book—of which I didn't comprehend a word. Desperately trying to appear busy.

He's unusually quiet today, hardly speaking at all. Each pass of the living room is the same—the searing heat of Enzo's gaze like a brand across my skin when he glances up from his phone or the Sports Illustrated he's reading. He just watches me from his spot on the couch, like he's expecting me to crack first. *He's going to be waiting a long time.* I would give him credit for the space he's giving me, but it feels intentional—like a predator giving their prey just enough rope to walk themselves into a trap.

"I'll be back in five minutes," he announces, breaking the silence as he slips on a pair of loafers. "I'm going to run across the street to pick up dinner. Try to behave while I'm gone."

"Don't count on it," I mutter, but he's already out the door.

As promised, he returns within a few minutes with a white plastic bag in one hand and a bottle of wine tucked under his arm. The mouth-watering aroma of Chinese food follows his every step—ginger, garlic, and something spicy. Against my will, my stomach growls angrily.

"Good. You're hungry," he teases, unpacking the paper cartons onto the white granite of the island. "I didn't think to ask what you liked before leaving, so I got a little of everything." He opens a cabinet and pulls out wine glasses, promptly pouring two generous servings of a deep red Grenache.

The food is surprisingly good—although I am starving and would eat anything right now. That tiny peanut butter and jelly sandwich I had at lunch didn't quite tide me over. We eat in silence, the two of us perched at the kitchen island. It's almost peaceful.

Almost.

"You always this quiet, princess?" Enzo asks around a mouthful of rice.

"You always so cocky?"

"Yes." He chuckles smugly, somehow lifting the heaviness that's been hanging in the air since I got here. We pass the takeout containers between us, the conversation growing easier as the evening progresses—and I am suddenly feeling far too comfortable with him. *It's the wine. It has to be the wine.*

"Rude!" I playfully scoff when he inadvertently insults my well-worn black leggings. "You're one to talk. You're literally a walking Italian mafia cliché."

He lowers his chopsticks and stares at me with a slightly gaped mouth. "What the hell is that supposed to mean?"

"The suits. The silk ties. The fancy shoes." I wave a hand at his outfit. "The only thing missing from your Tony Soprano starter kit is the velour tracksuit and a cigar."

He glares at me, clearly insulted. And I can't help myself. I burst out laughing. A loud, obnoxious howl rising from my belly. I haven't laughed like this in days. Weeks, maybe. But it feels good, even if it is in front of him.

Shaking his head, he watches me with an unreadable expression. I try to place it as I finish the rest of my wine— amusement, maybe. Interest. Hunger.

I reach for the bottle, and his hand lands over mine when we both grab it at the same time—the lightheartedness of our meal immediately fizzling out. It's just a brush of his skin against mine. But it's electric—a spark that travels up my arm and settles somewhere deep in my core. The way he stares back at me, it's like he knows *exactly* what he is doing to me. I tear my hand away, nearly spilling the bottle of wine.

"It's late... I should probably go to bed," I blurt, standing abruptly from my stool, almost toppling it as well.

Enzo leans back in his barstool, arms folded across his chest and that damn smirk on his face again. "It's only eight thirty. But if you're *that* eager, princess..."

"Alone!" I snap, feeling a warmth caused by something other than the wine flushing my cheeks.

He chuckles softly. "Sure."

I head toward the spiral staircase, fighting the urge to look back at him over my shoulder. But I don't need to see him to know he's watching. His gaze is boring through my skin.

When I reach Cillian's room, I lean against the back of the door and let out a shaky breath. *Two days.* Cillian will be home in two more days. If I somehow survive the next forty-eight hours alone with Enzo Roseti and his smug, maddening, too-pretty face, it'll be a goddamn miracle.

Eavan has been hiding out in Cillian's room most of the morning, only coming down once for coffee and toast. *At this point, I'm growing certain she lives on a diet consisting solely of bread and jelly.* I haven't seen much of her, but still, she hasn't left my thoughts since she walked away from the island last night. And it's fucking maddening. Her sweet floral scent is still nestled in my lungs. That big, hearty laugh of hers is playing on a loop in my ears. And I swear, I can still feel her skin brushing against mine.

She finally wandered downstairs about two hours ago, dressed in a T-shirt and still wearing those too-tight leggings I can't pull my eyes from—stomping around with heavy feet and even heavier sighs. After aimlessly perusing the kitchen cabinets and fridge, then tidying up an already pristine apartment, she finally settled on grabbing a book to read.

The mid-afternoon light shifts across the hardwood floor, drawing my attention from my newspaper back to her. She's sprawled on the couch and looks like she's seconds away from combusting from sheer boredom. Her legs are dangling over the armrest, and the book she was reading is resting on her chest—although I can fully understand how Cillian's boring philosophical drivel isn't holding her attention.

She exhales another exasperated sigh. "Seriously," she whines, sitting up and pushing her hair out of her face. "Is there *anything* to do around here? Who doesn't even own a television? Or a laptop? Board games, even?"

"I've got something that'll keep you occupied," I taunt, suggestively arching my brow.

Her eyes narrow instantly. "Nope." She draws out the word and pops the P as she rolls her eyes. "Do you *ever* get tired of hearing yourself flirt?"

I don't answer. Instead, I cross the room and stop in front of her. She leans back into the couch as I bend over her until we are close—*too close*. I reach out and slip a finger under her chin, lifting her face until those gorgeous emerald eyes meet mine. Her breath catches—the tiniest hitch—and that adorable pink flush creeps over her cheeks.

With my voice a deep, gravelly whisper, I ask, "Can you promise to be a good girl and listen to me?"

Her eyes go wide—a mixture of shock, need, and intrigue staring back at me. She swallows hard, the gulp audible, and I feel her pulse kick under my fingertip.

"Yes," she chokes.

I lean a fraction closer—any further and my lips would be on hers. "Grab your shoes, princess."

Her eyebrows scrunch together, and confusion floods her features. I can practically see a question forming on her tongue. "Cillian said I can't leave the apartment," she mutters, cautiously.

I shrug. "Cillian isn't here." That's all it takes. She dips under my arm and launches herself from the couch like a kid who's been told they're going to Disney World. Her excitement is palpable, bouncing up the stairs two at a time with her long red locks swaying behind her.

Within minutes, she comes back down in a pair of heeled booties that make her legs look a mile long and a short denim jacket tossed over a knee-length floral dress that hugs every curve she's got. *Fuck, she looks good.*

One hand on the knob, I pause at the front door and stare down at her. "Don't make me regret this. You will not leave my side for a second." She sassily bats her eyelashes and flashes me a coy smile in response. "Say it," I demand.

She sighs dramatically. "I will not leave your side for a second," she parrots, a devilish grin pulling at the corner of her mouth. "Because you're totally overbearing and completely obsessed with me ."

Taking a deep breath—and struggling not to roll *my* eyes—I pull open the door. As we step into the elevator, I glance at her sideways. *I'm so going to regret this.*

"Where are you taking me?" she chirps as I push the button for the lobby.

"There's a bookstore down the street. You clearly like to read. I figured you would like something that doesn't involve your brother's taste in existential dread." She laughs, and her face momentarily lights up. *I fucking love that sound.*

The short walk is casual and comfortable. As promised, she keeps pace beside me, occasionally brushing against my arm like she doesn't notice she's doing it. This temporary change in scenery has come with a matching change in her attitude. She's smiling, bubbly, and I haven't caught so much as a glimmer of her usual bratty defiance.

By the time we reach the bookstore, she's practically buzzing. She walks with purpose between the shelves, following the signs straight to the romance section. *Of course.* I hang back, arms crossed and leaning against the end of the shelf, watching as she picks up book after book with ridiculous covers—shirtless, muscular men and titles full of suggestive plays on words. *Okay, some of them are pretty clever.*

"I see you have a type," I tease when she picks up a book with a dark-haired man wearing nothing but sunglasses and a six-pack.

She glares at me, putting the book back on the shelf. "What? Strong, emotionally available men who pine for their women for hundreds of pages."

"That sounds horrible." I feign disgust.

"It's vulnerable," she corrects, playfully sticking out her tongue. "Maybe you should try it sometime, instead of being an arrogant flirt."

I shake my head at her, but I'm smiling uncontrollably.

By the time we leave the bookstore, she has three books tucked under her arm and a satisfied glimmer in her eyes. Her happiness alone was worth paying for. We're about a quarter of a block from the apartment, nearing a busy intersection, when a couple with a stroller accidentally cuts in front of me. I pause to avoid colliding with them. And just like that, Eavan is ahead of me. *Too far ahead.*

"Eavan!" I call, watching her step off the curb. Slipping between cars stopped at the traffic light, she glances over her shoulder and shouts, "It's fine! The building is right there. I'll meet you upstairs."

"No!" I shout, my pulse surging. "Wait!" But she doesn't stop. By the time my foot hits the curb, she's disappearing into the crowd on the other side. A stream of speeding cars separates us, and I teeter between the sidewalk and approaching cars—jaw tight and heart hammering.

"Fuck," I mutter.

The second the light flicks yellow, I step into traffic. Cars honk. Brakes screech. I dodge between stopped and slowing cars—my only focus is getting across the fucking street.

By the time I make it into the building's lobby, my chest is heaving. Not from running. From the red-hot anger currently coursing through my veins. "Eavan!" I shout her name, spinning in a slow, desperate circle as I scan the large open lobby. *Nothing.* It's quiet. Empty. *Too empty.*

I bolt toward the elevator bank and slip into a cab just as the doors start to close. Ignoring the woman inside, I slam the button for my floor. My reflection in the metal doors looks like a stranger. Wild eyes. Tight jaw. Struggling to contain my fury.

She didn't listen.

She never listens.

But this time, it wasn't cute. It wasn't bratty in a way that gets under my skin. This was reckless. Dangerous. She walked away from me without a thought—without any hesitation—like the entire city isn't a threat to her.

She promised she would listen. But, then again, she also *promised* she would stay by my side. She doesn't get it—the responsibility her brother gave me to keep her safe. They were simple rules to make sure she was protected from all the threats she doesn't know about and can't see coming. But she thinks she's clever—that this is a game. It's fun for her to push boundaries and test my limits. *But her life isn't a game to me.*

This time, she went too far.

With every floor that passes, my anger bubbles more, fiery and sharp, behind my ribs. Because this isn't about control. It's not even about rules. It's about *her*. About giving her what she needs. Someone to teach her how to listen. How to behave.

I rub my clammy palm against the thigh of my pants as I watch the final few floors pass. By the time the elevator dings and the doors slide open, every cell in my body is bristling, tense with frustration and... need.

Leaning against the wall beside the penthouse door, I wait for Enzo to come up the elevator to let me into the apartment. I tap my heel against the floor and absently flip through one of the books Enzo bought me. I'm pretty sure he would've let me pick however many books I wanted with shirtless men on the cover without any judgment—well, maybe *some* judgment.

Still, it was nice. Getting out with him. It was... fun... and surprisingly easy.

I expected Enzo to be right behind me. I glance at the elevator and sigh, eagerly waiting to confirm I survived the big, scary crosswalk without him holding my hand. Chuckling to myself as the elevator dings, I lift my gaze as the doors open and my pulse stutters.

Enzo is not amused—not even close. As he steps out, his jaw is clenched and his eyes are narrow—something dark simmering behind them. He doesn't look like the man teasing me in the romance section, not more than twenty minutes ago. This version of Enzo is furious.

"I told you not to leave my side," he sternly reminds, stalking toward me—his breathing heavy and nostrils flaring.

The mood shifts instantly, and my shoulders tense. "It was just across the street." I shake my head, blinking at him. "I came straight up—"

He doesn't give me time to finish. He steps forward, swipes to unlock the door with one hand, and pushes it open with the other—the gesture is sharp and precise. His hand presses against my back, guiding me through the door without another word, and it closes behind us with a dull thud.

"I told you to wait," he admonishes, walking me toward the kitchen.

I set my books and jacket on the island. Spinning around—feeling defensive even though I'm not sure I did anything wrong—I snark, "You're seriously mad about that?"

"I'm *seriously* trying to keep you safe. To keep you alive."

A nervous laugh erupts from me—because I don't know how to react to him right now—as I step toward the living room.

"It was maybe fifty feet. What? Did you think I'd get kidnapped in broad daylight?"

"Eavan," he barks in a tone that causes me to stop cold. "You have no idea what you're playing with when you act like this. No idea what it does to me."

My mouth opens, but nothing comes out. Before I can respond, he wraps his hand around my arm—not tight, but firm. It isn't rough. It isn't mean. But it's not gentle, either. He starts walking, and I stumble once, trying to keep up with him, my boots clicking against the hardwood as he practically drags me across the living room.

"Enzo, what are you doing?"

He doesn't answer as he tugs me toward the couch. He sits down and yanks me toward him—and I brace for a scolding in that low, quiet tone he's perfected. But he doesn't pull me to the seat beside him.

I let out a gasp. The sound catching in my chest when he drags me across his lap. "Enzo!" He steadies me—one hand braced at my waist and the other resting on my back—and my body tenses from head to toe. I don't fight him, but I don't relax either.

"You push every boundary you're given," he gruffs. "You think it's all fun and games. Just a little *playful* bratting. But what happens when I'm not there to protect you? When someone else is watching—someone who doesn't have your best interests in mind?"

"I'm not helpless. I can take care of myself." I try to twist, to look up at him. "And you aren't my father."

"You're right, princess..." He rubs his hand along my waist and over my hip. My cheeks burn, and I'm not sure if it's embarrassment or guilt... or something else entirely.

He's quiet for a second. I feel his heavy breaths whisper against the back of my neck, steady but tight as his hand roams lower on my hip. It slides over the swell of my butt cheek and lifts the skirt of my dress to bare my ass—my entire body immediately growing rigid.

"You didn't listen to your father..." His hand cracks against my panty-covered skin, and a breathy, startled cry blows over my lips. "But you will listen to your Daddy."

Enzo's rough palm dusts over my still-warm skin, and I'm completely frozen with shock. I want to fight. To push myself from his lap. To scream, *I'm not a fucking child.* "You need this to learn how to behave, don't you?" he asks, roughly palming my ass. I open my mouth to shout 'no,' only to surprise myself when I silently nod.

"You promised me that you'd be a good girl." He spanks me again, and the burn radiates across my ass cheek. My heart slams against my ribcage, and I struggle to catch my breath. "But you weren't a good girl, were you?"

Before I can answer, he swats twice in quick succession, my skin on fire from the repeated strikes. With one hand resting on my searing flesh, the other slides up my back and tangles in the hair at the nape of my neck. He fists it just hard enough to pull my teary eyes up to meet his gaze. "Do you even care how

I felt when I saw you disappear into that crowd?" he asks, his eyes riddled with fear.

I swallow hard at his question. I hadn't stopped to think about that. He's not just mad. He was *scared*. "I... I didn't mean to upset you," I mutter, my voice much smaller than intended.

"I don't like it when you don't listen." He shakes his head, his tone softening as he tenderly rubs his hand over the heat of the palm prints I'm certain he's left behind. He's no longer holding me down. I could get up if I wanted to. But despite my complete and utter vulnerability, I don't move. *I don't want to.*

Enzo's fingers dip beneath the thin fabric of my panties, and he slides his hand over my ass cheek. His fingertips teasingly rest at the crease of my upper thigh. With his chocolate eyes locked on mine, he whispers, "Tell Daddy you're sorry, princess."

"I'm sorry," I reply, the words cracking on my lips when his fingertips slowly inch toward my inner thigh.

The corner of his mouth ticks up the tiniest bit as he slides further toward between my legs. "No." He shakes his head, softly demanding, "Say it."

Locked on his gaze—adrenaline buzzing in my veins from his hand lingering where no man has touched me—I open my mouth and can't hold back the words that tumble out. "I'm sorry, Daddy." *Daddy...* The word echoes in my head and flutters between my thighs.

A pleased smile spreads across his face, and the hard edge in his eyes completely fades. "That's my good girl." Enzo's hand slides fully between my thighs, and his fingertip swirls at the slickness around my entrance before gingerly pressing it slightly into me. "Daddy likes it when you're a good girl."

I tense at the foreign sensation of his digit rubbing around my entrance and teasingly inching in and out of me. He immediately stills and he urges, "Relax for me. I'll be gentle."

"I... uh... I ummm..." I stammer, feeling the heat of the embarrassment over my complete lack of experience creep up my face and flush my cheeks. *Twenty-two years old and I've barely kissed a man, let alone had one put his hands in my panties.* "I've never..."

Enzo pulls his hand from between my thighs, lifts me from across his legs, and into his lap until I'm straddling him. He places his hands on my hips beneath my dress, and his thumbs draw leisurely circles on my bare skin. "Shit. I didn't know, princess. I don't want to do anything you aren't ready for," he softly insists, easing my nerves and tenderly pressing his lips to mine.

"We can go slow." He peppers the words against my lips. Wet, languid kisses pass between us, his tongue licking against the crease of my lips. I part them slightly, and he slips his tongue between them. It swipes against mine, massaging it gently, causing me to whimper with need into his mouth—a devilish chuckle rising from him as he pulls back from our passionate kiss. *It's like he can read my mind...*

Enzo's warm breath blows across my already flushed cheeks when he leans toward my ear. His short beard tickles my cheek, his lips dust against the shell of my ear, sending goosebumps up my spine. "If you want this, you need to tell Daddy what you want."

His demand leaves me at a complete loss for words and my heart pounding. I don't know what I want... *Lies. I know exactly what I want.* His hands on me again. To feel his lips press against mine. For him to tear my panties from me and slide more than just his fingertips inside me. I just don't know *how* to ask for it. "I... Can you..." I'm thankful his cheek is still pressed against mine and he can't see the embarrassment painted across my face. *Don't overthink it, Eavan... He's waiting for you to say it just as much as you want to speak it.* "I want you to... make me yours... to be my first."

"That's not how good girls ask," he whispers, sliding his scruff along my jaw as he pulls back from my ear. "They say please."

"Please..." I beg on an exhale before correcting myself. "Please, Daddy."

Enzo's hands slide up my sides, lifting the loose skirt of my dress with them. "Are you sure?" he asks, his hands resting at the sides of my chest. Unable to speak with his dark eyes locked on mine, I timidly nod my response. His hands slide higher, pushing my arms over my head to rid me of my dress. He drops it to the floor—leaving me in nothing but my panties and a pair of booties—as his eyes rake down my less-than-perfect body. "Fuck, you're beautiful, princess."

His heated gaze sets my skin on fire—his hands dusting over my flesh only further igniting me. My chest heaves as his hands slide up my back until they tangle in my hair. Using his light hold, he slowly pulls me toward him.

His soft, full lips press to mine, and I melt into him as he takes my mouth again. This kiss is far less gentle than the first, and I struggle to draw a breath as he plunders my mouth. My tongue dances with his, and I grind onto his lap to relieve the ache between my thighs.

Enzo peppers kisses along my jaw and down my neck—licking and sucking to my collarbone. He pulls my hair firmly, forcing my back to arch and pushing my heaving chest into his face. I gasp when he sucks my breast into his mouth, swirling his tongue around my nipple. The tingling sensation flitters through me, eliciting a need between my thighs like nothing I've ever felt before.

As though he can sense my desire, his hand slips from my hair, down my body, and between us. "Your little panties are absolutely soaked, princess," he hoarsely whispers, rubbing over the damp fabric. Enzo shifts his weight, and I'm suddenly on my back with him half on top of me. His hands slip up and down my inner thigh as he presses his lips back to mine. Slipping his fingers beneath the thin damp cotton, he pulls my panties to the side and rubs through my pussy lips. I moan into his mouth and push into his touch, wanting—*no, needing*—more of him.

His slick fingertips circle around my clit, and every touch causes my pulse to race faster as I quickly lose my breath. The tension from his touch builds low in my stomach, and I fist at his shirt, desperately needing him to bring me over the edge. "Your little pussy is so fucking wet for Daddy," Enzo groans against my lips, and I can hear the approval in his tone. His thumb rubbing over my clit, he presses a finger to my entrance. "Practically begging for me to be inside you."

He eases his finger into me, and I tug at my fistfuls of cotton to drag him back to my mouth. Sliding it leisurely in and out of me, he curls it toward my stomach, and the tightness in my core explodes through me. I come hard—harder than I ever have alone—as he swallows my cries. He pulls back from our kiss, lingering so close that his words vibrate against my lips, "Does my sweet princess like when I play with her tight pussy?"

"Mmmmm," I moan, lost in euphoria with my hips rising to meet his light thrusts.

"Yes, Daddy," he sternly corrects. His warm, wet tongue drags up the side of my neck until his lips are against my ear. "Yes, Daddy. Please, Daddy. More, Daddy. Harder, Daddy," he gravelly whispers between full deep thrusts of his finger. "That's how good girls answer, isn't it?"

"Yes... Daddy," I breathlessly answer.

"Good girl." Enzo kisses along my jaw, making his way back to my lips. "We need to make sure this tight, virgin pussy is ready to take my cock," Enzo softly insists. He kisses me hard and deep, stealing my breath and swallowing my whimpers as he eases a second finger into me. It's so much, but it also feels so good. Plundering my mouth, he thrusts them slowly and steadily until I'm practically writhing beneath him. "Are you going to come again?" he asks, thrusting deep and dragging his fingers along my walls.

My back arches from the couch again when he diligently curls and plunges his fingers inside me—my legs quivering and squeezing around his hand—and I scream, "Yes, Daddy!"

He withdraws his digits from me, sliding over me with a satisfied smile. Gripping my panties, he rises from the couch and pulls the damp fabric down my legs. After removing them and my booties, he haphazardly tosses everything to the floor—my shoes each hitting the hardwood with a thud. Enzo grips his white V-neck shirt at the nape of his neck, pulls it over his head, wipes his fingers clean, and drops it next to my panties.

My eyes roam down his body as he towers over me, standing next to the couch. I reach for the deep V protruding from his waistband as he undoes his belt and lowers his zipper, drawing my attention to the massive bulge at the front of them. He pushes his jeans and boxer briefs down his legs, and

I nearly choke when his hard length springs free. *That's going inside me?!? There's no way!*

"Relax, princess," Enzo softly urges, clearly seeing my wide eyes and gaping mouth. "You'll love how good I'll feel inside you." He quickly rids himself of his pants and climbs onto the couch. Settling between my thighs and pulling them over his hips, his weighty dick rests against my core as he presses his firm, bare chest against mine. "I'm going to stretch out your tight little pussy, but you can take it." *Stretch it? That thing is going to split me in two.* He reaches between us and presses himself to my entrance, promising, "I'll go nice and slow."

He eases forward, and a strangled groan blows over my lips when he enters me. It doesn't hurt, but it also falls a little short of being pleasurable. Stilling for a second, he rubs his knuckles along my jaw. "That's it, princess. Just breathe." True to his word, he inches forward, giving me time to adjust to the strange sensation of him stretching me wide and completely filling me. "Let Daddy all the way inside you."

His hips press against the back of my thighs, and I realize that I have somehow managed to take all of him. *And, miraculously, I'm not split in two.* "You feel so fucking good wrapped around my cock." He pulls back, and I clench with nerves, afraid he's going to slam back into me. *I might not be experienced, but I heard my share of horror stories from girls when I was in high school.* Cupping my face, Enzo presses his lips to mine. "I'll be gentle. Until you're ready for more. I promise."

Not once pulling his deep brown eyes from mine, he works himself in and out of me slowly, dropping kisses across my lips. With every stroke, I relax, and the feel of him sliding into me grows increasingly enjoyable. *Really fucking enjoyable.* "Such a good girl," he praises, slightly increasing the speed of his thrusts, "taking all of Daddy's big cock."

My fingers knead the knotty muscles across his back, digging into them as he repeatedly slides the entirety of himself into me. His lips trail up down my neck—sucking and lightly biting as he drives into me. "It feels so good..." I tangle my fingers in his hair as he travels along my throat. My clit throbs and I quiver around his length. "I'm gonna come, Daddy..."

"Don't tease me, princess," Enzo groans against the crook of my neck, palming my breast as his thrusts grow more zealous. "Come all over my cock." My body follows his command without hesitation. Screaming out in pleasure, I fist my handful of his hair and rake my nails across his back. He hisses against my neck and drives into me so hard and deep it almost hurts. *And I like it...*

"Ugh... I'm not gonna last, princess, if you keep coming like that." Crashing his lips against mine, Enzo claims my mouth as he plows into me. He swallows my moans and screams as he makes me come again. And again—and I don't know how much more I can take.

Breaking our kiss, Enzo props himself on his forearm beside my head. He wraps my leg around his waist and thrusts ungodly deep. Repeating the motion over and over until he's taking me hard and fast. Every drive is blissfully painful, and I claw at his back as breathy screams billow from my lungs. He doesn't relent, pulling a string of violent orgasms from me until my whole body is quivering uncontrollably.

Suddenly, he stops and pulls from me before vigorously fisting his thick length until streams of cum shoot from the tip. They spray over my pussy and stomach. "Fuuuuck," Enzo breathlessly grunts, rubbing his hand over the thick head and drawing out a few final drops of his release, letting them drip onto my skin. "Mine," he gravelly whispers, rubbing his tip through the creamy white splatters, thoroughly smearing them over the lips of my pussy. "Who does this perfect little cum-covered pussy belong to?"

Still struggling to catch my breath, I answer without hesitation, panting, "Daddy... It.... Belongs... To... Daddy."

Eavan's hair is the first thing I see when I wake, struggling against the bright sunlight to open my eyes. A wild, soft tangle of coppery red hair draped over my arm and splayed across the pillow behind her. Her cheek rests lightly against my chest, her breaths slow and even—the faint rise and fall of her chest syncing with mine. One of her hands is splayed across my ribs, and the other is tucked between us like she's meant to be here. Like this isn't completely and utterly wrong.

I glance down at her and then stare at the ceiling with my jaw tightening. *I shouldn't have done this.* Everything in me is screaming it. Joking and flirting with her was harmless. *Or so I lied to myself.* She is Cillian's sister. *His little sister.* And not just in that overprotective way some guys throw around; I know firsthand that he'd kill for her. He already has. Cillian is my best friend. He's fucking family. One of two people in this world who have had my back through more chaos than I can count. One person in my life that I'd never want to betray. *But I did.*

I can't say it was an accident. I can't say it happened without thinking. Because the truth is, I *did* think. I thought about it too much. I knew exactly what I was doing last night—every single second of it. *Both times.* From pulling her over my lap, to cleaning myself from her, and eventually falling asleep with her in my arms. It's what I've been thinking about since he paraded her in here with that perfect ass draped over his shoulder. It's what I've been dying to do since the first time she opened those pouty pink lips of her bratty little mouth. *She needs this as badly as I do.*

Staring down at her asleep with my half-numb arm beneath her, I try to tell myself I don't want this, but I can't bring myself to believe the lie. Because even though I know I crossed a line—one Cillian might kill me for—there's a part of me that doesn't regret a damn second of it.

Eavan stirs slightly, nuzzling closer to me. Her breath blows across my collarbone, and I swear my heart skips a beat. Settling back into me with a quiet sigh, her hand slides across my stomach until it's resting flat against my chest.

She shifts again, murmurs something too soft to catch, and her hand tenses. I'm flooded with guilt, knowing that Cillian is going to find out. Because as much as I know this was wrong and shouldn't have happened, all I can think about now is how much I want it to happen again.

I shut my eyes and draw in a slow, deep breath trying to calm my rapidly growing cock. And I'm not proud when my thoughts immediately drift back to last night and the way she looked at me when I marked her as mine. How easily the words "yes, Daddy" fell out of her mouth. And how unbelievably perfect she felt curling against me as we talked until the moon was high over the city.

I should get up. Put some space between us, because I should be the responsible one and not let this happen again. *It can't happen again.* Not if I have any hope of salvaging what's left of my conscience or my friendship with her brother. But I can't bring myself to do it. Her presence quiets something in me I didn't know *needed* to be silenced.

Her long lashes flutter, and her bright emerald eyes slowly open. "Morning," she groggily whispers as her gaze meets mine. And just like that—I know there's no going back. I'm already in far too fucking deep.

"Good morning, princess." I slide my arm from beneath her and pull her under me.

"Again?" Her laugh is coy.

"Daddy can't get enough of your perfect little pussy." When I drag her hand to my hard cock, her eyes widen, and she wraps her hand around it. I kiss her lips, her chin, and then pepper a trail down her neck to her collarbone as she lightly fists my cock. "And I still haven't had the pleasure of tasting you." My lips travel over her ample breasts—pausing briefly to suck on both of her already taut, rosy nipples—and down her stomach. Reaching her pussy, I press my face to her and inhale her sweet, musky scent—a feral growl of need rattling in my chest. *She smells like fucking heaven.*

Spreading her pussy open, I can't help but lick my lips at the sight of her glistening pink flesh. I run my tongue from entrance to clit, loving the way she reacts to my touch. "You taste so fucking good," I groan against her plump lips. Swirling my tongue, I lick and suck at her until her arousal is dribbling over my chin and her hips are bucking against my face. She writhes against me as she cries out her release, and I need more.

Wrapping my arms around her thighs, I hold her wide and pull her back to my mouth. I feast on her relentlessly—unable to get enough of her throbbing clit or her delicious taste. Her hands claw at the sheets and thread through my hair—her thighs shaking violently in my tight hold as I pull another orgasm from her.

I loosen my tight grip and leisurely stroke my cock as I sit between her thighs—relishing in the fully satiated look of euphoria on Eavan's flushed face. After affording her a moment of reprieve while I wipe her arousal from my face with the back of my hand, I pull her into my lap. "Are you too sore to climb on Daddy's cock?" She shakes her head, and I firmly grip her voluptuous ass and lift her from my thighs. Holding her up on her knees with one hand, I grip my rigid cock with the other and press it to her warm, wet entrance. "Show me how much you love the feel of me inside of you."

My hands glide up her back as she tentatively lowers herself over my thick shaft with a cracked groan. She drops over the last few inches, quickly burying me to the hilt, causing my head to snap back with a groan. She's so fucking tight around me; it feels like I almost don't fit. Cupping her ass, I guide her movements—showing her how to work herself over my length. I kiss along her neck with a pleased moan as she eagerly follows my silent instruction.

"Yes. Just like that, princess," I mumble against her throat when she swirls her hips. My hands roam over her soft skin, my lips and tongue sampling every inch I can reach with them, licking the salty sweat from her skin. Her movements grow erratic, her hips sputtering as she struggles to maintain her rhythm. "Don't stop," I groan. "Make yourself come on my cock."

"Yes, Daddy," she pants.

"Rock your hips for me and lift that perfect ass a little as you ride me," I instruct. Grabbing her ass, I help her grind her hips faster and vigorously slide herself over me. *And fuck... she does it so fucking well.* "You feel so fucking good," I grit through my teeth, desperately fighting my need to come before she does. Her already tight pussy constricts around me seconds before her head falls back with a guttural cry. Watching her eyes roll back and her lower lip quiver in bliss as she squeezes my cock like a vise, I nearly spill into her.

"Fuck," I grunt, gripping her ass so hard I'll be surprised if she doesn't bruise. Holding her tight to my hips and staying buried deep inside her, I lift us from the mattress just enough to twist and pin her to it beneath me. I drive into her without abandon, taking her hard and fast—wanting nothing more than to fill *my* tight little pussy with cum. *Needing desperately to fill her.*

Sweet, pained whimpers blow over her lips as I fuck her. She comes again, her heels digging into the back of my thighs, and her nails painfully dragging through the flesh of my upper back. My hands roughly fist her hips, holding her firmly beneath me. Grunting through every violent thrust, I fuck her even harder as she repeatedly unfurls—unable to push away this foreign idea of breeding her.

The thought of watching me drip from her tight little pussy flashes through my thoughts and it does me in. I drive into her with a roar, pulling out a second before spilling inside her —my release spraying onto her upper thigh and the sheets beneath her. That was close. *Too fucking close.* Stroking her face and pressing my lips to hers, I struggle to catch my breath and try to understand this sudden compulsion to finish inside her. A risk I have never taken with a woman before Eavan. *Fuck, she's the first woman I've ever slid into bare.*

"Let's get you cleaned up," I insist, when our racing hearts have slowed. I help her from the bed and immediately notice the barrage of fingertip-shaped bruises forming across her hips and ass. "Fuck, princess"—I rub my hand over the marks I left on her—"Did Daddy hurt you?"

"No, Daddy." She vigorously shakes her head, looking down at the source of my concern. "You didn't hurt me."

The smell of Eavan's shampoo lingers in the air as I step through the open doorway, the subtle mix of honey and something floral I can't quite place flooding my nostrils as I walk into Cillian's bedroom. I pause just inside the bathroom, watching as she wraps a white towel around herself. Her back is to me, her copper-red hair clinging to her shoulders in damp waves, and water is still dripping in lazy streams down her porcelain skin.

She turns, catching my gaze tracing over her curves and memorizing every perfect inch of her. She doesn't shy away— instead, a small smile pulls at the corner of her mouth. I match it and tease, "I still think we could've saved water and showered together."

"I wanted to get clean during my shower. Not dirty." She smirks, walking past me with an overzealous sway in her hips. It causes the tightly wrapped towel to part slightly, garnering me a peek at her hip. My amusement at her playfulness fades the moment my eyes land on the bruises. Faint—but unmistakable—and scattered like ink dots on her thighs and the curve of her hips. My stomach knots with guilt, knowing I marred her perfect skin.

I reach out, and my fingertips brush over one particularly dark mark about the size of the pad of my thumb. She twitches under my touch, and I'm uncertain whether it's from pain or surprise. "Are you sure I didn't hurt you, princess?"

She glances down at the bruise I'm tenderly rubbing my thumb over and shrugs. "They don't hurt. Really," she insists. "I don't even know they're there unless I look in the mirror." I let my hand fall away—not satisfied, but unwilling to argue about them. Accidental or not, I left them on her, and I hate not knowing if I was too rough with her.

"Get dressed and come downstairs. We need to talk about a few things."

She stops in her tracks, the towel clutched tighter to her chest, and her brows furrowing, alerting me that my tone might've been a little too gruff. "Is something wrong? Because I swear, I'm perfectly—"

"No, princess." I lean in and press a soft kiss to her forehead —hoping to comfort her in a way I don't know how to with words. "Nothing's wrong. There are just a few things we probably should've talked about before we had sex last night."

"Oh." The single word sounds more curious than understanding as she blinks at me. "We can talk now. While I get dressed. It's fine."

"No. Get dressed," I repeat, stepping back to give her space even though I don't want to. This isn't a conversation we need to have with her naked when my thoughts would be on anything but what we need to talk about. "I don't like to have to repeat myself," I gruff walking toward the door. "We'll talk downstairs. With clothes on. I'll go make coffee and find us something for breakfast."

In the kitchen, I pour two mugs of coffee—black for me, cream and too much sugar for her—as she dresses upstairs. By the time she makes her way downstairs and into the kitchen, I'm smearing the last of the jelly over her toast.

She's fucking radiant—effortlessly. Damp hair twisted into a messy bun on top of her head, my dress shirt hanging off her shoulder, and another pair of black leggings that might as well be painted on. *Fuck, I hate how badly I want to touch her again.*

Eavan climbs onto the barstool opposite the island from me and eyes the plate I slide toward her. "I'm downstairs. I have clothes on. Can we talk now?" she sasses with dramatics and an exaggerated sigh.

"Such a brat," I mutter, shaking my head. "And if this weren't so important, I'd let you know *exactly* how much I dislike that attitude and sharp tongue of yours."

Trying to hold my focus, I take a sip of my coffee instead of bending her over the counter and painting her round ass red with handprints. "I don't trust myself with you," I admit. "You make me want to do things... risky fucking things. If we're doing this, there are at least two things we need to be responsible about—a safeword and birth control." She watches me, chewing on her mouthful of toast and unable to respond. "I'll run out in a bit and grab condoms," I add, waiting for her reaction.

She swallows and shakes her head. "You don't need to."

"Yes. I do." I overemphasize each word, my thoughts drifting to how compelled I was—*and still am*—to come inside her.

"I've been on birth control since I was fifteen." Lifting her borrowed shirt sleeve, she shows me the small scar on her inner arm just above her elbow. "My father had two of his goons with muscle hold me down so a doctor could insert it. Two years ago, they did it again, so it could be replaced with a new one." She lifts her toast from her plate and leans forward with her elbows on the granite. "He couldn't be certain he could keep me pure, that the men he kept at my side day and night wouldn't take advantage of me. But he could damn well make sure to try and pass me off as a virgin bride."

Her confession throws me. I stare back at her and blink, not certain which part stuns me more—her casual account of the assault or the fact that it occurred at the hands of her own father. I see fucking red—heat creeping up the back of my neck and blood turning to lava at the mere thought of someone having the gall to put their hands on her. I could fucking kill him—if I hadn't already put a bullet in his chest.

"That's one," she says, drawing me back from my thoughts. "So... safewords?" Her voice ticks up an octave, the concept clearly foreign to her.

"A safeword," I correct, pleased she's taking this seriously. "A single word, or hand signal when you can't speak, to let me know you're at your limit. That I'm being too rough or pushing you too far."

"Wait?" She scrunches her face in confusion. "Why wouldn't I be able to speak?"

I try to hold back my chuckle at her naivety. "It's hard to speak when you have a cock buried deep in your throat. Among other reasons." Her eyes blow wide at my statement, and it's accompanied by a silent gasp. "Pinching me hard —*really hard*—three times will let me know." She nods her understanding. "But you still need an actual safeword."

"No, I don't need one." The genuine trust in her statement catches me off-guard as she shakes her head. "A week ago, I probably would've thought you'd kill me on sight," she confesses softly with warmth sparkling in her emerald eyes. "Now, I don't think you're capable. Not only could you never do that to my brother, but I'm certain you would never hurt me."

"It's not just for you. It's for me, too. To ensure I don't cross a line with you. I can't hurt you like that. Even by accident.

And if I ever did… it would break me, princess. This isn't something that I'm willing to compromise on."

I lift my cup and take a sip as she lets out a heavy sigh. "Fine. If you insist… *Cillian*."

I choke on my coffee, droplets of it spraying across the counter. "You cannot seriously pick your brother's name as your safeword."

"It's *my* word, right?" she quips. "And I'm pretty sure if I scream it, you'll stop… *and* he'll come running." A wicked and triumphant smirk spreads across her face, like she just won a game I didn't even realize we were playing. I can't help but chuckle. *She's right, though…* I don't think a thing in this world would take me from hard to flaccid quite like her screaming her brother's name while I'm thrusting into her.

"Cillian is another thing we need to talk about." My tone is serious, killing the lighthearted mood.

She immediately shakes her head. "No."

"Did you seriously just tell me no?"

"Very clearly," she sasses, leaning back in her barstool. "Cillian isn't back until tomorrow morning. I don't want to waste today arguing about him. Or us—whatever we are. Or figuring out how to explain to him that I'm a grown-ass woman and not a delicate little doll he needs to protect. I just want to spend today with you."

It's not fair, the way she says it. And it's like she knows I won't say no. *And she's right.* I don't want to spend today talking about her brother or the reality of what's going on outside this apartment. I want to spend it with *her*.

I exhale, willfully giving in. "All right, princess. What do you want to do?"

She lights up, leaning forward with an excited sparkle in her eyes. "A real date," she responds. "You. Me. And whatever we are right now."

"And what *are* we right now, Eavan?"

"Two people pretending the rest of the world doesn't exist."

"I'm not letting you out of this apartment again." I shake my head, watching the excitement in her eyes dim. "We can have a date here. If this is our last night alone, I don't want to share you with the rest of the world." It's a half-truth. I don't want to share her, but I also can't risk repeating yesterday's excursion.

"Whatever you say, Daddy," she flirtatiously brats.

"Careful, princess," I warn. "Or you might not be able to sit by our date tonight."

The day drifts by in lazy stretches—slow, sweet, yet entirely too quickly. We spend the hours wrapped in each other. Cuddling, teasing, and kissing between bouts of laughter that make my stomach ache.

Enzo and I find ourselves on the couch, my legs thrown across his lap while his hands roam up and down my calves in long, unhurried strokes. I've forgotten what it feels like to be tense and nervous around him. The man who terrified me less than a week ago feels so far away from the man currently dusting his fingers over my skin.

He glances down at his watch and then back up at me as he lightly taps my calf. "You should probably get ready."

"For?"

"Our date, princess."

I stare back at him, surprised. "I thought you said you weren't taking me anywhere."

"I'm not." That infuriating, sexy smirk tugs at the corner of his mouth. *That damn smirk is becoming my kryptonite.* "We're staying in, but I still plan to give you the night you deserve. You've got an hour. Then I expect you in the hall outside your brother's room, wearing a pretty dress for me."

I lean forward, practically tackling him to plant a big, wet kiss on his lips. "Thank you," I murmur against his mouth as I pull back. He palms the sides of my face and drags me back into him for a deep kiss that leaves my heart fluttering.

"One hour," he reminds, helping me from his lap.

I head upstairs and hear him banging around in the kitchen. *He cooks?* I somehow imagined Enzo as a guy who survives off takeout—or protein shakes and intimidation. *Oh God. What if he doesn't cook?* My concern about crunchy pasta smothered in ketchup is mitigated a few moments later when a rich, savory aroma wafts up the stairs. It smells so delicious that my stomach actually growls.

I dig through my meager section of clothes in Cillian's closet. When he went and grabbed my things, he didn't exactly fill a bag with date-night apparel—more like gym attire and a handful of casual dresses. With my limited options, I settle on the little black strapless dress I came here in. It's simple, yet hugs all the right places while still leaving a little to the imagination.

With my hair curled into loose waves and my makeup light but sharp, I slide the dress on and smooth it over my hips. My fingers tremble with a little anticipation as I pull on my strappy heels—nerves, maybe? *Ridiculous, Eavan... he's already seen you naked.* I pause before the full-length mirror to take in my appearance, wanting to look exceptionally good for him tonight.

I step into the hall, and the scent that greets me is decadent—creamy and earthy. Enzo is resting against the wall, waiting for me. His tailored navy suit fits him like a sin—the burgundy, jacquard, silk tie barely loosened at the neck. My feet root in place like I've suddenly forgotten how to walk. Quickly pushing upright, his eyes rake over my body. He crosses the short distance between us and takes my hand, squeezing it gently. "You look fucking incredible," he whispers, drawing me close enough to place a chaste kiss against my cheek.

"You clean up well yourself." I struggle to get the words out through the sudden tightness in my chest.

"Not like a Tony Soprano starter kit?" he teases, leading me down the hall toward his room.

"Did I seriously just get all dressed up to go to your room?" I snark.

He glares down at me, opening his bedroom door and warns, "There's still time to ensure you can't sit comfortably for our date tonight." He leads me past his bed and toward the open door to the balcony. My eyes are drawn to a soft glow on the other side of the threshold, and I audibly gasp at the sight. The Manhattan skyline stretches beyond the balcony, hazy and golden in the distance as the last of the sun sets over the horizon. Lounge chair cushions line the stone floor, covered with soft throws and surrounded by flickering candles. Dozens of them. *He was apparently quite busy when I thought he was playing on his phone today.*

Sitting in the middle of the pillows and candles—dinner. Enzo guides me toward the little area he's set up for tonight and helps me to a pillow. Taking the cushion across from me, he pours the wine and urges me to try the food before me. Savory and perfectly cooked mushroom risotto.

I shovel in a second—and third—forkful, moaning with each delectable bite. He licks his lips, watching me enjoy the meal he made, and the look on his face borders on indecent. "This is delicious," I finally praise between bites, chasing a mushroom across my plate with the tines of my fork. "I didn't know you could cook."

"There's a lot you don't know about me, princess," he responds, flirtatiously with a hint of smugness. His tone softens and he shares, "My mom taught me before she died."

I can't hide the smile that spreads across my face, not that I want to. Reaching over our plates, I lightly cup the side of his face and run my thumb over the sexy as hell scar in his eyebrow. "Start here."

His cheek presses into my hand as he smiles. "This?" He rests his fingers on my thumb and drags them through the scar. "I got this the day I met your brother and Nik. We all attended

Crestfallen Prep, so I knew them in passing. But with who I am... who they are... we were far from being friends. Or even acquaintances. On a dare from some friends, I stole the headmaster's Buick. Security shot at me, and I accidentally drove his sedan straight into the building when they put a slug in my shoulder."

I've seen the scar of that bullet wound, but this story isn't quite how I imagined him getting it. Far from it, actually. "You're kidding?" I scoff, shaking my head as he finishes the Pinot in his glass. Lifting the bottle to refill it, he tips it toward me, in a silent question. I shake my head, and he places the bottle back beside the plates between us.

"Not in the slightest." Rolling his stemless glass between his hands, he muses, "Straight into the gymnasium. My *friends* who dared me were nowhere to be found when I realized my leg was pinned in the crash. But—"

"Cian and Nikolai?" I interrupt.

"For some reason, they pulled me free and got me home. Probably kept my ass out of juvie," he shares with a lighthearted chuckle.

My eyes pull from his, flicking toward the scar. "So that's from the accident."

"No." His tone is suddenly less jovial and reminiscent. "That's from my father beating the shit out of me when an O'Brien and a Romanov brought my injured ass to his doorstep."

"Oh," I softly exhale, realizing his father wasn't too different from my own.

As though he didn't just drop a massive bomb, he continues, "And the three of us... We've been thick as thieves ever since."

He tells me more stories from his childhood—some about my brother that he probably shouldn't. The wine dwindles, and Enzo moves closer to me as we talk. I lean back into the bed of cushions to get more comfortable. "You surprise me, Enzo," I confess, watching the candlelight flicker when a soft, warm breeze blows over the terrace.

"How so?"

"You're... different from what I expected. Softer."

"I'll take that as a compliment, princess."

"It is," I promise. "I like this version of you."

He leans closer, and his chocolate eyes burn when they catch the light from the candles. "You're the only person who's ever seen this side of me."

I stare back at him in silence, wondering how we got here so fast. And why it feels like exactly where we're supposed to be.

Enzo finishes the last of his wine and leans back beside me with one hand behind his head and the other leisurely dusting along my upper thigh. Rolling toward him, I rest my head against his shoulder and curl my legs under me. "I still can't believe you managed to plan all of this in under a day."

"You said you wanted a date, princess."

"I was thinking pizza and a movie." I laugh softly. "I didn't expect a candlelit dinner under the stars."

"I don't do things half-assed, Eavan," he firmly responds. He turns, fingers brushing my jaw as he tilts my face toward his. He stares down at me, and my heart flutters. "Especially when it comes to you." Pressing his lips to mine, he kisses me gently. No urgency or need—just tenderness. His hand slides around the back of my neck, and his thumb rubs against my jaw as he takes his time tasting my lips.

The softness of his silk tie brushes against my bare skin at the neckline of my dress when I press my body to his. He parts his lips lightly, and his tongue teases mine with a deliberate slowness that leaves me whimpering into his mouth with need.

Our kiss growing more passionate, he rolls toward me, pressing me onto my back and leaving him resting half on top of me. His hand slides along my thigh, hooking under my knee, and lightly parting my legs. His knuckles dust over my skin—leaving a wake of goosebumps—and he mutters his instruction against my lips, "Spread wide for Daddy."

CHAPTER 15
enzo

Eavan's legs fall open as I drag my knuckles from her knee toward her upper thigh—her already short dress pushed up to her hips leaves very little to the imagination. Upon reaching the apex of her thighs, a pleased groan rumbles in my chest. I brush across the lacy fabric covering her pussy and run my fingertips against the thin material, tracing the length of her slit and pressing it lightly into the warmth radiating at her center. "Do you like these panties, princess?"

"What?" she murmurs when my question catches her off-guard, only to get her answer as I shove my fingers through the delicate material—shredding it as I rip them from her body.

"Enz—" I cut her admonishment short when I plunge two fingers inside her, "oooh."

Her arousal coats my digits as I thrust and curl them relentlessly inside her, demanding an orgasm from her. She spasms around my fingers, and I know she's teetering at the edge. I slide my fingers from her and listen to her displeased grumble as I lift them to my mouth. Slipping one between my lips, I suck the sweet, tangy taste of her from it with a delighted moan. "Is that how you're supposed to answer me?" I ask, pressing my other arousal-coated digit between her lips. With my finger massaging her tongue, she's unable to answer. Mercilessly, I press it deeper, I make her swallow me down to the knuckle before pulling back enough to allow her to speak.

"No," she hoarsely guffs.

"No, *what*, princess?"

Staring up at me with defiance in her eyes and struggling to hold back the wicked smirk pulling at the corners of her mouth, she brats, "No. It's not."

My jaw tightens, and I roughly cup her chin, demanding her attention. "Are you sure you want to play this game?" I gravelly whisper, loosening the knot of my tie. "Because Daddy's feeling generous if you want to change your answer."

Her insolence unwavering, she obnoxiously rolls her eyes. "No. It's not how I'm supposed to answer you."

Having given her enough chances, I yank my tie over my head and grab both her wrists as I climb over her. She struggles beneath me as I pin her to the cushions we're lying on.

Straddling her waist, I slip the noose over her hands, cinch it tightly around her wrists, and tie a quick knot around the metal spindle at the balcony's edge. Eavan struggles against the binding—further tightening the knots—as my fingers dust down her arms to the tantalizing cleavage at the neckline of her dress. Dipping my fingers beneath it, I fist the seam with both hands and quickly tear it in two down the front until her cute little black dress is nothing more than a tattered scrap of fabric, leaving her bound and naked beneath me with a shocked gasp flying over her lips.

Her mouth gapes, and before she has a moment to wield that bratty tongue of hers, I climb from her and roughly roll her onto her stomach. My palm connects with her curvaceous ass and a beautiful, startled yelp tumbles out of her. "Is this what you need, princess?" I ask, pinkening her pale skin with another firm swat of my hand. I swing again, my palm radiating as I leave my print on her. "Are you bratting for my attention or my mark? Is it because you're afraid you won't get either after tonight?"

I spank her again, hard enough to sting but not enough to leave a second handprint. After rubbing over the warm, pink skin of her ass, I lean over her and press my lips to the back of her neck. "You'll get both." I sweep her hair back from where it's hanging over her face. "I'll bend your perfect little ass over the kitchen counter and paint it red if I think you need it," I rasp before pressing my lips to the shell of her ear. "I will spend the rest of the night ensuring you can't sit tomorrow if you need me to. But I'd much rather spend it making sure you can't walk."

She swallows hard, her gulp audible. I place a soft kiss just below her earlobe before pushing myself back up to my knees. My palm slides along the length of her spine and over the swell of her ass, settling atop the lone handprint I left on her and roughly squeezing it. "Your choice, princess. Are you done being a brat?"

"Yes, Daddy." Her breathy response is soft and timid, laced with emotion over the elephant in the room. We haven't discussed how or when we're going to break the news to Cian —or what we're going to tell him—leaving us both a bit anxious about tomorrow.

"That's my good girl." I hastily undo the buttons of my shirt and carefully toss it beyond the surrounding candles. I unfasten my belt and zipper with the same urgency, splaying my pants just enough to pull my cock free. Spitting into my hand, I quickly smear it over my tip and drive the entirety of me into her—guttural cries billowing from both of us.

I pull out before plowing into her from behind, her generous ass softens the harsh blows of my hips. She cries out in pleasure with every deep, demanding thrust, hurdling her toward her release. I drive into her, burying myself to the hilt as her orgasm explodes through her. "Yes! Daddy!" she breathlessly screams, her nails digging into the cushions beneath her.

"Shhhh, princess." I urge, slowing to long, languid thrusts. "We wouldn't want the neighbors to hear you and find out what a naughty girl you are. No one else needs to know how much you like all the dirty things Daddy is doing to you."

With my chest pressed to her back, I kiss her neck and shoulders.

Wrapping my hand around her throat, I ease her face from the soft cushions, forcing a beautiful dip of her spine. "You're so fucking gorgeous." I turn her face over her shoulder, and sloppily kiss her, my tongue dragging along her jaw as I make my way to her neck. Licking and sucking along its length, I pause to feel the thuddy beat of her pulse against my tongue, before continuing over her shoulder. She moans and lifts her ass into me as I kiss down her spine, slowly pulling out of her as my lips inch lower.

"You wear my handprint so well." I pepper the words against the fingertips of the deep red mark I left behind. Nudging her legs wider, I press my face against the back of her thighs and lap at the sweet nectar dripping from her. I feast on her until she's a writhing mess—my cock growing more rigid with every orgasm she has on my tongue.

I manage—with a struggle—to rid myself of my pants and boxer briefs. And when I carefully roll her over, her hips lift to meet me when I sink back into her. "Such a needy little pussy," I teasingly groan, taking her with long, deep strokes. She's so sensitive that her body reacts to my every thrust. Sweat beads along her hairline and upper lip. I lick the saltiness from above her mouth and crash my lips against hers. Kissing her until we're both breathless, I pull back with a groan. "Fuck, I could fill you right now..."

"Fuck, I could fill you right now…" Enzo abruptly slowing the speed of his thrusts. "But first, I'm going to spend the night edging myself with your tight little cunt. Fucking you until you're begging me to stop."

He palms my breast with one hand and kisses the other, his fingertips and tongue teasing my nipples in tandem as he quickens his long strokes. His thrusts are rough and relentless, driving us both to the brink. My whole body tenses, the pleasure at my center ready to explode. Enzo sucks hard at my nipple, and the increased sensation is my undoing—my release detonates, my muscles twitching and gasping screams flying from my lungs.

While I struggle to breathe from coming so hard, Enzo fucks me through my euphoria, quickly pulling another orgasm from me. He slams into me—his chest heaving—stilling his hips entirely. "I love fucking you, princess." Kissing the words along the length of my neck through his heaving breaths, he lightly thrusts his hips again.

Enzo demands orgasm after orgasm from me as he uses me to edge himself—repeatedly fucking me hard and fast before stilling until he's ready to do it again. I fist the silk binding me to the railing, ferociously pulling at it as another blissfully painful release shoots through me. Slamming into me, Enzo roughly grips my hips and pulls me tight to him. "Look at you," he grits, clearly in agony and struggling not to come. His hand brushes over my face, pushing back my damp, matted hair as he reaches above me and undoes the tie restraining my wrists. He kisses each of them, placing them each gently beside my head. "So beautiful. Drenched in sweat from being Daddy's perfect little fuck toy. I can't wait to see how breathtaking you are when you're dripping with cum."

"Please, Daddy," I implore, with both exhaustion and need, wrapping my heavy arms around his neck.

Enzo circles his hips, eliciting a breathy groan from me. "You don't have to beg, princess. I can't stop thinking about pumping my babies into you." With his hands tangled in my knotted hair, he kisses me sloppily and swallows my cries as he drives into me without abandon. My thighs shake violently against his hips—each thrust dragging against my overstimulated nerves. "Be a... good girl... and take... all of...

Daddy's cum," he pants between vigorous thrusts, his face contorting in a mixture of pain and pleasure.

Wrapping my legs around his waist, I pull him into me as I come—demanding what he's promised me—and he groans, "Fuuuuuuck." His rigid cock throbs inside me, twitching as it spurts his warm release into me. He crumples on top of me, leisurely thrusting through his cum. Burying himself deep, he wraps his arms around me and holds me tight to him as we lie in silence. My breathing matches his, and I can feel the racing thud of his heart slowing as his cock grows soft inside me.

A cool breeze blows over the balcony, prickling goosebumps along my sweaty skin and causing me to shiver. "You're getting cold, princess," Enzo whispers, with a tinge of concern in his tone. He sits up and pulls me into him, rubbing over my arms. "Come on. Let's get you inside so I can take care of you." Before I can protest, he scoops me into his arms with ease, as though I weigh nothing. With my arms slung tightly around his neck, I squeeze a bit too tightly, worried he might drop me. He tightens his hold and insists, "Relax. I've got you."

He stares down at me as we cross the room, gently lowering me onto the bed when we reach it. The satin sheets are cool, and I flinch as they brush against my skin. Enzo returns to the balcony, quickly extinguishing the candles and pulling the door shut. I watch him move through the dimly lit room— the moonlight accentuating his breathtaking naked form—as he heads into the bathroom.

When he returns, he kneels beside the bed with a wet cloth in hand. His expression is soft as he brushes the hair from my face. "Let me clean you up, princess." I nod, warmth blossoming across my cheeks even though there isn't an inch of me he hasn't seen. It's the intimacy of how he meticulously cleans the sweat from my face before tenderly wiping away the cum smeared across my upper thighs.

After quickly cleaning himself as well, he tosses the towel into the hamper. He climbs into bed beside me, and his arm slips around my waist, pulling me into him. His chest presses to my back, and we curl together like two pieces of a puzzle. We lie in silence, my eyelids growing heavy.

"Are you worried about tomorrow?" Enzo mutters against the back of my shoulder.

"Yeah," I admit, my stomach tightening a little with uncertainty. *How do you tell your brother you're sleeping with his best friend?* "A little."

Enzo exhales slowly, pulling me closer to him. "We'll tell him when the time is right," he says softly. "It doesn't have to be tomorrow."

I chew on my lip with nerves. "Do you think he'll be mad?"

He hesitates. "Yes. At first. He'll get over it, though."

I sigh heavily and drape my arms over his, which are resting on my chest. "It's just... I don't want to lose him... Or you."

"You won't. He'll be mad at me. Not you." His voice is steady—confident. His lips press to the back of my shoulder, and he promises, "And you definitely aren't losing me. I'll do whatever it takes to make him understand that you're mine."

"Maybe don't use the word 'mine.'" I laugh softly and kiss his forearm.

"But you are." He loosens his tight hold and rolls me toward him. Cupping my face, he places a soft kiss against my forehead and another on my nose. His chestnut eyes meet mine, and even in the dim moonlight, I can see the warmth in them. "You are mine."

"Yours," I whisper, kissing the underside of his chin and nuzzling my face into his chest.

He lets out a contented sigh, his fingers tracing lazy circles on my back. "You should get some sleep. I know you're tired."

"Being Daddy's fuck toy is exhausting," I jest, feeling Enzo's chest vibrate against my face when he laughs.

"But you do it so well." His fingers dust along my spine as a lazy smile pulls at the corners of his lips. "Like you were made for me."

"You're just saying that because you want to sleep with me again," I tease, with a playful slap on his chest.

"No," he replies, brushing his thumb along my jaw. "I'm saying that because it's true." He doesn't try to justify his words. He merely holds my gaze, his eyes saying so much that his lips aren't. "Get some sleep, princess."

I settle into him again, head tucked under his chin, body curled into his. His hand dusting tenderly over my back, long and slow strokes, lulling me closer to sleep. My ear pressed to his chest, I listen to the solid, strong beat of his heart beneath me and find myself growing slumbersome again.

"I'm glad you're the one who had to stay with me, Daddy," I murmur, already half-asleep.

"Me too, princess," he whispers.

The front door closes hard enough to rattle through the apartment, yanking me from sleep like a slap to the face. I jolt, blinking against the bright early morning sunlight pouring through the windows.

"Enz!" Cillian's voice booms through the apartment, deep and unmistakable.

"What?" I shout, still groggy, and my voice rough with sleep. My yell causes Eavan to grumble, stirring against me. "Shit," I mumble under my breath.

Eavan.

And her brother—already pissed off about something—is downstairs.

My groggy haze clears instantly, and I sit up, my pulse spiking. Eavan shoots upright, the blanket sliding off her bare chest and panic flashing across her face.

"Cian?" she whisper-shouts, scrambling to glance at the clock on the nightstand. "Shit! Enz! They weren't supposed to be back this early."

"I know," I mumble, throwing off the blanket and hopping out of bed. Eavan is right behind me, tripping over my discarded pants and scrambling across the room, scouring for her clothes.

She finds what's left of her dress and the shredded, sad remnants of her panties from last night—lifting them both and glaring at me accusingly, like I'm the reason she can't put them back on this morning. *I mean, she's not wrong... and I'd do it again in a heartbeat.* I open my mouth to apologize, but she shakes her head with a smirk and drops them back onto the floor. *Clearly, she isn't that upset.* She grabs my gray dress shirt from last night and slips it on, quickly buttoning only what's necessary. I have to force myself to turn away and avoid admiring how good it looks on her. *Not right now.*

I yank on a pair of gray sweats—without bothering to find boxers first—and grab a T-shirt from the dresser. In a few quick strides, I've crossed the room to where she's standing and cup her face, dusting my fingers over her cheeks. "Wait a few minutes," I softly instruct, "then come downstairs."

She nods her understanding.

"Maybe stop by your room to change your shirt," I add, letting a grin spread across my face. She looks down and groans, realizing that she can't exactly parade around the apartment in my clothes without arousing suspicion.

"Shit," she exhales.

"And obviously I like it, but... maybe also a really quick shower to wash off the smell of me. I'll cover for you." I press a kiss to her forehead, hoping to comfort her. "It'll be fine, princess. I promise."

She's chewing at her lower lip—her adorable nervous tell—when I pull away. I grab my phone, finding five missed calls from Cillian, and shove it into my pocket as I cautiously open the bedroom door. Finding the coast clear, I slip into the hall and shut the door behind me. As my nerves start to get the better of me—worried that he somehow knows—I swallow hard before stepping from my door.

I take the first step down the stairs and immediately spot Cillian at the bottom, fists clenched at his sides and about to head up. "What the fuck?" he snaps. "You don't answer your fucking phone?"

"It's 7:00 a.m.," I huff my reply. "Like a normal person, I was still fucking sleeping."

Cillian doesn't look convinced. His face is tight, and his eyes are bloodshot, like he hasn't slept in days. "I need to wake Eavan. This concerns her, too."

"I've got it." Heading back into the hallway, I bang on his bedroom door—knowing it's empty—and raise my voice enough to carry to my room. "Save some water for the rest of us, princess." My words are laced with faux annoyance. "Your brother is back and waiting for you downstairs."

Watching me from the bottom of the stairs with his arms crossed, he sarcastically mutters, "Glad to see the two of you got along while I was gone." *If only you knew, brother...*

I follow him into the kitchen, where Nikolai is already nursing a cup of coffee like it's the only thing keeping him from committing homicide. Automatically, I grab two mugs from the cabinet filling both of them. I am about to grab the cream and sugar before I realize my mistake. "You wanted one, right?" I offer the cup I poured for Eavan to Cillian. He nods, and I slide it across the island to him.

"We haven't heard from either of you in days." I prop my elbows on the edge of the counter and sip my coffee. "Are either of you going to fill me in on what the hell happened?"

Nikolai doesn't look up. "It's probably best if we wait for Eavan." *That doesn't make me feel any better.*

"Wait for me for what?" she asks, walking toward the kitchen. Her hair is dripping wet, and she's wearing a short T-shirt dress—and I exhale a sigh of relief as she slips seamlessly into the conversation.

Cillian pulls her into a hug, squeezing her tighter than I've ever seen him hold anyone. "I'm sorry I had to leave," he apologizes. "Did Enzo treat you okay?"

She answers without hesitation, "He was exhausting to be around, but he took good care of me." I shake my head, fighting against the smile tugging at the corners of my mouth. *Exhausting… That's one way to put it.*

She takes the farthest barstool from me, like she knows being close to me would make it impossible to hide our secret. She's right. I wouldn't be able to keep from touching her. It's already hard enough to keep my eyes off her.

"How was your trip?" she questions, folding her arms.

I echo her, my voice sharper. "Yeah. How *was* your trip? What the hell happened?"

Cillian leans against the counter, jaw clenched. He glances at Nikolai for a moment before speaking. "Everything seemed fine when we first got there," he shares. "We were straight with them—told them we're not looking to get into the trafficking game with them. They acted like they understood."

"But?" I ask.

"But they aren't nearly as understanding about Eavan."

My gut twists. I already know what he's about to say. "What do you mean, *not understanding about Eavan?*"

Cillian's jaw clenches so tightly that I'm surprised he doesn't chip a tooth.

"Davit Sargsyan has a twenty-year-old son," Nikolai answers for Cillian. "They still want the merger between our four families. Which means they still want—"

"Me…" Eavan finishes his sentence, her voice barely audible. Her eyes flick to mine, wide and full of fear.

I want to go to her. Pull her into my arms and tell her it'll never happen. Swear to her that I'll burn the world down before I let anyone lay a hand on her. But I can't. Not with her brother standing three feet away from us. "No," I roughly blurt, unable to stop the word from spilling from my mouth.

Cillian's eyes snap toward me. "What do you mean, no?"

"I mean, it's not happening. We're not selling her off like she's a fucking chess piece," I snarl, my blood beginning to boil. "They only want her to force our... *your* hand in taking on our fathers' promises."

"You think I don't know that?" Cillian snaps. "You think I didn't want to put a bullet between that bastard's eyes when he demanded her like she was an object?" Cillian drags a hand down his face. "We're not agreeing to shit. But we need a plan."

"No plan that involves her," I huff. Eavan sits quietly, her eyes staring at the floor like she's trying not to unravel.

"Agreed." Nikolai's response is quiet but firm. "We just have to figure out how to walk away without starting a war."

If a war is what it takes to protect her. A war is what these fucking assholes are going to get.

I lean back in my seat, willing her to look at me. Just once. I need to let her know she's not alone. That no matter what happens, I've got her. *She's mine, and I will protect her.* She lifts her eyes, and the second those emerald orbs meet mine, I'm gutted. She is terrified, but trying desperately to hold herself together in front of them.

I can't touch her. Can't comfort her. Can't do a damn thing to ease the fear coursing through her veins. But I feel it all the same, in my gut and my chest, with my nails digging into the palms of my tightly bound fists.

I take a slow sip of my coffee, willing myself to stay composed. To think. Because if I let rage speak for me, I'll say something I can't take back.

Nikolai paces, rubbing the back of his neck. *There's more... And it's worse.* Nikolai never fucking paces. "We need to make sure she's not alone. Not ever without someone close by," he says, mostly to Cillian, though his eyes flick toward me, too. "They didn't say it, but the implication was clear. If we don't cooperate, they will act without our permission."

My throat tightens, and I feel like I'm suffocating. "Kidnapping?"

Nikolai nods. "We've seen how they operate out there—behind the curtain of a party neither of us wanted to attend. If they take her, being forced to marry might seem like it would've been a blessing." My fist now clenches so tightly at the thought of her being tossed into a sex trafficking ring that my nails pierce my palm, filling it with blood.

"The three of us can protect her. We can keep her safe." Her eyes flick to mine, and I know she hears what I'm really saying: *I'll protect you. I'll keep you safe.*

My brain can't seem to comprehend the reality before me. I hear the words, but they don't feel real. Arranged marriage or the skin trade—either way, getting raped until there's nothing left.

This can't be my life. I went to bed, wrapped in Enzo, and happier than I've ever been in my entire life. I thought my biggest hurdle was going to be telling Cillian what happened while he was gone. Instead, my world is crumbling, and they're all trying to decide how to keep me safe.

My hands won't stop shaking. My stomach is in knots and feels hollow at the same time. I grip the edge of the island, physically holding on to something to prevent myself from spiraling. I stand up slowly, my knees buckling—the movement taking far more effort than it should. I need air. I need space. To be anywhere that isn't this kitchen with three sets of concerned eyes boring through me. Somewhere Enzo isn't, so I'm not compelled to wrap myself in his arms for comfort.

"I'm gonna go out on the terrace," I manage. "Just for a minute."

Cillian pushes his stool from the island like he's going to follow me, but Nikolai grips his shoulder and shakes his head. "Let her go," he insists. "Give her some time." Cillian exhales a heavy sigh as I walk from the kitchen, but he doesn't move.

I don't look at Enzo as I leave. I can't.

When I step onto the terrace, the crisp morning air assaults my skin. It's brutally cold, but exactly what I needed. I walk to the rail and lean against it—over it a little further than I should. Staring blindly into the city skyline, I fight the urge to cry. A battle I do not win. Tears trickle down my face uncontrollably at the thought of the life the three of them are trying to protect me from.

Their conversation grows loud, and I glance over my shoulder to find all of them animatedly imparting their stance on the matter. Enzo catches my stare, and his harsh expression quickly softens, his eyes suddenly filled with pain. He turns to my brother and Nikolai, shouts something I can't make out, and throws his hands in the air before storming from the kitchen and through the living room.

Not wanting him to see me crying, I turn my eyes back to the city. The door slides open behind me, and I know without a doubt it's Enzo. He moves quietly, his bare feet not making a sound on the terrace stones. I startle when a blanket is draped over my shoulders—thick and warm—his hand lingering on my shoulder. Standing far too close, he dusts down my arm, slow and gentle, until his hand finds mine. He squeezes it and reassuringly whispers his promise, "I'll kill them all to keep you safe."

I don't doubt a word he says, and his conviction is terrifying. Returning his grip on my hand, I close my eyes and fight the urge to bury my face in his chest. "Don't say that."

"Why not?"

"Because I know it's true..."

He lets his hand slip from mine—his fingertips holding onto me as long as possible, like it's physically painful for him to let me go—and his silence says everything I need to know. I lift my head to find him sitting on a lounger a few feet away from me. His eyes are dark and stormy, filled with something I don't have a name for. Something that both calms and unravels me.

"I'm scared," I whisper.

"You're allowed to be, princess. You don't have to pretend to be okay. Not with me." Enzo shifts in his seat, turns away from me, and focuses his attention on the sprawling skyline. From the kitchen, with the distance between us, we probably look more like two strangers than lovers. "But I promise you... I'm not going to let anything happen to you."

As much as I want to believe him, I know the world we live in. It's bloody and ruthless—these brutal men always get exactly what they want. I pull the blanket tighter around me, like it's going to keep me from falling apart, and lean into the railing. Enzo's head falls solemnly to his chest when I softly sob. "Fuck," he mutters. "It's fucking killing me not to be able to wrap my arms around you. To give you just a moment of comfort."

"God... I want that, too," I sigh. *I need it.*

"I'll tell him." Enzo looks at me, and he's serious. *So fucking serious.* Like he's already decided that we are worth it, regardless of the consequences. "I'll take his wrath. Because I'm not walking away from you."

"I'm not walking from you either," I softly insist. "But we can't. Not right now." It's not because I don't feel the same way he does. Or because I don't believe in us. Because, as ridiculous as it is for how little of a time I've known him, I do. *It's Cillian I'm worried about.* "He can't deal with us right now." Glancing through the windows, I find him pacing back and forth like he's trying to wear a groove into the hardwood floor. He is distraught about the predicament our father has left him. One that I know hits too close to home.

I was too young to remember it or even understand it when it happened, but this situation with the Armenians is far too similar to how we lost our mother. Taken by a Balkan gang trying to find a place in this city, thinking they could use her as a bargaining chip to force our father's hand. Only, they grossly overestimated how much he loved his wife—not nearly as much as he loved his empire.

My thoughts drift, and they're dark. "Do you know how our mother died?" I ask, choking around the knot in my throat, worrying that I'll meet the same fate.

Enzo shoots up from his seat and quickly closes every inch of distance between us—my question clearly striking a nerve. Towering over me, his heated breath blows from his flaring nostrils and over my face. *He's too close...* My eyes dart into the apartment, making sure Cillian isn't watching. "Don't look at him. Look at me," Enzo barks, demanding my attention without laying a finger on me. "I know you're scared and overwhelmed right now, so I'm going to let that go. But I do not appreciate your downplaying of what I feel for you, princess. *I* am *nothing* like your father."

"Enz..." I mutter, my heart breaking at how upset he is—how hurt.

"You are not discardable. Do you understand me? I would walk away from everything this second if it meant I didn't need to worry about your safety. And if you can't see that yet, then I'm clearly not doing a good enough job of showing you."

He slips his hand inside the blanket and leisurely drags his knuckles along the curve of my hip. "You're mine, princess," he whispers, his dark chocolate eyes locked on mine and his gaze searing through my soul, as his ire subsides. "Nothing in this world will keep me from you. Not your brother. Not some fucking Armenians. Nothing. Understood?"

"Yes." I nod, swallowing down the tightness in my throat. "Yes, Daddy."

My fingers rest against the curve of her hip, under the thin throw blanket I wrapped her in. It's reckless, but I can't bring myself to pull my hand away. It clings to her like the late-spring frost on the metal railing running the length of the terrace.

A turn of Cillian's head and this moment—our secret—will be over. Worse than over if he finds me standing close enough to press my lips to hers. Yet, I can't stop touching her. Three days ago, I caved—putting my lips and hands on her for the first time. *Three fucking days.* That's all it took for her to become the center of my universe—a fucking gravitational pull I can't tear myself away from. I've barely gone more than a moment without having her soft skin against my hands or pouty lips pressed to mine.

"I'll wait to tell Cian," I murmur, keeping my voice low and fighting the urge to dip my head to taste the lips lingering below me. "Because I get where he's at right now. We can wait until things settle *a little* with the Armenians. But I'm not sneaking around forever, princess."

"Thank you," she whispers.

I nod, barely. "It's too cold for you to be out here dressed like that," I gruff. "You need to head back inside."

"What about you?"

"You go first." I lightly tap her hip. "I'll be right behind you." I let my hand linger a moment longer—another second of her touch I can't sacrifice—then slide away and tuck it into the pocket of my sweats.

As I instructed, she walks from me to head inside, pausing at the glass door to glance over her shoulder. *Fuck... That look.* The things I would give for those loving green eyes and the way they look at me. *Like she knows she's mine.*

Pacing slowly along the railing, I count to one hundred and hope the cold will knock some sense back into me. Everything about her—*us*—is reckless. Messy. Risking absolutely everything, especially now. But if I'm being honest with myself, I don't care.

A few minutes later, I slip back inside the apartment, finding the tension filling the room as thick as it was when I stepped onto the terrace. The scent of coffee still hangs in the air, mixing with the faint smell of leather from the still-new couches. I fill a mug with the last of the pot, the nutty dark liquid radiating heat against my palm as I carry it into the living room.

Cillian is slouched deep into the cushions of the couch, his face weary and eyes heavy, exhausted from both the situation with the Armenians and his travels. With the blanket still wrapped tightly around her, Eavan is sitting beside him. I take a seat at the other end of the sectional and settle in like it's just another morning.

"You all right?" Cillian asks, glancing at me.

"Yeah." I sip my coffee. "Just needed a little air." He watches me for a moment longer than necessary, like he's waiting for the rest of a sentence I'm not saying. The words I promised Eavan I would keep to myself a little longer. Letting out a heavy sigh, he leans back into the couch.

"I'm not leaving again," he promises Eavan, his voice lower and more solemn. "Not unless I have absolutely no other choice."

"You don't have to protect me from everything." Eavan shakes her head at him before her eyes momentarily dart to me. She's not saying it, but she knows. He doesn't have to, because I will.

"I'm your brother," he mutters. "It's something I should've been doing a much better job of."

"And I love you for it, Cian." Her eyes glance my way again, quickly. "But you're not alone in this, okay? This isn't all on you."

Cillian nods, his eyes flicking between the two of us. "I know."

The quiet that follows is laced with discomfort. *My discomfort.* I sip my coffee to fill the silence, but my thoughts keep drifting to her. The way she looked at me before she went inside. The way her skin feels against mine. And how I don't know if I'll survive keeping this secret and not having her touch whenever I want.

Nikolai walks downstairs with wet hair and clean clothes—a renewed vigor in his step. He drops onto the couch beside me and leans forward with his elbows on his knees. "We need to talk about security," he insists. "This place has been our little secret for years, and we've been lax as fuck."

"You're right." I nod, having already gone down this trail of thought myself.

Eavan got upstairs without a problem. A polite nod to the doorman, a short ride in the elevator, and she was standing at our front door. Reinforced or not, if she made it up here that effortlessly, anyone could. The thought turns my stomach—knowing how easily someone could get to my princess.

"I'll make a call to the building manager," Cillian informs us. "Tell him we'll pay whatever it takes to install more security— restrict elevator access, lock down the floor, the whole thing."

"I know some guys," Nikolai adds. "Ex-military, special

forces. Real disciplined. Don't ask, don't tell kind of guys. Not the kind to flinch if things go sideways."

I shake my head—*that so doesn't mean what he thinks it does*—and raise an inquisitive eyebrow. "Mercenaries," I clarify. "How the fuck do you know guys like that?"

He shrugs. "Where the fuck do you think the guns come from? You think they fall off trucks and walk themselves in?"

I chortle. "With your luck? Maybe."

Cillian doesn't even crack a smile. "We stay inside for now," he insists, eventually. "If they're watching us, we don't give them anything."

"We can't," I remind him. "The meeting with all our families is supposed to happen tonight. They're all waiting for us to provide confirmation and a location. It's been days since our fathers' untimely passings, and this meeting has to happen tonight.

"He's right." Nikolai agrees. "We need to know where they stand. If they're gearing up to make a move, we need to be prepared."

"They've all been quiet. Too quiet," I add.

"They're waiting to see what we do." Cillian nods in agreement. "We put it off long enough to deal with the Armenians. We can't make them wait any longer. Can you get a few of your guys here by tonight?"

"Yeah." Nikolai pulls his cell phone from his pocket, promptly making the arrangements we need.

She shifts on the couch, drawing her knees to her chest under the blanket. She's been quiet for the last few minutes, just listening. For it being so early in the day, she already looks tired—worn at the edges. I want to tell her to lie down, because I know she won't unless someone makes her. But I can't.

"I'm gonna grab a shower," I mutter, rising from the couch. Walking the length of the sofa toward the spiral staircase, I run my hand along the back of it and ever so slightly brush my fingers against the back of Eavan's shoulder when I stride past her. She's motionless as she lets out a soft exhale.

The water in the shower is blistering hot, but it doesn't burn out the restlessness crawling under my skin. I brace my hands against the tile wall and let the steam choke the bathroom. Images of Eavan in my bed flit through my mind, and I find my hand wrapping around my cock as though I have no control over either of them.

Closing my eyes and pressing my forehead to the cool shower surround, I aggressively fist myself from base to tip. It's a sore substitute for where I had planned to bury my cock this morning—one last time for us to be alone together before Cillian and Nikolai came home. Wanting to fill my sweet little princess full of cum and knowing that even if I couldn't touch her, she'd be spending her day feeling me drip from her. Finishing quickly and wasting my seed when it spills over my hand, I breathlessly mutter, "Eavan..."

The soles of my dress shoes echo heavily against the hardwood as I descend the stairs, and the cold steel of my Glock presses against my ribs beneath my suit jacket, a silent reminder of the world I live in—and of the stakes tonight.

Eavan stands alone in the kitchen, her fingers lightly rolling the base of her stemless wine glass along the granite countertop where she stands at the island. The hem of her skirt grazes the curve of her thigh, and for a second, I forget everything else.

I cross the space between us like a man possessed. She looks up as I reach her, surprise flashing in her eyes as her mouth starts to speak. I crash into her, lifting her effortlessly and roughly placing her on the counter. My mouth finds hers with violent urgency, swallowing her gasp as I crash my lips onto hers.

The faint taste of Merlot on her soft lips ruins me. My hands fist into her red locks, pulling her tighter, needing her closer. She grips the front of my suit jacket like she's holding on for dear life, and I wish I could stay here. Between her knees. Tasting her. Claiming her.

"I've been thinking about these lips all day, princess," I breathlessly whisper, my forehead pressed against hers. "All fucking day just trying to find a moment alone with you."

Pulling at my lapels, she drags me back into her. I don't fight her—I want to be lost in her, no matter how reckless it is. "Not touching you is fucking unbearable," I groan, kissing her again. Slower this time, but deeper. So fucking deep that I'm leaving a piece of my soul in her as I plunder her mouth.

One of the bedroom doors slams upstairs—*shit*—and I begrudgingly break away from her. Still panting, my hands reluctantly slip from her hair and slide down her body as I lower her to the floor. Her toes barely brush the hardwood before I step back. I position myself on the other side of the kitchen island just as Nikolai appears at the top of the stairs. Immediately followed by Cillian.

Eavan's cheeks are flushed, and her lips are swollen. Her eyes burn into mine as Nikolai and Cillian join us in the kitchen. *God, I want her again.* Every part of me aches for her. I turn my attention to them as they step up to the island. "We ready?"

"Yeah," Cillian responds, sweeping around the island and pulling Eavan into a brotherly hug. "There are guys outside to keep an eye on you until we get back. We might be late. Okay?"

She squeezes him back, her eyes never leaving mine as she insists, "Be careful and come home safe."

I nod. Just enough that she knows that I intend to uphold that promise.

"If we're done with all this mushy family shit, let's go," Nikolai barks.

The last of us to leave the kitchen, I walk close to Eavan—too close—and let my fingers trail across hers. Just a whisper of contact. Our hands curl together for the briefest second, sending a bolt of electricity zipping up my arm. Her breath hitches, and I agonizingly slip my fingers from hers, pretending that my entire body doesn't ache, leaving her behind.

The ride into Chelsea is quiet. Just like the last time. No music. No unnecessary conversation. Just the roar of the engine and the anticipation humming beneath our skin.

Cillian sits shotgun, tapping his hand against his knee. Nikolai drives, and his face in the rearview is emotionless, eyes sharp, watching every car we pass like he's memorizing license plates. I sit behind him, my ringed fingers bouncing off my thigh. This isn't just a meeting. This is *the* meeting to forge our families together.

Nikolai pulls to a stop before a vacant but familiar warehouse. His family has used it for years—gun running and interrogations. Tonight, it has a different purpose. It's our boardroom.

Arriving before the men of our organizations, we step into the dimly lit space, and our footsteps echo against the concrete of the vast empty building. The faint scent of oil, metal, and dust clings to the air. No chairs. No table. Just the three of us standing in the middle of the room.

One by one, they start showing up—Irish, Italian, Bratva— their eyes darting between us and at each other as they file in with suspicious glances. The growing crowd is filled with grumbles and muttered threats, a few of the men already reaching for the grips of their pistols. None of them were told what tonight was. They don't know why they've been summoned to this meeting of rivals. But they showed up, which means they're smart enough to know that, individually, we're in charge of our families now.

"What the fuck is this?" someone shouts with a thick Irish accent.

"Is this some kind of joke?" An unfamiliar Italian-accented deep voice billows through the crowd. "We're supposed to meet with *them*?"

The noise rises like a wave—accusations, curses, and questions—building to a deafening level. "Enough!" I shout, my voice slicing through the chaos in the room, everyone falls silent and their eyes shift toward me.

"Why the feck should we listen to you, asshole?" a voice growls from the back.

Cillian steps forward, flanking my right side. "Because you're listening to *us*."

Nikolai moves to the left, his expression as tight as his grip on the gun tucked into his waistband. One wrong move and he'll paint the walls with someone's blood—where everyone can see it. "*All* of us."

Eyes widen and breaths are held as the three of us stand shoulder to shoulder—unshakable. I glance around the room, making eye contact with every man who dared show up tonight. Some look nervous. Others are confused. But none of them speak.

"There are no Italians," I begin, voice low but steady. "No more Bratva. No more Irish. Those days are over. As of tonight, there's only one family. *Ours*."

Shock rolls through the warehouse like a tide. "Bullshit!" someone spits. "You can't fucking do th—"

Without hesitation, Nikolai draws his gun and fires a shot before the man can finish his sentence. The dissenter crumples to the floor as the single shot echoes off the metal walls. The silence that follows is absolute—our message is crystal clear.

"We can do anything we fucking want," Nikolai coolly retorts, tucking his pistol back into the waistband of his pants.

"You think this city can survive divided?" I ask, stepping forward and filling the silence with purpose. "We've spent years killing each other, wasting time, wasting resources. It ends tonight. You're either with us, or you're a fucking ghost by morning."

"This is a new world," Cillian adds. "You fall in line, or we erase you. Plain and simple."

"We aren't asking for your loyalty," I continue, watching the sea of nodding and uncertain faces. "We're fucking demanding it. Our fathers are dead, and *we* are taking their place."

"We are going to rule this fucking city," Nikolai finishes, his voice like gravel.

A low voice cuts through the crowd—Marco, one of the older soldiers under my father, steps forward with hesitation etched across his face. His hat is clenched tightly in his hand, eyes flickering between the three of us, like he's still trying to decide if it's safe to speak his thoughts. "What about the funerals?" he asks quietly. "Your father built this life for us. He deserves something."

The silence that follows is sharp. Cillian shifts slightly, but I hold up a hand before he can say anything. My eyes lock on Marco's. "There aren't any funerals," I answer, calm but firm. "They were cremated. All three of them. No names, no services. Ashes scattered before sunrise." A few people look around, unsettled—it wasn't the most Catholic thing to do. Someone opens their mouth to protest, but I keep going. "We don't know who was behind their deaths. Not yet. And until we do, we're not publicly putting all our families in one place for someone to take another shot. We're not giving anyone the chance to finish what they started."

"You want to honor them?" Cillian barks, his eyes sweeping across the room. "Then merge our families together. Take everything they built and make it stronger. That's how you fucking honor them." *Let them, because the three of us aren't.*

For a long moment, the crowd is silent and unwavering. Then someone in the back—an older man from the Irish family— lowers his gaze and nods. Then another. And another. We didn't ask for permission. We fucking took it. We are the kings of this city now. Three devils at the head of one family —united, ruthless, and unchallenged.

The meeting ends with a quiet acceptance. Our men filter out slowly, whispering and murmuring among themselves. As the last man leaves, Nikolai mutters, "That's fewer dead bodies than I was expecting."

"It's early," Cillian exhales. "There's no way they all just roll over and obey."

He's right. And fuck do I hate how right he is. "This is just the beginning," I agree. We're going to be fighting a war on multiple fronts—disgruntled family members and the Armenians.

And all I can think about is her. *Eavan.* The way her lips felt against mine, and the way her fingers curled into my jacket like she never wanted to let go. We may have just claimed the city, but I'd give it all away for one more kiss.

A loud, boisterous peal of laughter from outside the apartment jolts me from my sleep. My eyes snap open, heart racing, and I find myself alone in the dim, quiet living room. It takes me a second to place the noise that startled me awake —Nikolai's guys in the hallway. If they're going for inconspicuous, they're failing miserably. They were quite animated in their conversations all night, and apparently, they didn't tire as morning rolled in.

Sitting up, my neck immediately protests having fallen asleep on the couch and the position I twisted myself into—one arm wedged under my head and my legs tangled in something warm and soft. *A duvet.* Blinking away the last traces of sleep,

I recognize the smooth, black fabric immediately. It's from Enzo's bed. It smells like him, too—woodsy and sharp, with a spicy undercurrent of ginger. He must've covered me up.

That means, they're back.

My breath blows from my lungs, shaky and full of relief. I clutch the duvet tighter, pulling it to my face and breathing him in. It does nothing to relieve the aching longing in my chest. I wish desperately I were upstairs in his bed, instead of sleeping out here on the couch and pretending this blanket is enough. I want to be in his arms and surrounded by his warmth. I imagine his hands at my waist and his mouth at my ear, whispering the dirty things that make me melt for him. The way he kissed me before he left keeps looping in my mind —possessive and desperate. Like he couldn't stand the thought of leaving me behind.

I hadn't meant to fall asleep. I tried to stay up, to be ready in case anything went wrong. I'd paced the floors for hours, heart lodged in my throat, replaying every worst-case scenario I could imagine. Because no one woke me, I assume they're all here. All three of them. Safe. Alive.

Cillian is the first to make his way downstairs, quickly clanging around the kitchen. Likely making the one breakfast meal he knows how to—toast and eggs. Padding barefoot into the kitchen, I stretch my neck and rub my hand along the aching muscles. "And now you see why I'm so eager to get my bed back," Cillian teases.

"If this is how you feel every morning, I'm half tempted to give it back to you."

"Don't be ridiculous." Cillian cracks eggs into a bowl, whisking them as I fix myself a cup of coffee. "I'm reaching out to some contractors today to remodel the office and the guest bath. It'll be a little smaller than you're used to, but it'll give you space—privacy. And get me my bed back."

Nik and Enzo filter downstairs as though their stomachs are drawing them to Cillian's scrambled eggs. Nik grabs a cup of coffee and sips it at the island, silently scrolling through his phone. Leaning against the fridge, with his eyes locked on me, Enzo sips his black coffee. I pretend not to notice—falsely willing myself to believe that my pulse doesn't tick a bit faster every time I spy his eyes still on me. Not one of them says a word about the meeting last night. I want to ask, but I also don't want to know. The drama with the Armenians is more than enough for me right now. I don't know if I can handle any more.

Cillian plates breakfast for us all, and we take seats at the island—Cillian, then Nikolai, then Enzo... then me. Enzo's barstool is closer to me than it needs to be, and his thigh brushes against mine beneath the counter. Every little touch feels like a fire. His knee taps mine, and his fingers graze over my thigh, just beyond Cillian and Nikolai's view. Tiny fleeting moments, but I feel them everywhere. His touch causes my body to react instinctively—my heart racing, breath hitching, and the fluttering between my thighs.

Nikolai tells some ridiculous story about the time he and Cillian stole a truckload of vodka from down at the docks. Cillian—as expected—stays straight-faced, unimpressed with Nikolai's recollection of events. I smile on cue and laugh when I'm supposed to, but my entire focus is on Enzo—tracking every breath he takes and the subtle shifts of his body beside mine.

His fingers roam high up my inner thigh. My lips part and let out a tiny gasp before I can catch it. From the corner of my eye, his jaw clenches at my reaction to him. But the others are completely unaware—they don't see or say a thing. Reaching over me to grab the pepper, his lips press dangerously close to the shell of my ear, and he whispers, "You're driving me insane, princess. All I can think about right now is eating you on this counter."

Startled, I swallow hard and suck in a breath, squeezing my thighs together in a futile attempt to quell the desire he just ignited. He shifts back into his seat and sprinkles pepper over his remaining bites of eggs, a smirk tugging at the corner of his mouth like he didn't just set me on fire. *Asshole.*

I spend all day trying to get a moment alone with him, but it's impossible. This massive apartment feels too small—Cian and Nik are constantly wherever we are. Enzo is repeatedly pulled into calls—actually, the three of them are—pacing the apartment with that low, commanding voice that makes my skin tingle. Regardless of how busy or crowded we are, his eyes always find mine. Across the kitchen. Beyond the windows from the terrace. A glance. An ogle when he can. A spark that grows with every stare—until I'm *burning*.

Muttering something about needing a pen, I sneak into his room. It's a flimsy, transparent excuse. But I don't care. His room is dark, the curtains drawn tight. It smells like him—

stronger and more dangerous. I run my fingers along the edge of the mattress, my pulse suddenly racing.

I don't hear the door open behind me, but I *feel* him. I turn slowly, finding him standing in the doorway, framed by the fluorescent light from the hall. His eyes are locked on me, the dark chocolate pools full of ravenous hunger. He closes the door behind him and steps toward me, unhurried.

"What are you doing in here?" His voice is low. Controlled. Like a dam about to break.

"You know," I whisper so softly that it's barely audible.

"I know?" he teases and keeps coming.

He stops in front of me, so close I can feel the heat radiating off his body. He reaches up, brushing a strand of hair behind my ear, his thumb lingering on my cheek. "This is fucking hell," he exhales, his warm breath blowing over my face.

"I've been trying to get you alone all day."

"You think I don't know that, princess?" he murmurs. His hand slides to my waist, tugging me against him like it's nothing—a gasp blows from me when I slam against his firm body. His mouth hovers just above mine, close enough that I can practically feel his lips.

I fist his shirt and press onto my toes to close the distance between us. "They'll hear us."

"Let them." His lips brush my cheek, maddeningly close yet so far from where I want them. He dips his head, his lips feathering against mine as a crash erupts from the kitchen—both of us freeze as Cillian yells and Nikolai curses. "Later," Enzo groans softly, pressing his forehead to mine. Pulling back, his jaw is tight with restraint. "Go help them with dinner. They clearly need it."

Doing as he asks, I head downstairs to find complete chaos in the kitchen. "I'm not eating that," I huff, crossing my arms, taking in the burned chicken sizzling on the counter. "Maybe stick with the scrambled eggs a while longer before moving onto more advanced culinary skills," I tease.

"I'm not eating that either." Nik scrunches his face, swiping through his phone. "I have a strict rule about not eating anything I almost had to use the fire extinguisher on. I'm ordering us pizza."

The boys all tell jokes and ridiculous stories through dinner. It's easy and lighthearted—at least it appears that way. I'm still restless and burning from the inside out. An issue that only intensifies when Enzo meets my gaze across the table.

As it gets late, everyone retreats to their rooms—me to Cillian's with him on the couch again. I curl up in bed, wrapping myself in the blankets, my book open in my lap, untouched because the words are a blur. All I can think about is Enzo's hands on my thighs. His mouth on my neck. The way he keeps looking at me like he's seconds from losing control.

The apartment grows dark and quiet, but I don't sleep.

I wait.

For one more stolen moment.

Hoping. Aching. Burning.

TWO DAYS LATER

Lying awake in bed, my hands laced behind my head, I stare up at the ceiling and listen to the soft, distant hum of the city beneath us. The apartment is completely silent, except for the steady and occasional loud snoring of Cillian, completely passed out cold on the couch in the living room.

I've lain here for an hour with my door open, both waiting for the silence and hoping desperately that the urge to storm into Eavan's room would pass. The ache for her definitely hasn't dwindled. Every minute that I've waited has only fueled my need to stride down the hall. After two days of stolen glances, and fleeting touches, I'm fucking hard as hell at the mere thought of putting my hands on her soft body.

Fuck it!

After sliding from bed, I step into the hall and walk to Eavan's room. I pause to glance into the living room to ensure Cillian is asleep before gripping the knob and silently pushing it open, slipping within the darkness cloaking the room. Closing it behind me with barely a click, I stand in the dark shadows of the corner for a moment and watch her. "Are you awake, princess?"

"Enz..." She groggily whimpers my name into the darkness, barely roused awake.

"I'll take that as a not really," I mumble to myself with a smile, clinging to the wall like it's the only thing keeping me from doing what I want. Taking what I need. She rolls onto her pillow, the movement pulling at the blankets and causing them to slide from her hip. The moonlight filtering through the floor-to-ceiling windows dances over her alabaster skin. She groans my name again, and I find every bit of restraint draining from my body with each passing second.

Locking the door and stripping off my clothes, I climb onto the bed and slip beneath the covers. A soft, raspy moan rattles from her as I press against her. "Please, Daddy," she murmurs so softly I almost don't hear it above the rustling of the sheets as I pull them over us.

"Are you dreaming about me, princess?" I ask, a smile tugging at my lips. Gingerly, I roll her onto her back and settle between her thighs without waking her. I rest my rigid cock against the warmth of her wet pussy. *Apparently, it's a really good fucking dream.* Dipping my head, I brush my lips softly against hers and swipe her hair from her face. The touch startles her awake, and she sucks in a startled deep breath. I clamp my hand over her mouth seconds before she releases it in a scream. "Shhhh. It's just Daddy," I soothe.

"Enz? What are you doing here?" she grumbles sleepily against my palm as I slowly pull it back from her mouth.

"You need me so badly, you're in here dreaming about me fucking you. So excited at the thought of it, that my tight little pussy is ready for me to slip my thick cock inside you without me even touching you." I arch my hips backward until the head of my cock is resting against her dripping entrance. "And I can't go another night without you."

"Daddy..." She gulps nervously.

"Daddy isn't asking, princess," I hoarsely whisper, gathering her wrists above her head and lightly pinning them to the mattress. "Do I need to hold you down and force myself into that tight little hole? Or are you going to be a good girl and let me play with what's mine?"

Her eyes darting to the locked door and tugging against my hold, she pleads, "We can't."

With her hands in my left hand, I grip her hip with my right and ease myself inside her. *Fucking perfection.* "No, princess. We *shouldn't*," I softly correct, inching deeper as she struggles to take me. "Now, be a good girl and let Daddy stretch you out so I can fill you up."

"They're gonna hear…" she gruffly whispers, her brows furrowing in worry as I sink inside her.

"If you don't want them to know what a naughty girl you are, you better be quiet," I grit, burying myself to the hilt and stifling my own moan. "Do you think you can be quiet while Daddy fucks you?" Biting her lower lip and staring up at me through her lashes, she timidly nods. She's wrong—and I plan to prove it—but her gesture is hot as fucking hell.

Easing back, I slam the entirety of me into her with a single fast stroke. She lets out a gasping squeak as I bottom out inside her. I repeat the motion, steadily increasing the speed of my retreat until I'm driving into her to with sheer feral need. Her whimpers and cries grow louder with every brutal thrust. "You said you were going to be quiet for Daddy," I pant, lacing my fingers and clamping my hands over her mouth and nose, muffling her cries and stealing her breath as I take her even harder. "We wouldn't want anyone to hear the beautiful noises you make when you come for me."

I fuck her savagely, needing to feel her quivering around me. Starved for oxygen, her orgasm comes hard and fast. The screams of her release heat my palms, and her entire body detonates beneath me. I thrust deep and still, buried to the hilt, enjoying the rhythmic convulsions of her walls around my cock.

Letting my laced fingers slide apart, my hands slide down her ruddy cheeks. Her chest heaves as she sucks a few desperate breaths into her starved lungs. "I'm sorry if I was too rough, princess," I mumble against her lips, pressing my forehead to hers. "I've been thinking about making you come for fucking days, and I couldn't fucking wait anymore."

I drag my tongue between her lips and ease it into her mouth. Taking my time, I kiss her slow and deep—my hands roaming her body with my cock buried deep inside her. My kiss travels along her jaw until my lips are pressed below her ear. "Daddy wants to fuck both your pouty lips tonight," I gravelly whisper in her ear, slipping my cock from her.

"I... Uh..." she stammers as I pull her up to her to a kneeling position and stand on the bed before her. With her lack of experience, I assumed she'd never sucked a cock before but her reaction confirms it. And I quite like the idea of being her first. Teaching her how to use her mouth to please me. *And only me.*

"I'll talk you through it," I encourage, stroking the side of her face and easing her onto her hands and knees. "Open those beautiful lips nice and wide for Daddy." She promptly does as she's told, the pale pink of her tongue darting out just far enough that the tip rests on her lower lip. With my hand wrapped around the base of my shaft, I place the head on her tongue and watch as her lips instinctively close around it. "Lick and suck the tang of your greedy cunt from me," I instruct, pressing an inch more into her mouth so that my tip is resting on the flat of her warm, wet tongue.

She slowly licks at the underside of my shaft and lightly sucks her arousal from me. Her tongue swirls around my tip, and my hips buck forward from both the surprise and the finesse of her movement. "Fuck, you're being such a good girl for me," I praise as she begins tentatively bobbing her mouth over the first few inches of me. "Opening so wide for me. And so fucking eager to learn how to suck my cock."

With my hand lightly cupping the back of her head, I guide her movements—helping her to take me slow and steady. "Always so eager to please me," I pant through labored breaths. "Is there anything you wouldn't do for me?"

She slides her mouth up my shaft until my head is resting against her lips. "No, Daddy." Her words vibrate against the sensitive tip of my cock. "I want to be a good girl for you."

"You look so fucking beautiful on your knees with my cock in your mouth." I dust my fingers along her jaw. "I can't wait to teach you how to swallow me down your throat, so I can use this hole how I please, too." She teasingly suckles on my tip, staring up at me with widening eyes. Reaching over her, I run my hand down her spine, my fingers trailing to her last virgin hole as she continues to suck me. "This one, too, princess."

After pulling from her mouth, I press my lips to hers. I kiss her tenderly, my tongue slipping between them, as I ease her onto her back on the mattress. "I'll try to be more gentle this time," I half-heartedly promise, kissing down the length of her neck and sliding my saliva-coated cock into her pussy. A promise I don't know if I'm capable of keeping.

"I fucking love being buried inside you," Enzo groans against my neck, leisurely thrusting into me. "I can't get enough of you. And I don't know if I ever will."

As I stare up at him, I can't get enough either. Especially the way he looks at me—absolute adoration. Slowly closing the distance between us, he brushes his lips against mine and kisses me with the same languidity that he's claiming my body. There's no rush. Just slow, careful exploration—full of affection and desire. The connection we've ached for in the days since Cillian and Nikolai's return when we couldn't touch each other.

He worships me for what feels like hours, whispering his unfettered devotion—his hands and mouth explore my body as I come for him again and again. "Enz... Daddy..." I plead his name, the pleasure he's providing slowly becoming almost unbearable.

"Just a little more for me," Enzo peppers the words across my cheek, picking up his pace. "Can my good girl give me just a little bit more?"

I struggle to give him my answer, eventually squeaking out, "Yes, Daddy."

Holding himself above me on one arm, he beams at me with pride. His fingers slip into my hair and he tenderly lifts my head—steering my gaze to where our bodies meet. "Watch your sweet pussy swallow my cock," he demands, repeatedly thrusting every inch of his length into me. "Watch us as I fuck a baby into you."

My body reacts to his words in ways I can't even describe. Suddenly teetering at the edge of pleasure and pain again, I cry, "Please, Daddy."

"Are you begging for my cum, princess? Do you want me to spill myself inside you?"

"Yes..." I pant with need.

His already dark eyes burn with hunger, and he breathlessly grits, "Tell me. Tell me how much you want it."

"I want you to fill me," I groan, my fingers digging into the rippling muscles of his back. "Fill me until I grow round for you."

His eyes darken, and he drives into me without abandon. He slams into me for a few more thrusts and roars, "Fuck!" His cock throbs inside my quivering pussy as he violently spills into me. He lays my head on the mattress and engulfs me with his body, his lips immediately finding mine. His hand cups my cheek, and I rub my face deeper into his palm. "One day, princess..." he mumbles through our kiss, my heart swelling at the ridiculous notion. One he sounds so certain of.

His softening cock slides from me, and he rolls us both onto our sides. I press my hand to his chest, the steady beat of his heart pulsing against my palm. "This is crazy," I exhale, as much to myself as to him. Because it is. The two of us simply being together is preposterous. The speed at which I'm falling for him—*and him for me*—is absolutely absurd. But it doesn't matter how illogical it is, because there's no stopping it.

"Maybe," Enzo laments, pressing his forehead against mine and running his calloused hands along my back. The way he says it is so nonchalant—like it doesn't matter in the slightest. He pulls me tighter to him, and the world shrinks around us, to nothing more but the two of us wrapped in each other on this bed.

Pulling back from him just enough to see his face, I confess, "I missed you." I feel foolish the moment the words pass over my lips. *It's not like he was gone.* But since Cillian and Nikolai came home, things haven't been the same.

"I missed you, too, princess." He drags me back into him, pressing my face against his chest. "I fucking hate this. Having you right next to me and knowing that I can't touch you."

Lying together in the dark, the room grows silent as we cling to each other, stealing every last second of touch that we can. Both of us know he can't stay in here. The chance of getting caught is far too risky.

I fit against him, tucking into the space at his side, nuzzling my head against his shoulder with his arm wrapped around my back. "Enz?" I mutter groggily, fighting my heavy eyelids to stay in this moment with him. "Why'd you risk giving me your blanket last night?"

"You looked cold," he softly quips, placing a tender kiss against the top of my head.

"Seriously..." I press, trying not to fidget and make this more awkward than I fear I already have.

"Eavan, princess..." Enzo tightens his hold on me. "Are you trying to rationalize this? To make sense of me? Of us?"

I don't deny it. I can't.

"Wanting to be your Daddy goes far beyond sex and this insatiable need to have my hands on you," he discloses. "Yes, there's a physical side, but it's so much more than that. I want to care for you. Protect you. Guide you. Help you grow."

"And your handprints on my ass helps me grow?" I tease.

"Yes, my bratty little princess." I can *hear* the smile spreading on his face through his tone. "Discipline is a form of love, not punishment. It's to remind you that rules and structure are there for your benefit. And right now, most of them are geared toward ensuring I can keep you safe."

I swallow hard, my chest tightening at his reminder of the danger that I'm in. His fingers draw idle lines on the back of my arm—every touch grounding and easing the pressure in my chest—the tenderness undoing me.

My fingers move on their own, reaching for his. He doesn't hesitate. His hand closes around mine like it belongs there as our fingers lace together. I gently squeeze his hand and nuzzle closer to him.

He presses his lips to the top of my head and exhales slowly. "As much as I want to stay in here with you, I can't."

"I know." As much as I hate it, I can't argue. Cillian would kill us if he walked in on this.

Holding me snug to him, he lightly strokes my hair. "You should try to sleep," he murmurs.

"I don't want to." I shake my head, fighting both my grogginess and his instruction. "I don't want to fall asleep knowing that I'm going to wake up alone."

"You need to," his voice is soft and tender. "I'll stay as long as I can. And know that I hate the idea of sliding from this bed. It pains me as much as it does you."

I pour myself a cup of coffee as the events of last night replay in my thoughts, and I can't help but smile, still feeling the softness of Eavan lingering on my lips. The sudden warmth of my mug against my palm tears me from my thoughts.

When I turn from the coffee maker, I'm surprised to find myself staring across the kitchen at Nikolai. He's standing at the island, arms crossed and eyes narrowed—his eyes rolling over me with suspicion. "You're up early," I blurt, lifting the cup to my lips.

"Couldn't sleep," he replies, his tone clipped. "Had a lot on my mind."

I raise an eyebrow, adjusting my grip on the white mug in my hands. "And what's that?"

He steps further into the kitchen, his gaze never leaving me. "Last night. I heard you."

My stomach tightens, but I mask it and play it off. "No," I feign a scoff. "That ridiculous snoring was Cian."

Nikolai lets out a heavy exhale. "Don't play coy with me, Enzo," he whisper-shouts, so we don't wake Cillian, who's still sleeping in the living room. "Cillian is going to murder you when he finds out you're fucking his little sister."

I take a slow sip of my coffee, buying myself a moment to compose myself before responding. "How did you find out?"

"Find out?" He arches a brow, silently asking if my question is facetious. "It wasn't exactly hard to figure out. She was screaming 'Daddy' loud enough to wake the dead." He laughs. But behind the humor is a warning: If he knows, it's only a matter of time before Cillian puts it together. And when he does... *Yeah. That's a bloodbath waiting to happen.* Thank fucking God, Cillian sleeps like the dead.

Nikolai leans in slightly, his voice dropping to a low grumble. "You know that sleeping with Cian's little sister is fucking foolish. Maybe one of the stupidest fucking things you've ever done."

I set the mug down with deliberate care, my eyes not once breaking his stare. "Maybe."

"Maybe?" he scoffs, shaking his head. "Are you fucking

serious? It's a betrayal, Enzo. You know damned well that Cillian won't approve."

His words cut through me painfully, because they're true. All of them. I know I'm betraying one of my closest friends. *My family.* But deep down, I also know that Cillian won't approve, and that goes far beyond Eavan being his little sister. He knows what kind of man I am. *Or was.* He knows about the countless, meaningless women who passed through my bed over the years. Why would he think that his sister would be anything more to me? Fuck... even *I* don't know why she's different. *But she is.*

Nikolai steps closer, his presence imposing. "He was really fucking clear when she got here, Enz. Eavan is off limits."

"I know..." I lean against the counter, crossing my arms with a heavy grumble. "But you don't understand."

"And you think he will?" Nikolai quietly snaps. "He'll find out. And when he does, that fallout... It'll be on you."

"She's worth it," I mutter into my mug.

He stares back at me in disbelief for a moment before realizing that I'm serious. "Then you'd better fucking tell him."

"We just need a little time." I push from the counter.

Raising his hands in surrender, Nikolai swears, "I'm not saying shit. That's not a fight I want to find myself in the middle of. But do yourselves a favor and don't sit on this."

I take another sip of my coffee, which suddenly tastes like ash. After pouring it down the drain, I leave the cup in the sink and walk from the kitchen with a gnawing tightness in my chest. Nikolai's words ring in my ears—sharp, smug, and deadly serious. *And entirely right.*

Climbing the stairs two at a time, I run my hand through my hair when I reach the landing. I don't bother knocking and quickly let myself into Eavan's room before Cillian wakes. I shut the door behind me and exhale hard, leaning against it like I'm trying to hold everything together.

Eavan is sitting up in bed with her legs tucked underneath her and a sheet draped loosely over her soft body. Her eyes still look tired, but she's alert. She glances at my face, and the faint smile that spread across hers when I barged into the room quickly fades. "What's happened?" she asks quietly, pulling the sheets tighter to her chest.

"Nikolai knows."

Her eyes blow wide. "He *knows*?"

My stare not leaving hers, I share, "He heard us last night."

"Oh my God," she whispers, a deep crimson quickly painting her cheeks. She tugs the sheets higher, over her mouth, and groans into them. "Please tell me he didn't say anything."

I push off the door cland cross the room to her. "He said *plenty*," I admit with a half-chuckle, sitting beside her on the edge of the bed.

Her eyes search mine anxiously. "What did he say?"

I hesitate. For a second, I debate sugarcoating it before opting to just tell her straight. "He made a few jokes. Mostly about how loud you were."

The scarlet covering her face deepens. "Oh my *God*, Enz!" she exclaims, mortified.

"And he made it really fucking clear that your brother isn't going to approve of us. Mostly because of me, which, based on how I lived my life before you, I can't fault him for." I reach for her hand and hold it firmly, quickly adding, "He's not going to say anything to Cillian."

She falls back against the headboard. "I want to disappear."

I lean forward, elbows on my knees, scrubbing a hand over my jaw. "It was only a matter of time. And last night was fucking reckless."

A faint reminiscing smile pulls at the corners of her mouth. Sitting from the headboard, she leans her face against my arm and quietly asks, "So, what do we do?"

"I don't want to stop this." I turn toward her and cup her round face in my hands.

"Me neither," she adds without hesitation.

"Then we need to be more careful. Until we decide it's time to tell Cian." I place a chaste kiss against her lips. "In the meantime, we have to hope he doesn't figure it out himself."

She draws in a slow breath. "You're not scared of him?"

"Terrified." I laugh. "If our roles were reversed, and you were my sister, I'd fucking kill either of them for sleeping with you."

She smiles, just a little.

"But I'd face worse for you," I add, kissing her again. "Hell, I'm already willing to fight the whole fucking Armenian mob for you. What's your brother too if it means I get to keep this?"

Her smile slowly blooms across her face, staying in place a bit longer this time. She shifts closer, curling her fingers into the hem of my shirt.

"I don't want to sneak around forever," she murmurs.

I lean in, pressing a kiss to her forehead. "I know. And we won't."

"But for now..."

"For now," I echo, begrudgingly agreeing to keep my promise to her. "We keep it between us. And Nikolai, apparently. I'll keep him in check."

"Do you think he'll actually keep his mouth shut?"

"I do." While he is loyal to us both, I truly believe he'll keep his word. "He doesn't want to be caught in the middle. He'd rather Cillian just kill me," I deadpan.

"That's not funny."

Eavan watches me for a long moment, eventually leaning into me again and resting her head on my shoulder, her fingers still gripping the edge of my shirt like she's afraid I'll disappear.

I'm not going anywhere. No matter what.

It's been a week since Cillian and Nikolai came back from Armenia. A week of tiptoeing, fleeting glances, and stolen touches when no one is looking. A long week of pretending. Enzo and I have mastered the art of stealing seconds. A quick whispered word when we pass in the hallway. Passionate kisses tucked behind a closing door. We live in a haze of nearly getting caught during the day, only to find ourselves hidden away with limbs tangled together under the moonlight.

It's not enough. We both want more. But right now, it's all that we've got.

Having learned that, like my brother, Nikolai can't boil water without burning the building down, I have been cooking for us the past few nights with Enzo's help. A new ritual that's really just an excuse to be left alone together. One that neither Cillian nor Nikolai objected to—*well, Nikolai a little... in private to Enzo.* It gets us thirty minutes of closeness, A time for us to laugh and brush against each other as we move through the kitchen without drawing any suspicion from my brother.

I carry my bowl of finely diced vegetables to the stove, where Enzo is currently browning ground beef, and place them on the counter. He stirs it slowly while I lean against the counter beside him. We stand too close for casual friends—but just far enough apart that we can deny anything if it comes to it.

His hand slips behind me, his palm teasingly brushing the small of my back as he reaches for the bowl of vegetables. I glance up at him with a knowing smirk tugging at the corners of my mouth. He knows *exactly* what he's doing. "I swear to God, if you're about to start singing Sinatra again, I'm stabbing you with this wooden spoon," I murmur, keeping my tone light and playful.

Enzo chuckles, low and warm. "That's not very romantic, princess."

"Neither is your blood under my nails," I quip.

"You might be right." He dumps the vegetables into a pan sizzling with olive oil with a broad smile. Leaning closer and lowering his voice, he adds, "It might not be romantic, but I sure as fuck love it when those perfectly manicured hands of yours rake down my back."

I playfully elbow him in the ribs with a smile and roll my eyes.

His eyes darken slightly, and he gravelly whispers, "You know how I feel about that, princ—"

The rapid thud of boots hitting the hardwood floor echoes across the apartment, interrupting Enzo, as Cillian hastily makes his way down the staircase. My smile falters when he turns toward the two of us and prompts Nikolai to join us from the pool table. Enzo's jaw ticks, and he turns off the stove, stepping back enough to widen the space between us.

Cillian storms across the apartment with his phone pressed to his ear, his expression hard and unreadable. I know that look. It's one I have seen far too much of in the past couple of weeks. It's the same one he wore when he informed me that he had killed our father. The same one I stared at when I learned of the reason why. *Something is wrong.*

"This is a call for all of us," Cillian announces, his voice tight, almost choking on the words. He places the phone on the counter and hits the button to flip the call to the speaker. "Go ahead. We're all here."

A voice crackles through the phone—deep, gravel-thick, and unmistakably Armenian. *Sargsyan.* His voice alone sends chills down my spine. The room constricts around me, the air suddenly too thick to breathe—*I know exactly why he's calling*—and my stomach twists in knots at the thought.

"It's been a week," Sargsyan says, smooth yet venomous. "Have you made arrangements to send me what I'm owed? Or do I need to come and pluck that pretty little redhead from your penthouse apartment?"

I swallow hard at the immediate realization that he knows *exactly* where to find me. Without thinking, I reach beside me and grasp Enzo's hand. Even with Cillian a few feet away, he doesn't pull back. Instead, he grips it firmly and laces our fingers together, squeezing it protectively, silently letting me know he's not letting go. *Not just of my hand, but of me.*

Sargsyan continues, "It's a long flight, plenty of time for my men to ensure *all* of those virgin holes of hers are ready to be put to use when they deliver her."

My stomach flops, and I choke back the bile rising in my throat. "Fuck you," I spit, the words spewing from my lips before I can stop them. The phone falls silent—the whole apartment actually. It's so quiet that I can hear Enzo's heated breathing beside me.

"Feisty, are we?" Sargsyan darkly laughs, his chuckles slow and measured. "Good to know. I have a few clients who will really enjoy that. They'll want to know in advance, though, spitfire. Are you true Irish? Do you have a pretty fiery bush nestled between those thick thighs to match that beautiful hair of yours?"

Enzo's entire body tightens, his grip on my hand practically crushing me. I glance at him and find his eyes narrowed and his jaw trembling with rage. He's seconds from unloading on Sargsyan.

"We're not fucking paying," Enzo grits. "Cillian and Nikolai were quite clear when they visited you. Your deal with our fathers isn't happening. And that means we don't owe you a fucking thing."

Sargsyan tsks. "I disagree. I need to be compensated for wasting my time and the money I'm going to lose by not filling your city with my girls. And I think that little fiery bush seems like it's going to be a remarkable payment. See you soon, spitfire."

Enzo ends the call without another word, and my knees buckle. I hit the floor before I know I'm falling, and the firm hardwood floor slaps against my skin. Enzo is there in an instant, down beside me, wrapping his arms around my shoulders and letting me lean into his firm chest. "No one is getting you," he murmurs, voice fierce and low. "I—*we*—will protect you. Me. Cillian. Nik. We've got you. You've also got Gunnar, Damon, Jagger, and Hawk. We have you absolutely surrounded. You're safe." *But I don't feel safe.*

Cillian rounds the kitchen island, his face hollowed out, pain and rage burning behind his eyes. He crouches beside me and pries me gently from Enzo's arms. "I promise you," he whispers, holding me close to him. "They will never get you. We did things, deplorable fucking things to make sure of it. That won't be for nothing."

I nod, but I don't believe him. Not really. Because the world we live in doesn't run on promises—it runs on blood.

Cillian and Enzo both help me to my feet—looking at me like I'm a china doll. Turning my back on them, my legs still unsteady beneath me, I flip the burners of the stove back on. "Eavan," Cillian exhales. "What are you doing?"

"Finishing dinner," I answer matter-of-factly. "We all still need to eat." And I need to do something—*anything*.

Something to keep me busy so I don't scream or fall apart again. He watches me, but he doesn't argue. None of them do.

"Okay." Cillian gently squeezes my shoulder before leaving me to the simmering sauce on the stovetop.

Enzo stays in the kitchen with me, but the laughter and warmth of us cooking together have gone. "He's actually going to come for me, isn't he?" I ask softly, my gaze fixated on the pot I'm stirring.

"Yes." Enzo's answer is straight and honest. *I wish he had lied.* "I won't let him touch you. I swear it, Eavan. I will burn this city down before I let him take you."

The sauce bubbles over slightly, but I don't even flinch. I merely stir a little faster to keep it from sticking to the bottom of the pot. "Do you think he knows about us?" I ask.

"Sargsyan?" Enzo inquires with a knowing look, trying—and failing—to lighten the mood. "No, princess. I don't think your brother knows, but I do think his gut is starting to figure things out. We've managed to keep it a secret this long."

"Barely," I mutter. "When you kissed me in the hallway yesterday, we were *this close* to getting caught."

"Worth it," he retorts without hesitation.

I glance over my shoulder and meet his eyes. There's something in them that takes my breath away—not just want, but certainty. And for a moment, just a sliver of time, I forget about Sargsyan.

CHAPTER 26
enzo

"Where the hell have you been?" Cillian's voice cuts through the quiet apartment the moment I walk inside. I left mid-afternoon, and in hindsight, I probably should've at least lied to someone about where I was going. Walking toward his angered voice, I find him at the island—arms crossed, brows furrowed, and pursed lips.

Shit... He knows.

Footsteps echo on the hardwood floor behind me, and Nikolai unknowingly saves me from Cillian's inquisition. "We've got a problem." Nikolai steps between us, phone in hand, frustration carved into his already hard features. "There are grumblings happening among the ranks that we need to deal with."

Cillian drags his hand through his hair, mussing it. "Fucking fantastic," he grumbles sarcastically. "Let me guess, Fitzpatrick?"

"Fitzpatrick, Montano, Vasiliev, and a few others," Nikolai corrects. "The irony... They've been working together and stirring the pot since our meeting, calling our three-family merger"—he pauses to air quote—"unstable."

"They're testing us. Seeing how far they can go before we react," I opine.

"Then I guess we fucking show them." Nikolai smirks, the sudden glimmer in his eye showing that he is all too eager to tend to this problem. "They're meeting in a few hours."

"Sounds like we all have a meeting to get to," Cillian grouses, fists clenched at his sides. The ire in his eyes has only grown with Nikolai's news, and he looks like a man on the verge of snapping.

I glance toward the stairs, thinking about my princess who was resting in bed when I slipped out of the apartment earlier. "What about Sargsyan?"

"Gunnar has a tight perimeter set up. No one is getting into the lobby without them knowing about it," Nikolai informs us. "Between the four of them *and* needing a passcode to bring the elevator anywhere near our floor, no one is getting up here." The information does little to calm my unease. I know how fucking determined the three of us are. Four well-trained armed guards wouldn't do shit to keep me from something I wanted.

"The three of us. We have to go," Cillian grumbles. "We have to show that we're unified and strong—that we will not stand for anyone stepping out against us."

Nik's gaze flicks between us. "If killing our fathers wasn't enough of a statement, we'll have to give them what they're asking for."

Cillian nods in agreement. "I'm going to let Eavan know we're heading out in a bit and get ready."

Nikolai glances at me as Cillian walks up the spiral staircase. "You need to get your head straight before we walk into that meeting."

"I've got it handled," I gruff.

"Yeah…" he snarks with an eye roll. "Totally handled. You looked like you were standing before a fucking firing squad when I walked in." *He's right.* I don't know if Cillian knows, but we both know he's intuitive as hell. And if I know my friend, which I do, he's going to listen to whatever his gut is screaming at him. "And you need to fucking tell him already."

I leave Nikolai standing in the kitchen, heading upstairs to remove the reason I snuck out of the apartment from the pocket of my suit jacket. After stepping into my room, I close the door and pull the slim velvet box from beneath my suit. I run my thumb over the soft exterior, pushing at the latch to open it.

"I didn't know you were back," Eavan whispers, startling me as she slips into the room and quickly shuts the door behind her.

"Jesus Christ!" I exclaim, snapping the box in my hand closed and stowing it behind my back. "It's not safe for you to be in here."

"It's fine," she softly insists, reaching for me and tucking herself into my side like she was made to fit there. "We've got a few minutes. Cian is in the shower."

"You okay, princess?" I ask, knowing the answer. Her eyes still hold the fear that flooded her face during the Sargsyan's call.

"Better now." She nuzzles closer as I wrap my arms around her. Not missing a thing, she reaches for my hand and asks, "What's in the box?"

"It was supposed to be a surprise." I slide it before her and let her take it from me.

She opens it carefully, eyes widening as she sees the platinum chain. It's delicate and feminine. Hanging from it is a small, weathered charm in the shape of an antique skeleton key—simple, understated, and hiding a secret.

Her fingers tremble slightly as she lifts it from the box. "It's beautiful, Enz."

"Let me?" I take it from her and reach around to clasp it at the nape of her neck when she pulls her long red hair out of the way. Closing the clasp, I place a light kiss at the nape of her neck before she lowers her hair. The chain rests below her collarbone, the charm settling over her heart.

"It's perfect." She touches it gently. "But why a key?"

"Because it's to my heart, princess." It might be an omission of the truth, but it *definitely* isn't a lie.

Rising onto her toes, she places a light kiss against my lips. "You didn't have to get me anything."

"I wanted to." I lightly cup her cheek. *I need this.* Hidden in the charm is a micro-GPS tracker, triple-encrypted and military grade. I had Hawk help me with it after the call from Sargsyan yesterday. She'll never know I'm tracking her. But if anyone takes her, I'll have eyes on her location within seconds, chasing into the depths of hell to rescue her if I have to.

She rolls the key between her fingers as she stares up at me with those gorgeous eyes of hers. "I'll never take it off."

"Good." I cup her other cheek and pull her face up to mine. Her warm breath feathers over me as our lips meet delicately. Rubbing my thumbs over her cheeks, I pull her closer as her lips part slightly—an invitation I eagerly accept. My tongue explores the softness of her mouth, relishing in her like it's the first time I've had the pleasure of kissing her. While fisting my shirt, she moans into my mouth as our kiss deepens—both of us quickly growing needy for each other. A need we can't tend to right now. I pull back, both of us breathless, and I pant, "You should go. Before we get caught."

"Ok." She nods, begrudgingly walking to the door. Cracking it open, she checks to ensure the coast is clear.

"We can finish this later," I gravelly whisper, gripping her chin and planting one last kiss on her lips before she steps into the hall.

I take a minute to change from my suit into a pair of dark jeans, a Henley, and boots—something more fitting for this evening—before heading downstairs. Jagger is standing at the island with Nikolai and Cillian, a tactical arsenal spread out over the granite countertop. Cillian tosses a tactical vest at me as I join them. "Wear it. For all we know we're walking into a fucking setup."

"If it's a fucking setup," I grumble, strapping on the vest, "they bleed."

"Fuck that," Nikolai exclaims. "They fucking bleed no matter what."

CHAPTER 27
enzo

The night air is thick as we approach the old cannery in Greenpoint. The building looks days from being condemned, the rusted exterior and crumbling brickwork a testament to years of neglect after the factory closed. If it weren't for the two BMWs and the Lincoln parked before it, I would think we were at the wrong location.

Cillian, Nikolai, and I move with purpose, our steps deliberate as we enter the cannery. The heavy metal door creaks, announcing our arrival to the traitors meeting inside. The room falls silent, surprised eyes shifting toward us as we step further into the abandoned building.

Fitzpatrick, Montano, Vasiliev, and a couple of guys from all our families, whose names I don't know, all stand, their hands all reaching for their guns. "I wouldn't," Nikolai warns, pulling the charging handle on his AR-15 to load a round into the chamber.

"You think you can just waltz the fuck in here and dictate terms with us?" Fitzgerald, the apparent leader of this little rebellion, scoffs. "I don't fucking work for you."

Cillian's gaze locks with Fitzgerald's. "If you work for me, you work for him."

"Then maybe I don't work for you anymore," Fitzgerald retorts, his voice unwavering—a couple of the men behind him suddenly looking a little less convincing. "Maybe we all don't."

"Maybe you do. Maybe you don't," I lament, tapping the muzzle of my Glock against my thigh. "It doesn't matter. We're here to end this."

His palms resting on the table in front of him, Fitzgerald sneers, "End this? This is just getting started."

"No." Cillian shakes his head. "Whatever you all think *this* is" —he gestures at their little gathering—"it won't be going any longer than tonight."

Fitzgerald leans forward, his eyes narrowing. "You think you're the only ones with power? With connections? We have allies and resources."

"You don't." I laugh smugly. "You know our networks of

allies and resources. Men who would sooner take their own lives than dare cross the three of us."

The room is ungodly tense, the air thick with eluded threats. I step closer to them, and with my voice low but firm, I warn, "Make no mistake. This isn't a threat. It's a promise. No one is going to stand in the way of what we're building." The silence that follows is deafening, his comrades exchanging glances and weighing their options—some clearly realizing that they don't have a play here.

"Enz," Nikolai shouts. My gaze shifts from Fitzgerald to the target Nikolai is aiming his rifle at, just in time to see him—Montano, one of my father's trusted advisers—pulling the trigger of his pistol. The round hits me before I have a chance to react, knocking me to my ass on the concrete floor. Ignoring the searing pain in my chest, I raise my Glock and fire into the men above me. The loud pops echo around the building when Cillian and Nikolai join me in eliminating our threat.

The reverberations quieting, I lay my gun on the floor beside me and feel nervously at my aching chest. My finger dips into the bullet hole in my jacket. Pressing into it, the still-warm slug is lodged in the vest Cillian insisted I wear. "Thanks," I painfully exhale to both Cillian for the vest and Nikolai for the warning.

Pushing myself from the cold, hard floor, the metallic stench of blood mixing with the musty mildew in the air is thick enough to coat my tongue. Fitzgerald's lifeless body is slumped into the folding chair he fell back into. Montano's is on the floor, blood pooling from beneath his chin and the unsightly exit wound on the back of his head. Vasiliev and some guy whose name I'll never know lie crumpled against the nearby wall, each with a clean set of double taps to the chest, leaving no doubt about Nikolai's marksmanship.

Their bodies are still warm when I pull my phone from my jacket pocket and start snapping pictures. One of Fitzgerald's face—jaw slack, eyes wide, and blood splatter across his face. One of Montano and the deep crimson pool I plan to leave him in. And a final one of the two men slumped against the wall.

The photos are clear—brutal and sharp—with no ambiguity about what happened here. Resistance to our family merger will not be tolerated. The Kings don't negotiate—we execute swift judgment, fatally.

Cillian walks past me, wiping blood splatter from his face with a stained rag. "You got what you need?"

"Yeah." I nod, swiping through the images.

The three of us head toward the exit, stepping over sticky smears on the concrete. "Send them tonight. Make it known."

Oh, it will be known.

I flip through my contacts, adding a slew of burner numbers —former advisers, guards, and men who willfully bled for our fathers. I add anyone who might think they can exploit the power shift from the change in our family dynamic.

I attach the photos. No text—just the images. I hit send, giving them all a warning straight from hell.

The message will be received: Crossing The Kings is a death sentence.

No hesitation, no second thoughts.

I tuck the phone back into my pocket and step into the cool night air, the briskness cutting through my clothes. Nikolai lights a cigarette beside the G-Class, exhaling slowly as I approach. "They'll either fall in line," he pauses to take another long drag, "or it'll further drive a rebellion."

"Let them." I open the door and slide into the passenger seat as Nikolai grinds the unfinished butt of his cigarette into the asphalt with his boot. "We'll make examples of them, too."

I scroll through my contacts as we drive back to the apartment. There's one more warning I still need to send.

I call Vito Bonetti—my father's former consigliere. The man who taught me how to field strip a Glock years before I learned how to drive a car. The father figure who made sure I knew from a young age that there are only three kinds of men in our world: useful, obedient, and dead.

The phone rings a handful of times before Vito answers. "You shouldn't be calling me."

"I wasn't asking for permission."

"You've made quite the mess," he muses. "And I'm not just talking about tonight."

"That mess is what happens to men who cross us. You taught me that, Uncle Vito."

"I did." He sighs. "And you apparently have the balls to do what your father couldn't."

"I'm not my father," I gruff.

"No, Enzolito. You're worse." The phone falls silent for a second, and I'm left uncertain if that's an insult or a compliment. "So, what is this? A warning?"

"No. It's a courtesy," I insist.

"To the old heads still playing games in the dark. The ones watching and waiting for the three of us to fumble. Tell them we're not boys anymore. We're not asking. And we sure as fuck aren't sharing. This is our city now. And if they don't want to be six feet under, next to the men in the photos, they better decide who they stand with... quickly."

Vito's heavy breath blows through the phone. "I'll let them know, Enzolito."

Without another word, I end the call and shove the phone back into my jacket pocket. My finger snags the hole inches from my heart, and my breath catches for a second, realizing how close I was to not making it home.

To my princess.

CHAPTER 28
enzo

"Jesus fucking Christ, princess," I whisper-shout, stepping into my room and finding Eavan curled up in my bed. Quickly shutting the door behind me, I grumble, "Your brother and Nik are wide awake downstairs."

She drops the covers, revealing that other than the necklace I gave her earlier, the sheets were the only thing she was wearing. And suddenly, I don't care how risky it is to have her in my room. My eyes rake over her gorgeous naked body as she crawls toward the edge of the bed, her hungry stare not once faltering. "It's after midnight. He's going to assume I'm already in bed. And I am... Just not the one he thinks," she flirtatiously whispers with a smirk.

"You're getting pretty fucking brazen, princess." I cross the room and stand at the edge of the bed before her as she rises to her knees, unable to hide my smile. I love that she's finding this side of herself—so fucking confident with her sexuality.

"I was worried and needed to know you got home okay." She looks up at me like she knows something terrible happened tonight—like she can feel it. "People died tonight, didn't they?"

I nod once, dusting my knuckles along the soft swell of her rosy cheek. "They had to."

She reaches for me, her fingers slipping beneath my jacket and sliding up the front of my chest like she's making sure I'm actually here. Her fingertips reach the cool metal of the bullet lodged in the vest I'm still wearing, and her whole body tenses. "Enz?" she chokes.

Wordlessly I pull her hand from my chest and lift it to my lips, kissing her fingertips, and whisper against her soft skin, "I'm okay, princess." Tears well in her eyes as I place her hand back on my chest and shed my ruined jacket.

I grip the straps fastening the vest along my sides, and the loud rip of the separating Velcro fills the room. After lifting it over my head, I drop it to the floor with a thud and reassure her. "There's no need for tears."

Her hand presses to my chest, rubbing where the vest stopped the bullet from piercing my skin. With one hand gripping my shirt at the nape of my neck, I pull it over my head, leaving her hand resting against the bare skin of my chest—proving to her nothing happened to me. I cup her round face and promise, "Nothing in this world could drag me away from you."

My lips crash against hers, and I snake my arms around her, lifting her up to me as she wraps her legs around my waist. Our kiss grows deeper with every step as I carry her into the adjoining bathroom. I set her on the cool, dark marble of the bathroom vanity and fumble to unlace my boots as I continue to claim her mouth. "Fuck." I laugh against her lips, thoroughly regretting my shoe choice tonight. We break our kiss, and I quickly turn on the shower and crouch before her to untie my boots.

Her dainty feet adorably dangle from the counter as I rid myself of the heavy shoes. I glance up to find her thighs slightly parted, just enough to garner me an unfettered view of her pussy. "I need to taste you," I mutter, leaning onto my knees, gripping her hips, and yanking her to the edge of the counter. My lips press into the side of her left knee and leave a trail of kisses up her inner thigh as I drape her leg over my shoulder. I repeat the motion with her other leg, leaving her spread wide with perfect pink perfection resting inches from my lips. "Be quiet for Daddy and I'll let you come."

Without further warning, I bury my face in her and lap through the sweet tang of her pussy with a growl. A gasp blows over her lips as she leans back and presses her shoulders against the cold mirror behind her. Her hips swirl, and she silently grinds her clit against my tongue. I can't get enough of her reaction to my touch—every movement only makes me want to feast on her more.

"I fucking love the taste of you," I groan against her pussy between slow, sensual swipes of my tongue. Rising to my feet as I continue to run my tongue over her swollen clit, my fingers work swiftly to rid me of my pants. I push them over my hips and kick them down my legs as I pull her against my mouth. Her fingers lace through my hair, dragging my tongue *exactly* where she needs me, and she unfurls with a string of breathy whimpers.

"Such a good girl." I pepper my praise up her soft stomach with a trail of wet kisses. My cock presses against her slick entrance as I reach her lips and pull her into me, claiming her mouth. She mewls quietly into our kiss, our tongues wrestling as I coat hers with the sweetness of her arousal, and the bathroom continues to fill with steam.

I slide my cock into her with ease and wrap her body around me in one swift motion—our kiss silencing the beautiful fucking moan that rattles from her lungs when I fill her. The tiles have grown slick with condensation beneath my feet, so I carefully carry her into the walk-in shower. The water spills in gentle streams from the rainfall shower head above us, the fiery droplets cascading over us both, and the dense steam wrapping around us like a second skin.

A tiny gasp blows over Eavan's lips when I press her back to the cool, condensation-covered tiles of the shower. The water spills over us—down my neck, my spine, and between our bodies to where I'm buried deep inside her. Droplets trickle down her face, over the swell of her desire-flushed cheeks, and she looks almost too perfect to be real. "You're so fucking beautiful," I whisper, easing my cock from her nearly to the tip and slowly inch back in.

Her body pinned between me and the shower wall, I take my time and savor every leisurely thrust. Kissing her lips, her neck, and whispering into her ear, I keep her teetering on the edge. Her chest heaves, causing the ample swell of her tits and her pert nipples to slide along my slick skin. She squeezes her thighs and flexes her hips, trying to meet my thrusts— desperate for more.

My eyes meet her searing emerald gaze—the bright green pools full of lust and need. "Use your words, princess," I tenderly demand, dipping my face into the crook of her neck. I kiss over her warm, wet skin and suck lightly before licking up the side of her neck. My tongue dusts along the shell of her ear, and I draw her earlobe between my lips. I nip at it and drag it through my teeth as I let it go. "Tell Daddy what you need."

"Harder, Daddy," I groan, needing to finally come with him inside me. "Please."

Firmly gripping my ass with both hands, he pulls back and drives the entirety of himself back into me so fast and hard that I yelp when he bottoms out inside me. "Is this what you want?" he darkly asks, repeating the savage motion. I open my mouth to answer, but he slams into me again, stealing my breath. "Do you want Daddy to fuck your little pussy with his big cock?"

"Ye—" Ramming deep, he silences my answer, my back arching along the tiles I'm pressed to. His hips work hard and fast, my skin sliding along the wall as he gives me what I asked for. *More than what I asked for.* My thighs shake against his waist, and I squeeze my fingers into his shoulders, thrusts from coming.

"Your tight little pussy loves my fucking cock," he breathlessly grits against my shoulder. "Show Daddy how much you love it." As if on cue, my body gives him exactly what he's demanding. The aching pleasure at my center crashes through my body like a pulsing burst of electricity, with my broken, breathy screams being drowned out by the heavy spray of water.

Enzo maintains his punishing pace, the pleasure rushing through me continuing to come in waves. The sounds spilling from me are caught somewhere between a gasp and a scream as he pulls a string of unrelenting orgasms from me. My thighs shake uncontrollably against his hips as he continues to drive into me. I dig my fingernails into his shoulders, clinging desperately to him, unsure how much more I can take.

"Don't stop... princess," he painfully pants between his vigorous thrusts. "Keep... coming... on my... cock... as I... fill you." He thrusts as deep as he can go, a feral, breathy roar rising from his lungs. His hips sputtering against me, and his cock throbs as he spills his release deep inside me.

Still buried to the hilt, he presses his forehead to mine—his deep chestnut eyes boring through my soul—as we both catch our breath. "You are so fucking perfect, princess." The softly spoken, warm words blow over my lips. "So fucking perfect *for me.*" His lips press to mine, and he kisses me with a soft tenderness—a stark contrast to how savagely he just took my body—and I melt into him.

Not breaking our kiss, he gingerly pulls his softening cock from me and lowers me to my unsteady feet. He holds onto me tightly, to help maintain my unstable footing. Filling his hand with soap, Enzo quickly washes away his release now trickling down my thighs.

His hands not leaving my body, he walks us from the shower and dries me before helping me into his bed. He pulls me close to him—a place that has quickly grown to feel like home—and wraps both of his strong arms around me. With the sheets tangled around us, and his warm breath on the back of my neck, he whispers into the soft curve of my shoulder, "You're... I don't even have the words for you, princess."

Smiling into the pillow, I roll enough to tuck my face into his collarbone. I breathe him in—soap, warmth, and something unmistakably him.

The room falls silent, but it's not awkward. The quietness of being cocooned in him is comforting, unlike anything I've ever experienced.

"I know all of this has been fast... *really* fast." His voice is low and rough as he pulls me in tighter. "But... I think—" he pauses, his heart suddenly racing beneath my hand splayed over it—"I can't remember my life before you... Or imagine my future without you."

My breath catches, and I nearly choke on the sudden lump in my throat. It's not from fear, but from the sudden overwhelming flood of emotions. Because I'm falling for him. Hard. Faster than I ever thought possible, in the way that feels like gravity—inevitable and terrifying. I shift my weight and prop onto my elbow so I can look up at him. "Me too," I whisper, the two words cracking nervously off my smiling lips.

His face softens, and he lifts his head to press a kiss to my forehead so gently, like he's worried I'll break if he touches me too hard. I lie back on his chest, breathing him in and floating on the high of his confession.

His hand dusts leisurely over the length of my spine as we nuzzle together. "We have to tell your brother." My eyes snap open as his words shatter my emotional euphoria.

"What?" I exclaim, lifting my head, needing to see his expression.

His brows furrow slightly. "We can't sneak around anymore, Eavan. Cillian... He saved my life tonight. Literally. I can't keep lying to him about... *this*."

"You *promised*, Enz," I angrily whisper.

His hand stills on my spine, and he holds me the slightest bit tighter. "I know."

"No," I bark. Pulling from his arms completely, I sit up and vehemently shake my head. "You promised you'd wait until I was ready. That we'd have more time to figure this out. That *I* would have more time."

He rolls onto his side and pushes onto his elbows, his eyes not once leaving mine. "I did. And I meant it when I said it. But things changed tonight, princess. Cillian insisted I wear that vest to the meeting tonight. That vest is the only reason I'm lying in this bed with you right now and not in a hospital... or the morgue. All I can think about is how he's looking out for me, and I'm lying to him about us."

I shake my head. "He's going to hate me."

"No, princess," Enzo quickly rebuts. "He's going to hate *me*. I'm the one who crossed the line. I'm the one who's falling for his little sister. I care about you. So much. I can't keep treating us like we're a secret to be ashamed of."

"I'm not ashamed," I blurt defensively.

"I know." He reaches toward me and tenderly grips my thigh. "But that's how it will look if he finds out before we tell him."

My heart pounds against my rib cage as I stare down at him. I don't know if I can handle watching the fallout of the relationships that could be destroyed by our secret.

Ours.

Theirs.

And mine with my brother.

"I need you with me on this." He softens his voice, nearly pleading for my agreement. "It's for the best. We will tell him tomorrow. Together."

Unable to hold his gaze, I look down at my hands curling in the blanket over my lap. I want to beg for a few more days, but I know he's right. Every day we let this carry on as a dirty secret, it's only going to look like we knew we were doing something wrong, and my heart tells me there's nothing wrong about the two of us. "Okay," I whisper through the tightness in my throat. "We'll tell him in the morning."

Enzo reaches for me and pulls me back into his arms, and my body curls against his. "Thank you," he murmurs, his lips pressed to the top of my head. "I know it's going to be hard, but we need to do this."

I nod, uncertain what more to say—part of me already mourning the loss of our privacy.

He wraps both arms around me and tucks me into the crook of his chest. I listen to the slow, steady rhythm of his heartbeat and try to match my breathing to his. "We'll figure it out," he whispers. "No matter what happens tomorrow, you're mine."

I'm tangled up in Eavan as the sun starts to peek through the surrounding buildings. We move together, desperate and urgent, needing this final moment of secrecy. Thrusting into her, I groan, "Who does this sweet pussy belong to?"

"You," she moans. Her back arching from the bed, her tits pressing tighter to my chest as I work her to the brink. She breathlessly pants against my neck, "Daddy... It's Daddy's pussy."

"It's my pussy, princess. It belongs to me," I grit, wrapping my hand around her throat. Her pulse races beneath the tight grip of my fingers. "And my pussy is going to come for me, isn't it?"

"Yes, Daddy," she exhales the near-silent cry, her fingernails digging through my shoulders as she unfurls beneath me. Pinning her under me, I take her faster, needing desperately to fill her again.

"Enz," Cillian's voice calls through the door with a soft knock as he pushes it open. My chest tightens, and I fall onto Eavan, shielding her naked body with mine. "What the fuck!" he shouts, loud and thunderous. "Get off my fucking sister!" Mad isn't close to the appropriate word to describe his expression.

Fury.

Rage.

Homicidal.

I jerk back from Eavan, and she scrambles from me, grabbing the sheets and pulling them over her naked body. "Cillian..." I exhale, but it's too late, the damage has already been done.

His jaw is clenched, and the vein running the length of his neck throbs with his racing heart. Every heated breath he takes causes his nostrils to flare and his eyes—dark and narrow—lock onto me like a target. His brows furrow, accentuating the harsh lines on his face. Without speaking a word, his fury radiates from him—hot, volatile, and barely contained.

He grips my arm painfully hard and yanks me off the bed with explosive force. "Get the fuck away from her," he roars as I land bare-assed on the hardwood floor with a thud, the impact rattling my bones. "You've got some fucking nerve!"

he shouts, his tone raw and unrestrained. "She's my fucking little sister."

I push myself from the floor to my feet. "Your little sister... She ain't so little, Cian," I snark, the words slipping from my mouth before I can think about them. I regret them instantly. His fist connects with my jaw—pain exploding in my skull and my teeth rattling as my head whips to the side. I don't swing back. I don't want to fight him. *I deserve this*. This is what happens when you keep secrets... When you fall for someone you aren't supposed to.

"Don't you dare fucking talk about her like that," he spits, his face inches from mine as he tackles us both to the ground. Before I can fully recover, Cillian is on top of me. His knuckles come crashing down again, and this time I feel the crack in my cheekbone—my eye feeling like it's exploding.

I raise my arm to block the next punch, but the one that follows lands firmly, sending searing pain across my cheek and blood trickling from my lip. He's lost it. *Rightfully so.* From the cold, hard look in his eyes, it's clear there's no coming back from this fight until one of us taps out.

"Stop!" Eavan shouts, cutting through the chaos, but it does nothing to calm our scuffle.

"Put some fucking clothes on, Eavan," Cillian barks as I try to buck him from on top of me. "You let *him* touch you? *Him*? My best friend? Jesus, Eavan. Are you out of your fucking mind?"

She pulls the sheets tighter around herself. Her voice is small as she trembles. "It's not like that—"

"Oh really?" he snaps, smothering me with his body and pinning me to the floor. "Because it looks *exactly* like that."

"You don't understand—"

"No," he cuts her off with a growl. "What I *understand* is that you went behind my back. That you've been sneaking around like some desperate little—"

I shove him off me, grabbing his arm and twisting it behind his back as I roll him on top of me. My legs lock around his torso, and I tighten my grip. Snaking my free arm around his neck, I cinch it tightly around his throat. "You're her brother. You're *my* brother. And I know you're really fucking mad right now," I growl, trying to hold back my anger, "but if you ever fucking talk to her like that again, I'll break your fucking neck. Do you understand me?"

We struggle, both of us straining for control—control I'm not letting go of. My heart pounds, the blood rushing in my ears with every beat, and adrenaline fueling my tight hold on him.

Nikolai's broad stature fills the doorway, and he leans against the frame. "I see he found out," he muses, with a hint of humor in his tone.

"Are you going to do something?" Eavan demands, standing in the corner of the room, clutching the sheet around herself. She looks furious—livid, actually—but also terrified.

"Nope," Nikolai answers casually, a faint smirk on his lips. "Just let them get it out of their system." Eavan's eyes flick between us and Nikolai. Her expression is a mixture of disbelief and anger.

"I trusted you to watch after her. And *this* is how you repay me? Treating my little sister like some whore you picked up at a bar," Cillian shouts, his voice breaking with emotion and from the vise around his throat. His words fuel me, but they also hurt—because I know they come from a place of concern.

"I'm not treating her like anything," I snap back, crossing my ankles and flexing my feet to maintain my grip around his waist as he fights to free himself from the cage of my limbs. "Because it's not like that at all." I hold him tighter, squeezing my thighs around his waist to keep him in place. I've had enough. "I'm falling for her, Cian," I confess, almost whispering. "And you're not going to stop me. Not now. Not ever."

The words hang in the air, and Cillian actually looks at Eavan for the first time since this whole thing started. She stares at the two of us with sad, pained eyes—so full of tears that she's seconds from them spilling down her cheeks. "Stop. Please," she begs, and I'm not sure if it's directed at Cillian or at me. Maybe both.

"If you're going to calm down, I'll let you go," I offer, maintaining my tight grip on Cillian, still feeling the anger coursing through his veins. His breaths are harsh and uneven, his rigid body softens, and he stops struggling, muttering through gritted teeth, "We're not done talking about this."

"Yeah. I know." I release my hold on him and push him off me. "We aren't."

He stands quickly, his fists clenched white-knuckle tight at his sides. Turning on his heel, he pauses when he reaches Eavan. He shakes his head disapprovingly before muttering, "I can't even look at you right now." He storms away from her, his shoulder aggressively slamming into Nikolai as he barges past him in the doorway, muttering, "And I'll fucking deal with *you* later."

"Let him go," Nikolai insists, not bothering to hide the amusement in his voice. A bemused expression on his face, he blocks the doorway. "Give him a bit to cool off, so he listens instead of trying to take your head off again. Maybe to also change his shirt so he doesn't have your wet dick prints all over his back." *Of course, Nik would find this fucking funny.*

Eavan watches Cillian storm out, her eyes wide and breathing still shaky. She looks at me, her expression momentarily unreadable. I expect her to yell. To cry. To tell me I've ruined everything. *I almost wish she would.* She walks silently across the room. "Enz..." Her voice cracks with concern when she reaches me.

When her fingers brush just under the bruise forming on my cheekbone, I flinch. Not because it hurts, but because I don't deserve her tenderness right now. She pulls back instantly. "I wasn't trying to hurt you," she exhales, soft as the breath blowing over her lips.

"You didn't," I manage, forcing myself to meet her eyes. They're so damn full of worry that it makes my chest ache. Pulling her into me, I press my painful lips to the top of her forehead.

"I'm sorry," she mumbles against my chest.

"You have absolutely nothing to be sorry about, princess." Tenderly cupping her face, I tilt it up to mine. "You're worth it. Every second. Every bruise. I'd take his fists again if it means I have this—*you*. Out in the open. No more hiding."

Her lips part, but no words come out.

"I'd let him knock me down a hundred times, Eavan." I dip my head and press my swollen, split lips to hers. "Because nothing about us is a mistake."

It's been hours since Cillian stormed out of Enzo's room—and subsequently out of the apartment. Nik and Enzo have both tried calling him a handful of times—all three of us having an apology of some sort to give—but he isn't taking either of their calls.

With my legs draped over his, I sit on the couch tucked into Enzo's side. I rest my head against his chest, the touch grounding me. His right arm is wrapped around me, and he uses the other hand to try Cillian again. But it's yet another call that goes unanswered.

The front door slams shut, and I know it's Cillian before seeing him or hearing the heavy thud of his boots on the hardwood floor. He steps through the foyer doorway, and his eyes immediately land on the two of us snuggled together on the couch. "Really?" His voice is sharp, with a displeased edge. "We're playing fucking house now?"

The air thickens, and Enzo's muscles tense beneath me. I glance at his face to find his jaw tightening, but he bites his tongue and fights the urge to snark back at my brother. *Even though I know he wants to.*

As much as I hate confrontation, there is no avoiding this any longer. I take a deep breath and turn my attention to Cillian, stomping across the apartment. "Come. Sit," I insist softly but firmly, trying to keep things civil. "We all need to talk."

He huffs from the base of the spiral staircase, clearly still *very* irritated. "I said everything I needed to say earlier."

"Yeah, my fat lip and this black eye are both well aware of your stance," Enzo sarcastically quips with a smirk, not bothering to hide his bitterness.

"Stop it. Both of you." My voice trembles, and I struggle to sound calm. I turn slightly to see each of their faces, and it takes everything in me to keep from backing down. I need them to listen. Both of them. "Please."

Cillian stands motionless with his hand resting on the railing, his posture tense and eyes flicking between the two of us. There's a fierce battle raging behind his eyes. He lets out a heavy sigh and grumbles as he takes a seat at the opposite end of the large sectional. He's far enough away that it's obvious he still wants to distance himself, but at least he's willing to listen.

He glares at the two of us, and the anger is simmering beneath the surface of his usually calm exterior—the weight of his disapproval hard to ignore. "How long have you been sneaking around behind my back?" he asks a little too calmly, like he's holding on to some thread of control.

Without hesitation, Enzo answers firmly, "Since you went to visit the Armenian."

Cillian's eyes narrow, a vein in his temple pulsing with irritation. "Did either of you plan on having the decency to tell me?"

The question hits me harder than I expect, and my chest tightens. My gaze flicks to Enzo, and I can see the slight shift in his expression—*guilt*. "Out of respect for your sister," Enzo confesses, his tone low but steady, "I promised her I wouldn't."

Cillian scoffs, the sound laced with disbelief and frustration. "So you're *her* dirty little secret?"

"No," I snap, louder and more sternly than I intend. Slipping my legs from Enzo's lap, I pull from his comforting hold to face Cillian head-on. I refuse to let him make me feel small or treat me like some naïve little girl any longer. "You were dealing with enough, Cian. I didn't want to put this on your plate, too."

His eyes darken, and he shakes his head. "That wasn't your decision to make."

"Actually," I respond slowly, fighting the anger rising in *my* chest and taking a breath to calm myself, "who *I* sleep with and who *I* decide to tell about it are both very much my decision to make. The fact that you didn't let Father give me to the Armenians tells me you understand that, too. Even if you aren't willing to admit it right now."

The words hit him like a punch, and I can see his jaw tighten, the realization settling in that, while he has a right to be upset over our secrecy, he doesn't over our relationship. His posture shifts, and his shoulders tighten. "I don't like this," he mutters, the words filled with a kind of resignation that makes my chest ache.

"I've had an O'Brien man telling me what I can and cannot do my entire life," I continue, each word more daring than the last. "So, I'll be honest, I don't care if you like it, because I'm not asking you if it's okay."

Enzo shifts beside me, his hand resting on my knee, and his thumb brushing reassuringly across my skin. His voice is steady as he stares at Cillian. "It's happening. It's going to *keep* happening. She means something to me, Cian. *Everything* to me."

His words are a promise. To Cillian. And to me. I place my hand over his on my thigh and give it a light squeeze, silently echoing his sentiment.

Cillian looks between us, his anger still simmering but also tinged with something else—hurt, betrayal, maybe even a little bit of understanding. *It's hard to read him sometimes.* "On the bright side, you can have your bed back," I half-heartedly jest, trying to ease the discomfort between the three of us.

Cillian's eyes flick to me, but they don't soften. Instead, his lips curl into a cynical smirk. "After what I walked in on earlier? If it happened in my bed, too... No thanks. I'll stay on the couch."

"Yeah, about that..." An uncontrolled, quiet laugh, low and just a little bit mocking, rattles from Enzo. "We've done it here, too. Truth be told, there probably isn't a place in this apartment besides Nik's room that's safe."

Cillian runs a hand through his hair, clearly trying to suppress the surge of anger building inside him at the thought of his best friend fucking me enough to have tainted most of this apartment. He leans back on the couch, his arms crossing over his chest. His eyes flick to me again. "I just don't get it," he mutters. "Do you know what kind of man he is?"

Enzo sucks in a deep breath, the words slapping him in the face like they were intended to. "I do," I answer, squeezing Enzo's hand before he has a chance to spit a retort. "We don't have secrets. He's been more than honest about how he's lived his life. I'm not a little girl, Cian... You don't need to protect me. I know exactly what I'm doing *and* who I'm doing it with."

"Are we all kissing and making up?" Nikolai jokes, joining us from the terrace and unknowingly saving this conversation from souring again.

Cillian stands from the couch, and sucker punches Nikolai in the gut the second he steps within reach. He folds in half, struggling to suck in a breath. "That's for knowing and fucking keeping it from me," Cillian snarls.

"So, we're good?" Nikolai asks sarcastically, choking on a breath and stumbling to a seat on the couch.

"Yeah. We're good."

"I'm not asking for your blessing," I interject, my throat tight as I struggle to find the right words, "but I want your acceptance."

Cillian doesn't respond, his silence stretching out uncomfortably long. He sighs, a deep, heavy sound that carries with it a mix of frustration and concession. "It'll take me time," Cillian discloses honestly, his gaze focused on the two of us. "But if he proves his devotion to you, I'll happily give you both."

I know Enzo will give him what he wants. And all things considered, that's probably the best I can ask for right now.

"You might be my brother..." Cillian exhales, turning his attention to Enzo. "But if you hurt her, what I did to your face will feel like a kiss on the cheek."

"Understood, brother," Enzo responds with a nod, a faint smile tugging at his battered and bruised lips, knowing that this strain in their relationship will heal.

ABOUT A WEEK LATER

Blinking the sleep from my eyes, my hand instinctively reaches across the sheets for Eavan. My brows furrow, finding nothing but the cool satin where she should be. Sprinkles of spring rain fall against the windows, the light patter and hazy gray sky making it the kind of morning made for staying in bed... together.

I sit up slowly, scrubbing my palm down my face in annoyance, not enjoying waking up alone. *Not anymore.* I swing my legs over the edge of the bed and tug on a pair of sweatpants. Noticing the nail marks running down my chest

I run my fingers over them, reminiscing with a smile, and opt to cover them with a shirt before heading to find my princess.

The faint smell of coffee hits me halfway down the stairs. Coupled with the soft clink of mugs, I pause at the bottom step and lean against the railing long enough to watch her. Eavan stands at the counter, back to me, her hair twisted up in a messy knot, wearing one of my hoodies. Far too big, it hangs off her and barely covers her ass—leaving me wondering if she has anything on underneath it. She hums quietly while fixing a cup of coffee. *It's dangerous, how much I love her like this.*

I move silently, sneaking up on her like a shadow. Snaking my arms around her waist, I quickly tighten them and pull her back snug against my chest. She lets out a breathy scream, tensing for just a second before melting into me when I press my lips to her neck. "Daddy doesn't like it when you sneak out of bed."

She gasps, a mixture of shock and laughter. "Enzo—"

I kiss her again, slower this time, my lips lingering just beneath her ear. "I need you to come back upstairs," I groan, my voice raspier than intended. "Right now."

Her breath hitches, and I feel her smile against my cheek. She wriggles in my hold before turning around to face me.

"Someone's needy this morning," she teases, eyes bright.

I pretend to let her push me away, giving her a few inches of space before catching her wrist and dragging her back into me. "Have it your way, princess," I murmur, tipping her head to the side and leaving a slew of wet kisses along her neck. "We don't have to go upstairs first."

Her laugh turns into a light moan as my hands slide around her hips and over the generous curve of her ass, drawing her close and firmly pressing my hardening length against her.

"For fuck's sake," Cillian grouses, his voice still tired and already full of irritation. With my face buried in the crook of Eavan's neck, I laugh softly and slide my hands from her ass to her lower back. "You have a room," Cillian groans, taking a seat on a barstool at the island. "Use it."

"Trust me, brother," I grumble, without turning to face him. "I'm *trying*."

"Enz!" Eavan swats me in the chest, cheeks flushed with the heat of her embarrassment. She squirms out of my hold and tries to look composed, though her lips are still tipped upward, letting me know she's not entirely upset with my teasing. Eavan busies herself with the coffee machine as I hop onto the counter and stretch, watching her.

"I'm going to start charging you two every time I walk in on *that*," Cillian mutters, reaching for the mug Eavan is sliding across the island. "My therapy bill is already racking up."

I shrug. "Your fault for coming in without knocking."

"It's the *kitchen*," he snaps, trying desperately to hide his amusement and maintain a disapproving stance. "There is no door *to* knock."

I grin. "Fair."

Eavan, mercifully, changes the subject. "I'm making muffins," she says brightly. "Blueberry."

Cillian gives her a suspicious look. "What's the occasion?"

"Surviving another week in lockdown without strangling each other," she quips, pulling ingredients from the cupboard.

"Barely," he snorts, glancing at me—his eyes still harboring his annoyance over my relationship with his sister.

I jump down from the counter to help her, not because she needs it, but because I enjoy watching her work. There's something domestic and comforting about it—so unlike the world I'm used to—like if I stay in this moment long enough, maybe the outside world will stay away.

It isn't long before the scent of baking muffins drifts through the apartment, warm and sweet. Nikolai stumbles downstairs, sniffing at the sweet aroma—shirtless and his hair an absolute mess. "What smells like happiness?" he mutters, heading straight for the coffee like it's life support.

"Muffins," Eavan says.

"Possibly still with a side of murder," Cillian mumbles half in jest.

"Coffee." I smirk, glaring at Cillian. "And inappropriate kitchen behavior."

"Again?" Nikolai teasingly mutters. "You do know that you two have a very large and very nice room upstairs, right?" I snicker as he unknowingly repeats Cillian's sentiment. While they both might be correct, I can't get enough of her, and I will happily take her anywhere I can.

Eavan steps into the hall and opens the front door, her soft voice carrying into the kitchen. "Come on. You both can take a short break. Or at least protect me from in here."

Hawk and Jagger follow behind her as she returns to the kitchen—tall, stone-faced, and both carrying an arsenal. They pause at the threshold to the kitchen, unsure whether they're allowed in.

Hawk clears his throat, looking vaguely uncomfortable. "That's very kind, ma'am."

Jagger nods once. "Much appreciated, ma'am."

She hands each of them a muffin straight from the tray, and I swear they both look like they've just been knighted as they take the warm baked goods from her. She pours them each a cup of coffee, and I realize that she's silently thanking them for helping to keep her safe.

The kitchen fills with quiet conversation and the clinking of cups against the granite countertop. On the surface, everything appears normal, but I can see it—the way Eavan stares out the window and over the terrace with distant eyes. She hasn't been outside this apartment in weeks, and no matter how much she pretends otherwise, I know it's wearing on her.

The tray of muffins is reduced to nothing more than a few crumbs, and the coffee pot has been drained. Everyone starts to clear from the room—Nikolai mumbling something about a call, Hawk and Jagger returning to their post in the hall. Cillian stays at the island, scrolling through his phone, and Eavan sits beside me on the counter as I load the dishwasher. *My thank you for her breakfast.* After turning it on and drying my hands, I press myself between her knees and slide my hands along her bare thighs. "Want to get out of here for a bit?"

She blinks at me as though trying to ensure she heard me correctly. "What do you mean?"

"I mean," I answer slowly, watching her face, "you and me. A quick trip outside these walls. Assuming you can follow the rules. There's a boutique I know of nearby. It's privately owned and appointment only. No crowds. No risk. Just a change of scenery for the morning."

Her eyes go wide. "Seriously?"

"No," Cillian sharply answers for me with his arms crossed. "Absolutely not. We've kept her in here for a reason."

"I get that," I reply calmly. "But she's going stir-crazy. We're talking one hour... Two, tops. We'll take Hawk and Jagger, and she won't go a second without someone's eyes on her—"

"She's not leaving," he snaps, louder this time.

Eavan stiffens beside me, and something in my chest hardens. I take a breath, trying to maintain my composure. "Cian, I know what you *think* you're doing. And trust me, I understand why you're being so protective. But keeping her locked in here like a prisoner isn't protecting her."

His jaw tightens. "You don't get to make that call."

"Actually, I do," I curtly insist, stepping forward. "I want to keep her safe as much as you do, but I also want to ensure she's happy. And no one is going to keep me from giving that to her. She deserves a bit of normalcy."

He looks at me long and hard, mistrust simmering under the surface. Eavan shifts uncomfortably on the counter, and I squeeze her hand while maintaining Cillian's hard stare. "I'll take care of her," I promise. "I know you still don't believe she means something to me. That this is just some fling. But it's not. I swear to you that I will protect her with my life."

"Please, Cian," Eavan begs softly, batting her eyelashes at him like it's some play from the *How to Manipulate Men* handbook.

He lets out a heavy exhale and grumbles, "You take Hawk and Jagger. Back before lunch."

"Go get ready, princess," I whisper against Eavan's temple before brushing a soft kiss against it.

She grins brightly and darts from the room with the same excitement as the last time I took her out the front door. Cillian watches her go, waiting until she has disappeared upstairs before turning to me and threatening, "If anything happens—"

"I know," I interrupt him. "But nothing will."

The city feels different after weeks of watching it from behind glass or overlooking it from the terrace. It's quieter than I remember and smells different. Or maybe I've just forgotten what outside air smells like—food carts, garbage, and exhaust fumes. *It's weird that I missed it.*

Hawk and Jagger flank us like silent shadows as we walk down the street from the parking garage, never more than a few steps behind. Their presence isn't subtle—nor is the fact they're both heavily armed. That's the point. Anyone watching will think twice before trying anything.

Still, I tense every time someone gets too close or their eyes linger on me a little too long. In the back of my mind, I can't shake the thought that the Armenians are nothing more than an arm's length away, just waiting for their chance to take me like they've threatened. A threat we're all waiting for them to try to follow through.

As though he can sense my discomfort, Enzo reaches for my hand and laces his fingers with mine. He holds it tightly as we walk, his other shoved into the pocket of his jacket—likely wrapped around the grip of a gun hiding within it. "I won't let anything happen to you," he murmurs without looking at me.

I nod, with a hard swallow. "I know." I believe him fully when he says he'll do anything to protect me. My hesitation stems from the intrusive thought I can't seem to shake. *What if he can't?*

Enzo stops outside a glass-fronted electronics store, the door already open. The clerk inside gives a small nod when he sees Enzo, clearly expecting us. Jagger heads inside while we wait with Hawk on the sidewalk, returning a moment later and informing Enzo it's clear.

"A phone?" I raise an eyebrow. "That's not what you brought me out for."

"It is now," he insists, tightening his hold on my hand, tugging me inside. "Come on, princess."

"Enzo," I mutter, dragging my heels. "I don't need a phone. I don't even leave the apartment. Who would I text?"

"Me," he responds simply. "It's for when I'm not with you."

I roll my eyes. "You're always with me."

"Not always," he disagrees. His business with my brother and Nik pulls him away sometimes without warning. And while I try to pretend it doesn't bother me, I fight against the urge to unravel every minute he's gone.

He abruptly pulls me close—close enough to whisper into my ear. "And you'll pay for that one later. You *know* Daddy doesn't like it when you roll your eyes."

"Sorry, Daddy," I mumble my apology into his shoulder.

"Now, be a good girl and let me spoil you today. You deserve it."

He picks out a sleek phone and has the store clerk set it up in under ten minutes, ensuring his number is placed into the favorites so I can reach him within seconds.

"Now you can harass me all day, even from the next room," he teases as we walk out.

I slide the phone into my coat pocket, my cheeks warm. I'm not used to being doted on the way Enzo pampers me. "Thank you, Daddy."

He lifts our joined hands to his lips and kisses the back of mine. "This next part's more fun." His words vibrate softly against my skin. I follow his gaze to the painted storefront to my right with delicate lettering on the small sign above the door. *Lucullan Boutique.* The small display windows house mannequins in flowy dresses and barely-there silk lingerie.

"This is dangerous," I exhale with a smile, beyond eager to buy myself something new.

Enzo quips, "That's the idea, princess."

Inside, the shop smells like roses and fresh linen. A stylish older woman in an impeccably fitting, classic little black dress and perfectly styled hair greets us with a knowing smile. She offers me a mimosa and assures us both she and the store are solely ours for the hour—no other appointments, no interruptions. On such short notice, I can only assume it's a privilege Enzo has paid handsomely for.

Hawk and Jagger station themselves at the front and rear doors like sentries, arms crossed, silent as ever, as I trail my fingers along a rack of soft summer dresses. "Pick whatever you want," Enzo insists from behind me, his voice low and warm.

I glance over my shoulder with a smirk. "You sure you trust me with that?"

"I trust you with my life." He matches my playful tone, a coy smile spreading across his face. "And my wallet... Begrudgingly."

A smile plastered across my face, I start selecting things I like from the racks. A blush-toned wrap dress. A forest-green sundress. A sleek black cocktail number with an open back— even though I have nowhere to wear it. *Maybe someday when things are back to normal...*

Every time I hand something to the attendant, he follows behind with a little smirk, slipping something else into her hands. "I'm picking your lingerie," he states simply, when I notice the pattern.

I arch a brow. "Is that so?"

It becomes a game—one I'm increasingly losing. Every soft floral dress or outfit I choose is met with a more risqué counterpart: sheer panels, silk ribbons, lace that barely qualifies as coverage. I snag the lingerie from his hands before he can hand it to the saleswoman. Holding up the deep plum set, I snark, "This is see-through and hardly enough fabric to bother putting it on."

"Exactly," he says, not even pretending to be innocent.

While the matching set on the display next to us looks amazing, my curvy body looks nothing like the super-toned size-zero mannequin. "I'm *not* wearing that," I scoff, rolling my eyes.

"I'm buying it, because I know how fucking gorgeous it'll look on you," he insists, dusting his fingers down the length of my spine. "I'll prove it to you."

He takes my hand and leads me toward the dressing room at the back of the store. Ushering me into the small stall, he shuts the curtain and waits on the other side. I stand in the middle of the tiny room and stare at the sheer strips of fabric. I swallow hard, glancing between the risqué lingerie in my hand and my reflection in the mirror.

"I'm waiting, princess."

After stripping off my clothes, I fold them neatly and drape them over the navy upholstered chair in the corner. Inhaling a deep breath and releasing it slowly, I remove the tiny scrap of fabric—apparently panties to this designer—from the hanger, pull them up my thighs, and situate the tiny spaghetti straps on my hips. I step into the ribbons making up the teddy and attached garters, relieved to have seen the display mannequin to have even a semblance of an idea how this thing is supposed to be worn.

Trying not to overthink how this looks on me—*like a trussed roast*—I tentatively draw back the curtain separating me from Enzo. His eyes darken immediately, raking over every inch of my skin like a starving man. He doesn't move, but looks seconds from pouncing on me. "You look fucking irresistible."

"Fine, you can buy it," I nervously laugh, shaking my head and feeling my skin flush. With a tug of the curtain, I try to pull it shut. My movement is met with his firm hand wrapping around my wrist, tearing my grip from the fabric. Letting himself into the tiny dressing room, he pulls the curtain shut behind him.

Stalking toward me, he runs his thumb along his lower lip and backs me against the wall. "No, princess. I'm afraid Daddy is going to fucking ruin this one."

Enzo closes the distance between us, leaving only a breath of air between our bodies as he towers over me. "It looks even better than I imagined," he murmurs, more to himself than to me. His fingers skim my shoulder, slow and reverent, tracing the edge of the strap before dusting down to my elbow. The tender, intimate touch steals the breath from my lungs.

"You are so fucking beautiful," he states simply, like it's a fact. His hands settle at my waist, thumbs brushing over my bare skin, and he leans in until his forehead rests against mine.

My racing heart thunders in my ears. "This is so inappropriate," I whisper.

"No, princess"—a devilish grin spreads across his face—"what I still plan to do to you here is inappropriate."

Before I can argue, he abruptly uses his grip on my hip to spin me. He shoves my face into the mirror as his hands roughly grab my wrists and pin them to the mirror above my head. Adjusting his grip, he holds them firmly with one hand as the other runs down my body. He fists the delicate string running over my hip and tears the thin panties from my body as I gasp, "We're going to get caught."

Dropping the scrap of fabric to the floor, he hastily undoes his belt and lowers his pants. "Then we better make it quick, and you better be quiet." He tugs at my hips, pulling me toward him until I'm finding purchase against the mirror. Fisting my hair, he steers my gaze to our reflection. "I want you to see what you fucking do to me."

With my hair laced around his fingers and his other hand gripping the ribbons of the teddy at my waist, Enzo slams into me without restraint. My arms buckle at the force; his firm hold on me is the only thing keeping my face from slamming into the mirror.

He fucks me without abandon, demanding that we both come quickly. The pleasure building at my core is overwhelming, and I close my eyes as the swell of euphoria teases me. "Watch us," Enzo breathlessly demands, grasping my hair tighter. The pain radiating around my scalp is countered with the ungodly pleasure he's providing between my thighs. "Watch yourself come. See how much you love my cock stretching out your tight little pussy."

Struggling to keep my gaze on the mirror, I watch my expression gradually shift. My eyebrows draw together, and my lips part—the lower one trembling slightly as I let out a rushed, shaky breath. The flush in my cheeks deepens, and my mouth gapes wide, a breathy scream rising from me as Enzo hastily buries himself deep and throws me over the edge.

"That's my good fucking girl," he pants, drawing my attention from my reflection to his. Fighting against himself, his jaw is clenched painfully tight. His eyes are half-lidded, dark with focus, and flickering between control and surrender. Tension fills every line of his face, his lips pursing together and his heavy breaths blowing between them, sharp and uneven. His throat bobs with a swallow, and he bites down on his lower lip, painfully resisting the inevitable. A fight he can't win.

He slams into me with a savage roar, pulling so hard at the ribbons of my teddy that it tears at the seams. His eyes are glassy when they meet mine, and he exhales a series of heavy grunts before filling me with his release. Holding my stare in our reflections, he snakes his hand around my neck and pulls me into his chest. "Look at my cum dripping from you," he tsks, drawing my attention to the cum trickling down my thighs from where our bodies meet. He pulls from me, runs the head of his cock through the creamy trail and quickly buries himself deep in me again. While kissing along the side of my neck and sliding into me with deep, leisurely strokes, he breathlessly whispers, "Daddy's babies belong deep inside you, princess."

Pulling my face to his over my shoulder, his lips sloppily find mine before I can speak. His hands slide over my body, like he's memorizing every inch of me. "I'll never get enough of you," he mutters through our kiss, the words vibrating against my lips. "I don't know when this happened, but I'm pretty sure I'm in love with you."

His words catch me so off-guard; I'm left completely speechless as he tucks himself back into his pants and uses the tattered panties from the floor to wipe the remnants of his cum from my thigh. I try to find words to say something—anything—to let him know how I feel. "Guess I *will* be buying these after all," he teases, and my moment to return his sentiment has passed. He shoves the now-stained fabric into his pocket as I wriggle from the rest of the destroyed lingerie.

His hands not leaving my body, he tenderly helps me dress—the act somehow more intimate than him undressing me. "I can do that," I insist as he pulls my panties up my thighs.

"There's nothing in this world you can't do, princess." He stares up at me as he pulls them over my ass. "But I like taking care of you. So let me."

Enzo pulls open the thin curtain of the dressing room, and I smooth my tangled hair in the mirror before taking his extended hand. He leads me through the store to the saleswoman behind the counter, looking bemused. When we pass the display with the plum lingerie set, Enzo pauses to grab another in my size. Setting it on the checkout counter, he flatly insists, "Charge me for two of these."

"Two?" The woman arches her brow.

"Yes." He glances at me as he pulls a black card from his wallet and slides it across the counter. "There was a slight mishap with the other one in the dressing room. Respectfully, I insist on purchasing them both." *A mishap... Is that what we're calling it now?*

The older woman's gaze darts between the two of us—with the same unapproving scowl of my brother—as she runs his card, and an uncontrolled chuckle rises from me. "Sorry," I snort, quickly grabbing the bags and heading toward Hawk at the front door before embarrassing myself further.

"Ma'am." He reaches out to take the heavy bags from me. "Successful trip?"

"*A very* successful trip," Enzo answers for me, taking my hand. "I'm quite certain she's very satisfied with what she got." My cheeks burn hot, near certain that everyone within a five-block radius is aware that Enzo just fucked me senseless in the upscale boutique.

We cross the street, walking slowly, with Enzo's hand firmly on the small of my back. "Thank you." I smile, glancing up at him.

"Your sweet cries of pleasure are more than enough thanks, princess," he teases. "But if you want to formally thank me for fucking you, I guess I can oblige."

"You're incorrigible." I playfully swat his arm, loving the jovial way he's constantly toying with me. But also genuinely grateful for today, and him wanting to make me happy. Because he cares about me. *Because he loves me...*

His hand slides around my waist, and he pulls me closer to him—my hips lightly brushing against him with every step. "You deserve more than a life locked in that apartment. You deserve a full, rich life, princess." His lips brush the side of my forehead as we reach the G-Class in the parking garage. "And that's the life I plan to give to you."

ABOUT A WEEK LATER

I should be used to leaving by now, but the sight of Eavan curled up on the couch, wrapped in my hoodie, makes the idea of walking from this apartment nearly unbearable. Her hair is still messy from bed and her legs are crossed beneath her; she flips through the book in her lap that she's pretending to read. She hasn't actually looked at a page since I started putting on my boots.

"You sure you have to go?" Her voice is soft, and there is no denying the concern woven in it.

I step closer, brushing a hand over her cheek. "Unfortunately." I lean down and kiss her, slow and deep. I want her to taste the apology I don't say out loud. Her fingers tangle in the collar of my jacket for a second too long, like she's thinking of pulling me down beside her.

"Don't get shot," she mutters against my lips, her lighthearted tone trying to hide her sincerity.

"I'll try not to." My retort is only slightly playful.

"Not good enough," she grouses, brattily crossing her arms and sulking.

I walk backward toward the door, unable to pull my eyes from her. "I'll bring you home a black-market souvenir. Something with a questionable origin and no warranty." She grabs the couch pillow and hurls it across the apartment at me. I laugh, tossing it back at her and slipping out the door before I decide to stay.

Nikolai is already leaning against the G-Class when I reach the parking garage—his reflective sunglasses hide his eyes but not the shit-eating smirk that's far too wide. "What took you so long?" The smile somehow grows more as he razzes me. "Did she threaten no more sex if you skipped cuddles before leaving?"

"She didn't threaten," I snip, jokingly. "It was more of a plea with knives."

"A woman like her," he muses as we climb into the car, "well worth getting stabbed a time or ten."

"Shit, Nik." I smirk, turning over the engine and pulling from the parking spot. "Are you getting all sentimental and poetic on me?"

"Fuck," Cillian mutters from the backseat. "Do I have to worry about you fucking my sister now, too?"

Our ride is short—a little café in the center of Midtown. A highly populated tourist area with far too many people drinking overpriced espressos for this meeting to go south. The Armenians picked it—probably to ensure Cillian didn't put a bullet through their skull before taking a seat at the table.

Gunnar swept the place an hour before we got here. One exit to the front and a side hallway that leads to the kitchen. No visible security in the restaurant, but two men at a corner table haven't so much as touched their drinks. *Amateurs.* Scanning over the crowd, I barely recognize Gunnar. Dressed in a three-piece suit, with a laptop and various papers spread before him, he looks like the other nine-to-five schmucks filing this place.

"Mr. Roseti. Mr. Romanov. Mr. O'Brien." The man in his mid-thirties stands from his seat, chirping our names a tad too brightly. He's thin, forgettable, and fidgeting nervously with a napkin. "Thank you for agreeing to meet with me."

I slide into the booth, setting my phone and keys on the table without bothering to accept his hand. He laughs nervously, retaking his seat, and sliding deep into the booth as Cillian forces his way in behind him. "I'm Narek."

Nikolai gives him a charming smile and saddles a chair up to the end of the booth, relaxed like he's here to talk about real estate. "You know, Narek, there is a remarkable vodka tasting room down the block. We could have met there instead."

Narek blinks. "Uh... I guess. It's ten in the morning."

"Live a little." Nikolai winks at him. "It's five o'clock somewhere."

Unsure how to respond to Nikolai's relatively unhinged proposal, Narek looks like he wants to evaporate where he sits. His phone buzzes, and he apologizes before pulling it from his pocket, quickly scrolling through it, and placing it face down on the table between us.

"What is it you want?" Cillian huffs, reeling the conversation back in.

"Our people don't want more conflict," he says quickly. "We know about the... um... issue with Davit Sargsyan and... the girl. Those of us here in Brooklyn, we aren't involved in that." I stare back at him in silence, waiting for him to make the point he brought us here for. "If... I mean, when things come to a head with him—because they will—we don't want to be caught in the middle."

If Sargsyan actually comes, everyone will be caught in the middle

"Unless you are willing to entirely cut ties with your Armenian brethren overseas, that's not a promise I can make," Cillian responds flatly.

"Understood." He nods, clearly unhappy with my decision. When he reaches over the table to shake my hand, he topples the glass of water between us. He instantly grabs both our phones and my car keys before the puddle reaches them both. "Apologies," he says quickly, all of us slipping from the booth before the water spills over the table edge and into our laps. "Tight space."

I wave it off without a thought, extending my hand. "My things?"

"Oh... of... of course," he stammers, his grin lopsided, as he places them into my waiting palm. Nikolai's inquisitive gaze lingers on him as we walk toward the door, but I don't bother to ask.

We walk two blocks before Nikolai speaks again. "Well, that was productive."

"In what world?" I grumble.

"Okay, maybe not productive, but entertaining. Narek looked like he was about to piss himself."

Cillian shakes his head. "I don't know what it was, but something about all of that just didn't feel right."

"They're trying to keep the peace while buying time," Nikolai insists.

We pass a guy leaning against a kiosk, dressed like any other businessman, scrolling through his phone. But the screen has gone black, and he's not really scrolling. He's just watching the crowd.

"You see him?" I murmur.

"Yup." Nik and Cillian answer in unison.

"Think he's one of theirs?" I ask, casually glancing over my shoulder to see if he is following us.

"No." Nik shakes his head. "He looks too clean-cut. I'd put my money on him being a cop."

"Great... Just what we fucking need."

Back in the SUV, I check my phone. I tap into my messages, but the app flickers and crashes. *Weird.* I try again. Same thing. My brows furrowing, I power off the phone to reboot the device.

"Something wrong?" Nikolai asks.

"Must be a glitch. They make these things far too fucking smart now. Like they're trying to think for you."

We drive in silence for a while. Nikolai hums tunelessly, probably just to irritate me. Phone powers back on, and I flip open the texts without issue—or any new messages.

When I walk into the apartment, the first thing I see is Eavan's bare feet poking over the couch arm. She hears the door and pops her head up, beaming. "You're back early."

"We're just efficient." I pause in the kitchen to remove the Glock from my waistband and set it on the counter.

"Did you get me something shady and illegal?" she asks, and Cillian arches an inquisitive brow.

"I was going to grab the Mona Lisa while we were out," I playfully fib. I take a seat beside her on the couch, toss my phone onto the coffee table, and pull her legs over my lap. Her fingers find mine easily, like they belong intertwined with mine. "But did you know that thing is in Paris?"

"You're ridiculous." She chuckles, curling into me and resting her head on my chest. "Who would've thought the big bad mafia guy was a funny man?"

"Or such a generous lover." I drag her into my lap to taste her lips. My phone buzzes on the table, but I ignore it. I press my lips back to hers and kiss her slow and deep, just for a moment, forgetting everything but the two of us.

The apartment is quieter than usual, Nikolai and Cillian having ventured out to grab something to eat and probably have a few drinks. Rain patters against the windows, a steady rhythm that hums in the background. Enzo and I are draped across the couch, tangled in each other, like we have nowhere else to be. Because right now, we don't.

His arm is tucked beneath my head—his fingers combing slowly through my hair, twirling strands between them as if the motion soothes him as much as it does me. I lie half on my side, my chin resting just above his chest where I can feel the calm, even rise and fall of his chest.

His thumb brushes against my scalp. "Still with me?" he asks softly.

"Barely," I mumble, smiling into him. "You're too good at this."

"At what? Lying around like a lazy bastard? Or lulling you to sleep?"

"No, Enz..." I laugh quietly. "At making me feel safe." Even when I didn't know him like I do now, I felt protected when I was with him. He was willing to go the distance and do deplorable things in my name before I even laid eyes on his face—like the world sent him to take care of me.

"Did you mean it?" I wonder hesitantly. I've been trying to find a way to have this conversation for days.

He doesn't say anything, his fingers just keep running through my hair. When I peek up at him, he's watching me with an adoring gaze. Using his hand, he tips my face all the way up to his. "Mean what, princess?"

"The other day... At the store... When you said you loved me."

His eyes warm, and he lets out a soft, reluctant sigh as his thumb lightly dusts over the swell of my cheek. "Yes," he answers the lone word with absolute certainty. He lowers his face and places a gentle kiss in the middle of my forehead. "I haven't been able to stop thinking about what my life looks like with you."

I shift a little, repositioning to comfortably hold his gaze. "Yeah?" I ask curiously.

"Yeah." His thumb catches behind my ear. "About the beautiful life I want to give you."

"And what have you decided?"

He doesn't smile. Not really. But there's a glimmer of light in his eyes that wasn't there before. "I want a place. For just us. No Nik. No Cian. Just us," he shares. He drops another kiss against the bridge of my nose and half-teases, "So I can have my way with you anywhere I want."

"Enz." I laugh, shaking my head.

"I'm serious. I should be able to kiss the woman I love without two grown men grumbling about our public displays of affection."

I'm unable to hold back the anticipative smile. "That sounds... perfect."

"I think about it a lot more than I probably should," he admits.

I brush my fingers across the fabric of his Henley, tracing along the seam at the collar as I nuzzle back into his chest. "Does that scare you?"

"What?"

"Wanting to have something normal in your dark world?"

"No," he exhales. "You may have come into my world like a tornado, but you're the calm among my chaos, princess. I'm not scared of having a life with you." His lips press to the top of my head, and he pulls me tighter to him. "I'm fucking terrified of *not* having one."

I press my palm to his chest. "You're sure? It's not just because I'm locked in here with you... and happen to make excellent muffins?"

"That's 80 percent of it. The muffins." He laughs lightly at his clarification. "That and wanting to pump you full of babies."

"Do you actually want kids?" The words blurt from my lips uncontrollably—needing to know if his desire to impregnate me goes beyond the bedroom.

He tenses slightly and replies, "That's... a big question."

"I know." I immediately regret having asked. "You don't have to answer."

"I love the idea of filling you with babies and watching that beautiful body of yours grow round with our children," he admits sincerely. "I just... I don't know if I'd be good at it. The closest I had to a caring father was Uncle Vito... and I don't think you'd want me to teach our kids how to load a magazine before they go to preschool. But I'd try like hell, princess. I'd learn. I'd probably fuck it up and have to get better. But I'd try. Because they'd be ours."

"You'd be amazing." I sigh, tears pricking at my eyes, picturing the life he's been planning for us.

"You think?"

"I *know*." I run my hand over the perfectly groomed beard covering his jaw. "The way you care for me... I can only imagine how lucky a child would be to have even a fraction of that."

"Is that something you could picture? Something you might want?" He slips his hand over mine, lifts our laced fingers to his lips, and kisses the back of mine. It's such a small gesture, but it breaks something open in my chest.

"If it's with you... Yeah. I want all of it," I answer, trying to keep my emotions steady.

He leans in until our foreheads touch, and he vows, "I love you."

The words fill me with comfort. Knowing what he sees for us, this time they feel bigger, deeper—like a promise for the rest of our lives. My throat tightens, and I feel the familiar rush of everything I've been holding back. "I love you too, Daddy," I whisper without thinking. Because I do. *I really do.*

He exhales slowly, as if he's been holding his breath, waiting to hear them. With the gentlest shift, he moves, easing his weight above me and leaning down until his lips meet mine.

Our kiss is slow and intentional. His hand cups my face, and I wrap my arms around his shoulders, pulling him deeper. His tongue wrestling tenderly with mine, the two of us slowly grow breathless together.

His kisses trail from my lips to the edge of my cheek and down my neck. Barely lifting his head, his warm breath blows over my skin when he murmurs, "You have no idea how much I want this life with you."

A FEW DAYS LATER

Opening the wine fridge nestled under the kitchen counter, I reach in for the bottle of Sauvignon Blanc. The wine bottle clinks softly against the countertop as I set it down and pull out two glasses. I'm about to pour a glass for both me and Eavan when heavy footsteps approach behind me. I turn in time to see Cillian step into the kitchen.

The air in the room suddenly feels thick and heavy—this thing between us is still not settled. "Hey, Cian." I push the glasses aside and lift the bottle from the counter. His eyes flit between me and the two glasses, and I can feel the judgment in his gaze. The two of us haven't had a proper conversation about everything. We've actually been ignoring the elephant in the room and avoiding each other since the day he caught me balls deep in his sister and he bloodied my face over it.

"Enzo." His greeting is flat and guarded, a far cry from the joviality he used to address me with. I slide the cork back into the bottle, my fingers moving with a practiced ease, as the room falls into an uncomfortable silence for a moment. "I didn't know you were..." He stops, shaking his head like he doesn't even know what he's trying to say. His expression hardens, and I can't blame him.

What I did... What Eavan and I did—hiding our relationship from him, keeping him in the dark—has been hard on him. And our relationship. We all know that.

"I'm getting a glass of wine for Eavan," I share, forcing a casual tone and setting the bottle back on the island.

"I can see that," he mutters dryly—a chuckle almost escaping him.

"We haven't really had a chance to be alone since... everything happened." I stumble a little through my words. "But... for what it's worth... I want to officially apologize."

Cillian's brows furrow, and he crosses his arms over his chest before leaning against the counter. His eyes narrow slightly, and he gruffs, "Oh yeah? For what exactly? Sleeping with my sister?"

"No," I laugh, the reaction a mixture of amusement and discomfort. "I'll never be sorry for that." The muscle in his jaw twitches, and I can't help but smirk at his reaction, knowing my answer has completely caught him off-guard. I shift my weight, holding his gaze. "But I am sorry. Sorry that I didn't tell you. About Eavan. About us."

His expression softens slightly, the tightness in his shoulders easing as he uncrosses his arms. "I just... I don't get it." He shakes his head. "You're my best friend, Enz. My brother. You and Eavan... Out of nowhere..." His words trail off as he tosses his hands up in exasperation. They fall to his sides, and he mutters. "It feels like I was the last to know, and I can't help but wonder why you felt you couldn't share that with me."

The words stinging, I swallow hard. *I let him down.* "I didn't mean for it to happen this way. Fuck... I didn't mean for it to happen at all. And when it did... I just... I didn't know how to explain it. I fucked up. I should've convinced her to let me tell you sooner."

His eyes search mine as though he's trying to verify the sincerity of my words. He lets out a heavy exhale, his shoulders slumping in resignation. "You're not the only one who fucked up," he confesses, breaking the silence. "Eavan and me... We have our own shit... I'm not exactly blameless for her thinking I'm not capable of seeing her as anything more than the little girl she was when I left home."

"I'm not willing to give her up. Not in the slightest. But I don't want to lose our friendship."

"We're not friends, Enzo." Cillian shakes his head, and the words hit me like a punch to the gut. "We haven't been friends for years. You're my brother. My fucking family. I can't deny that I was fucking pissed—and hurt because of the secrecy—but I get it. I do."

"We should've told you. And I'm sorry."

"It's done now," he laments, his voice finally easing. "I'm not mad. Well, not anymore. I get it. I just... I needed to hear that. From you." Cillian nods again and jests, "And maybe you could not force me to endure listening to the two of you at night again."

"We can pick you up some headphones," I lightly quip. "Or some earplugs."

He rolls his eyes, a small laugh rising from him. "Just, don't fuck this up, Enzo. If you hurt her, I will beat the ever-loving shit out of you... again."

"I would expect nothing less." I feel a sharp grin tug at my lips. My eyes wander behind Cillian to the terrace where Eavan is patiently waiting for me to return with our drinks. Her silhouette is framed against the fading light of the evening—her hair blowing slightly with the soft breeze. "I could never hurt her. And if I did, I'd deserve whatever you did to me. Probably worse."

"Good. I'm glad we're on the same page." Cillian wraps his arm around my back, and he pulls me close until our shoulders bump. After clapping me twice on the back, he steps back with a nod—a true bro hug. "You better get back out there before Eavan thinks you're avoiding her. Or that I've murdered you."

I turn toward the counter, finally pouring the wine. The distance between Cillian and me is still there, but it feels a little smaller now. A little more manageable. The bottle glugs softly, and as I pour the second glass, the door slides open to the terrace.

"Enz," Eavan calls from the cracked door, her expression showing her concern over finding Cillian was my hold-up. "Are you coming?"

"Yeah, princess," I answer with a smile, not wanting to deny her my attention for another second. "I'm coming."

"Be good to her," Cillian insists as I lift the two glasses from the counter.

"Always."

CHAPTER 38
eavan

The night air is cool, but not enough to make me uncomfortable. Except for the soft hum of the city below, its skyline lights dancing across the adjacent buildings, the terrace is quiet. It would be remarkably relaxing if I weren't constantly glancing over my shoulder, worried that I'm going to need to intercept a bloodbath in the kitchen between Enzo and Cillian.

Their conversation has stayed civil—at least it appears so from this side of the glass—but this is the longest they've spent alone since Cillian walked in on the us. I checked on them a few minutes ago and thought Enzo was coming, but something held him up again.

I lift my feet onto the terrace chaise and pull the blanket over them. The soft clink of glass pulls my attention to the sliding door, where Enzo is finally returning with our drinks. He has an odd grin on his face, and I can't quite tell if he's amused with himself or relieved.

"Mission accomplished," he announces, handing me one of the glasses—the moonlight reflecting on the surface of the white wine.

"Are you referring to getting the wine or not getting sucker punched by my brother again?"

"Both," Enzo chuckles, taking a seat on my chaise and wrapping his arm around me. "But honestly... The second one was definitely a toss-up."

I smile over the rim of my glass as I take a sip of the amber-colored wine. "So, how'd it go?" I ask seriously.

He reclines with a sigh, pulling me to the plush cushion of the chaise-back with him, taking a second to gather his thoughts. "I apologized," he states simply. "Told him I was sorry for not telling him about us sooner. For sneaking around behind his back, even if it wasn't meant to hurt him."

"And?"

"He didn't sucker punch me in the face." He laughs. I join him, the sound of our amusement dissipating into the night air. "And neither of us is currently in the ER. So, I'm going to call that a win."

He shifts to face me more fully, propping one arm on the back of the chaise. His tone more solemn, he shares, "He was actually decent. A little grumpy... as expected. Protective... of course. But I respect him. He loves you."

"He does," I agree, swirling the wine in my glass. "The two of you... Are you—"

"I'd say things are gonna be fine."

I glance up at the sky, trying to see the stars through city lights and pollution. "You ever just sit and think about how weird it is how all this worked out? Or is going to work out," I correct myself.

He hums, considering. "Weird, maybe. But not surprising. Something about the two us... We make sense even though we shouldn't."

"You're ridiculously charming." I nudge his side.

"I know." I roll my eyes at his cool cockiness, and he teasingly gruffs, "I saw that, princess."

I set my wine glass on the little table beside us and snuggle in closer. He reaches over me and adds his glass beside mine before pulling the blanket further around me. Breathing in the scent of him, I press my face to his collarbone—woodsy and comforting, a little like cedar and salt.

Enzo inches closer until the heat of his body is pressing gently against mine. He leans down, his dark hair falling a little over his forehead, as he stares at me with an intensity that causes my heart to skip a beat. His fingers dust gently along the curve of my shoulder, feather soft. I close my eyes and lean into him, letting the warmth radiating from him sink into me.

His soft lips dust along my skin, the gentle wetness of his lips and tongue replacing the light touch of his hand. He trails kisses over my collarbone and up the side of my neck. My heart races as his lips linger on the ticklish spot below my ear, sending a tiny shiver zipping down my spine.

Enzo's hand slides down my back, and he pulls me closer, fully pressing his rock-hard body against me. A tiny gasp flies from my lips when his hard length grinds against my hip. I turn my face toward him, just enough for our eyes to meet, and the intensity in his gaze takes me by surprise. His eyes are dark—almost black in the moonlight—an undeniable hunger raging behind them. It's a look that I have come to know all too well. One that causes me to lose control of myself in the best of ways.

He dips his head, and my breath hitches when he pauses a hair's breadth from my lips—teasingly making me wait for his kiss. "You're so fucking beautiful," he murmurs huskily, the deep vibrato sending flutters between my thighs. He closes the distance, and his lips brush against mine in a feather-light touch, pulling back when I try to take more.

His hand wrapping around my throat, he tightens the hold and crashes his lips against mine. I kiss him back, almost reflexively. Our lips and tongues move together in a rough, needy rhythm as his hands roam over my body with desperation—unable to get enough of me.

He breaks our kiss, both of us breathless, as he presses his lips back to the exposed cleavage at the low neckline of my shirt. The feeling of him kissing over my skin sets every nerve in my body on fire, and all I can think about is what it's going to take to extinguish the need he's currently igniting in me.

His lips brush along the shell of my ear, and he stills, his breath warm against my skin. "Eavan," he whispers, his voice low and dark. "I think I need to take you inside, princess."

A gasp catches in my throat at the way he says it—low, seductive, like a promise of what's to come when he gets me upstairs. Opening my eyes and meeting his gaze, I nod. "Yes, Daddy. I think you should."

Enzo takes my hand and pulls me from the chaise, not bothering to grab our glasses from the small end table before pulling me across the terrace. His palm not leaving the small of my back, he ushers me up to our room at the far end of the hall.

Enzo leads me into the room, and the door closes with a soft click the second he has me inside. Wasting no time, he pulls my loose maxi dress over my head and drops it to the floor. "Tell me, princess..." He presses his lips to my neck and walks me backward toward the bed. Rubbing his hand over my panties, he asks, "Did you ever play with this pretty pussy of mine before you had Daddy to take care of it for you?"

"Yes," I choke, his question catching me off-guard as the back of my thighs bump against the mattress.

"Show me," he gravelly demands in my ear, gently pushing me onto the mattress. Hooking his fingers under the thin fabric of my panties, he takes his time pulling them down my legs and over my feet before letting them fall to the floor.

Enzo grabs one of the two reading chairs from near the window and places it at the edge of the bed, directly in front of me. Upon taking a seat in it, his hand slides down my left leg. He lifts it from the floor and places my foot on the cushion beside his thigh. Repeating the motion with my right, he splays me wide before him, granting him an unfettered view between my thighs. His thumb dragging over his lower lip, he growls, "Show Daddy how you play with your pussy."

I swallow hard at his instruction. Lifting my fingers to my lips, I drag my tongue over them to coat them with saliva. Enzo watches intently as I reach between my thighs and run the saliva-coated tips through the lips of my pussy. I rub my fingertips from my clit to my entrance, repeatedly sliding them over the soft pink skin as it coats them with my arousal. Growing slick with need, I drag them in circles around my clit —my hips swirling to meet my own touch.

"Fuck..." Enzo moans, heavy breaths blowing from him as he watches me, his eyes flicking between my face and industrious fingers as though he can't decide which to watch. His eyes not leaving me, he undoes his pants and works them just far enough down his thighs to free his rigid cock. He wraps his fingers around his shaft and lightly fists himself.

His enjoyment only fuels my need, and I press two fingers inside me to the knuckle. I thrust them vigorously, desperately wishing it was Enzo inside me—needing the fullness of him. "You're so fucking close, aren't you?" he groans, knowing my body so well.

After pulling my arousal-coated fingers from me, I rub them vigorously over my clit and pant, "Yes, Daddy... so close..." My demanding touch is too much, and it quickly throws me over the edge. My release spills from me in a breathy groan, my thighs squeezing around my hand as I grind against the fingers pressed against my pussy.

Enzo grabs my hand, pulling me from the bed and onto his lap. With both hands now my ass, he lifts me high enough to press his cock to my entrance. "Now, be a good girl"—he drags me over him, filling me perfectly—"and show me how you fuck Daddy's big, hard cock."

My hands resting on his chest and my eyes locked on his, I grind over him. Every swirl of my hips draws groans and whimpers from us both, and he roughly palms my ass. The firm touch is a silent demand to ride him harder. I pick up my pace until I'm rocking over his length so energetically that I find myself becoming breathless. Sloppily kissing over my heaving breasts, he sucks one of my nipples and rolls the other between his fingers, and the added pleasurable sensation does me in. My head lolling, I cry out my release as it fires through every nerve in my body.

Enzo lifts us from the chair before dropping us onto the mattress. He barely misses a thrust as he adjusts between my spread thighs. He claims my mouth while taking me with fast, deep strokes—each leaving him grunting. And I love the raw savageness of it. I come explosively hard, clawing at his back as he plunders my mouth and swallows my screams.

Breaking our kiss, he stares down at me. "My sweet little princess"—he heavily exhales, drawing back his hips and slamming into me—"loves being fucked like Daddy's little whore."

"Yes, Daddy," I barely muster as he quickly ramps up his thrusts to a punishing pace again. "I love how you fuck me."

Gripping my inner thighs, Enzo pushes my legs wider. "I need to be deeper," he grits, driving the entirety of himself into me. "I want to fill every last inch of this perfect fucking hole. Spend the night pumping you so full of cum that it spills from you with every thrust."

"Please…" With my back arching from the bed and my hips rising to meet his, I beg, "I love the feel of your babies in me."

"Oh… fuck… princess…" Enzo pants, fisting the sheets so hard as he comes that they pop free of the mattress. His rigid length twitches inside me, pumping his release into me. Buried to the hilt, he tenderly kisses my lips and takes my mouth again as he slowly softens inside me. But he doesn't pull out. Instead, he flexes his hips, ensuring his flaccid length doesn't fall from me.

"I'm going to stay right here," he softly insists, his lips lightly traveling along the length of my neck. "My cock warming inside you until I grow hard again. So I can take you slow and tenderly, worshipping my perfect girl the way she deserves. Treating you like the princess you are."

My hand dusts along the side of his face, and I whisper, "I love you."

"I love you, princess. It's in my blood—like every part of me was made to hold you, care for you, and worship you. You're mine... My everything."

A FEW DAYS LATER

Cillian's Aston Martin hums beneath us as we drive down the FDR. Rain smears across the windshield in light streaks, and Fall Out Boy blares through the speakers as Cillian weaves through traffic—water sprays from the tires whenever he ventures too close to the shoulder. We've just finished dumping two bodies into the East River—two more men who thought it wouldn't be a death sentence to cross The Kings—and need to put a little distance between us and our disposal.

I lean back in the passenger seat, my thumb flicking across the phone screen out of habit. Or boredom. My text messages load slowly. *Probably shitty service because of the weather.* The thread with Nikolai glitches when I open it, then loads a handful of old messages at once. *Weird... Maybe it's time for an upgrade.*

> You get back okay?

NIKOLAI
> Still alive. Just walking through the door.

> I've also just been instructed to order Chinese food for dinner.

I chuckle softly to myself. *She is pretty fucking persistent when she wants something.*

> Jesus. She's circled enough fucking entrées on the menu that we're apparently going to have a buffet.

> And be eating leftovers for the next week.

I glance at Cillian. "Your sister has decided we're having Chinese for dinner."

"Dumplings," he blurts, abruptly changing lanes. "Make sure it's the steamed ones, not the fried."

I shoot Cillian's request to Nikolai. Then add in a request for crab rangoons. *Apparently, it is going to be a buffet.*

> Jesus. She's circled enough fucking entrées on the menu that we're apparently going to have a buffet.

And be eating leftovers for the next week.

Really, Nik? The same messages? Because that's not an obnoxious way to get a response at all.

I got it! Way too much food.

Cillian pulls to a stop at the gate for the parking garage, and my phone buzzes again.

You okay?

I shake my head and grumble, "Apparently, this is what having a little brother would've been like."

Yeah. All Good.

Just parked.

Hawk called.

Same black SUV has circled the block twice in the past ten minutes

Same one he saw yesterday

I grind my teeth and squeeze my phone a little too hard. *It was only a matter of time.*

Sargsyan?

The plates are for a rental. So, definitely not one of our guys.

> Make sure he gets eyes on the nearby buildings.

> And keep Eavan off the terrace.

Already on it.

His response comes as Cillian and I are walking past Gunnar and into the apartment. Eavan pads across the living room toward me, damp-haired and wearing a tiny pair of pajama shorts with one of my T-shirts. "Everything okay?" she asks, her eyes scanning over my face.

"Yeah," I lie too fast, not wanting to worry her. Based on her suspicious expression, I'm certain she catches the slight edge in my tone. I lean in and kiss her temple. "Just some work stuff, princess," I skirt the truth, wanting to confirm the threat before unsettling her. "I'm gonna go change before dinner gets here. I'll be back down in a second."

She smiles, small and guarded, her lips momentarily parting like she wants to argue. But she doesn't. But worry flickers in her eyes as she offers to get me a glass of wine while I change.

Nikolai follows up the stairs behind me. His voice low, so Eavan doesn't overhear, he shares what I already know. "If they're circling enough to concern Hawk... they're not scouting. They're waiting."

They know what they want and where to find her. They're just waiting for us to give them the opportunity. "I know," I groan on exhale as we reach the top of the stairs.

When I reach my room, I sit on the edge of the bed and stare blindly at the dark windows. I drag my hands down my face, thinking about all the ways things could go wrong, all the ways we could fail her... And worse, all the ways I could lose her.

I watch them from my seat at the corner of the kitchen island, perched with my wine glass sitting loosely between my fingers, the rim of it catching the soft kitchen lights. The scent of takeout—dumplings, skewers, teriyaki, and some spare ribs that no one asked for but everyone keeps eating—hangs in the air, mixing with the smoky hint of bourbon and the sweet perfume of the Shiraz I'm drinking. There's food everywhere. *Too much food.* Silverware clinks and takeout containers trade hands like poker chips.

Nikolai sits at the opposite end of the island, one elbow braced against the granite counter, swirling vodka in a glass like he's narrating a classic novel. He's halfway through retelling his version of the accident that somehow bonded the three of them. He's in full storyteller mode—animated, with hands flailing as he speaks.

"And then," he pauses for the utmost dramatics, "Enzo comes barreling through the fire doors in the headmaster's Buick."

Cillian snorts, chewing through a mouthful of dumpling. "Screaming like a little girl"—he glances at me—"no offense. Because he was pinned in the car."

"I was *not* screaming like a girl," Enzo insists.

"Enzo was stuck," Nikolai continues his story, a broad smile spreading across his face. "*Not* screaming like a girl." I can't help the full-bodied laugh that tumbles from me.

"Fuck all of you," Enzo playfully snips. He is leaning back, one arm draped across the back of my stool, his other hand wrapped around a glass of wine from the bottle we've been sharing.

"We pulled him free. His shirt was soaked with blood, and tears were *definitely not* streaming down his face." He winks obnoxiously as he recounts the events. "And then the two of us dragged his sorry ass home."

"Lies," Enzo waves dismissively. "*Almost* complete and utter lies."

Cillian wipes his hands on a napkin and sends a mock glare down the island. "And I've been stuck with the two of them ever since."

"Come on, brother." Enzo grins, nudging him with a foot under the counter ledge. "You love it. Your life would be boring as fuck without us."

"Love it?" Cillian arches an eyebrow. "No. I've just developed an impressive level of tolerance and emotional numbness."

"Therapy would be cheaper," I jest, taking a sip of wine.

"I'm sure it would," Nikolai agrees, raising his glass. "But it wouldn't be nearly as fun as shooting people." All I can do is shake my head at his statement.

They're ridiculous, the three of them. There's something disarming about watching them like this, bantering over chow mein and overpriced alcohol. This is a far cry from the tension-filled rooms just a week ago when Cillian was barely speaking to Enzo and Nikolai was stuck in the middle, refusing to pick a side. And I thought I was going to lose Cian and Enzo.

I can't help but think of all the years I missed out on this—or something like this. After Mam died, Father might as well have locked me away in a tower. Sure, I left home for school or to go shopping, but I never really had friends—not like this. No one wants to hang out with the girl with two armed men practically attached to their hip.

Part of me is insanely jealous of Cian and this secret brotherhood he hid from me—*from everyone*—nearly his entire life. He was out here living this rich, full life while I was practically kept under lock and key. I'd resent him for it, but I can't. Not after learning the type of man our father truly was, and the position that put Cian in. And while he might not have been a good man, I know that at least some part of my brother is living with the fact that he murdered his own father to keep me safe. *And for that, I would forgive him for anything...*

Nikolai refills all of our glasses—because apparently we're testing the limits of the human liver and resigning ourselves to one hell of a hangover tomorrow. He points his chopsticks at Cillian. "You still haven't admitted I saved your life."

"That's because you didn't," Cillian refutes, somehow having room to shovel in yet another dumpling. "You tripped and shot a guy by accident."

"So... you accidentally saved his life?" I muse.

"Still counts," Nikolai shrugs. "Dead is dead. At the end of the day, *I* pulled the trigger and *you're* still here. So, you're welcome."

The three of them erupt with laughter as the music from the Bluetooth speaker shifts to something soft and contemporary. I take another sip of wine and glance across the island at the leftovers we won't finish, enjoying the way the men laugh with full bellies and unguarded mouths.

It's rare to see them like this. The warmth in how they interact is palpable—teasing each other, not out of malice but years of shared history. Their friendship is deep-rooted, built over years of countless memories. It's the kind of bond that rivals companionship. The three of them are truly family *—brothers.*

I glance at Enzo, my heart swelling with something I can't quite put into words. He's grinning, his dark eyes glinting in the dim light as he listens to Cillian and Nikolai banter. There's contentment in his smile, and I wish I could keep him like this—light, happy, and unburdened. Not weighed down by his concerns for my safety or the stress that comes with taking over a city.

His fingers interlace with mine in my lap, and I turn to find a smile splitting his face. It's not from the ridiculous stories being told at the other end of the island, because every bit of his focus is suddenly on me. He gives my hand a tender squeeze before lifting it to his lips and kissing the back of it. Glancing at me over it, he mouths the words, 'I love you.'

CHAPTER 42
enzo

ABOUT A WEEK LATER

Cillian and I spent the day visiting our businesses and making sure all the strip clubs are still running smoothly with the new mixed-family management. I dropped him at a restaurant down the block to grab takeout for him and Nikolai.

The second I step from my G-Class in the parking garage, I can feel it. *Someone is watching.* My eyes dart between cars—and occasionally over my shoulder—as I walk toward the elevator bank. I tread past a black Suburban parked in the shadows, and something about it doesn't feel right. I glance at the plate and my stomach drops. It's the same one Hawk noticed circling the building five nights ago.

My gaze rises over the hood, and even in the dimly lit interior, I spot the man in the backseat. He looks up and our eyes meet —both of us immediately realizing we're fucked. My heart rate skyrockets.

I race toward the driver's door as he clamors over the center console to get behind the wheel, yanking it open before he can turn over the engine. As I pull him from the driver's seat by the lapels of his jacket, he throws wild fists. A solid punch lands against my jaw, and I grunt in pain as I throw him to the concrete. He scrambles to get to his feet while reaching for his waistband—for a gun I didn't notice at first.

Driving at him with the full weight of my body, we hit the side of the Suburban with a loud thud, denting the rear panel as I tackle him against it. The impact causes him to drop his gun, and it clatters against the ground at our feet. With my forearm shoved into his throat, I pin him to the side of the SUV with the full weight of my body and grit, "What the fuck do you want?"

He stares back at me with dark, cold eyes, not a word passing over his lips. I shove into him again—any harder and I'll likely collapse his windpipe—and pull my gun from the waistband at the back of my pants. He grunts when I jam the muzzle into his gut.

"Who the fuck are working for?" I snarl, painfully grinding the gun into his stomach.

His expression is stoic, and his eyes are full of conviction as he stares back at me, unwaveringly. "Fucking kill me," he spits, unable to hide the tinge of Armenian accent.

Fuck this...

"By the time I'm done, you'll be wishing I had," I snarl, yanking him from the side of the SUV and shoving him forward. Fisting the back of his jacket, I walk him the length of the garage toward the elevator with my gun pressed firmly against the nape of his neck. If he won't talk here, he will in the basement. *Everyone talks in the basement.*

The musty dampness and heating oil smells of the basement fill the elevator the second the doors open. Jagger is at the rear wall, his back toward us, his sleeves rolled up and headphones on, cleaning a weapon. He doesn't flinch when I shove the man out of the cab and drag him deeper into the cool space.

"Sit," I bark, throwing him onto a metal chair in the middle of the room, causing the legs to screech against the concrete. Jagger spins around at the sound, his hand pulling his sidearm from his hip with Wild West quickdraw speed.

"Jesus. That's how you get fucking shot!" he exclaims, lowering the pistol and slipping the headphones down until they're resting around his neck. His eyes roam over the man in the chair between us. "Who the fuck is this?"

"Don't know yet." Jagger hands me a few zip ties, and I bind the man's hands behind the chair and his feet to the legs. "Found him in the garage. Black SUV. Same plates as the one Hawk kept spotting."

Jagger yanks the headphones off and tosses them with his rag onto the workbench and strides over, his eyes sharp with intrigue. "Anyone with him?"

"Didn't see anyone else. But that doesn't mean he's alone."

The man shifts in the chair, testing the restraints. He eyes us both—me standing over him and Jagger circling like a wolf about to pounce.

"I know you've been watching us," I inform him. "Just know that this will go a whole lot easier for you if you explain why you've been spending so much time outside our building. And exactly what it is you're planning."

Nothing from him—not even a twitch.

Jagger throws a punch, and blood spews from the man's mouth. Without hesitation, a second lands just beneath his eye. He grumbles something in Armenian and Jagger chuckles. "Armenian. That narrows things."

Not holding anything back, Jagger plunges a fist into the man's gut—forcing every bit of air from his lungs. He chokes and sucks in desperately as another fist rattles his jaw, but still... nothing.

Jagger leans on his workbench, arms crossed, waiting impatiently to swing at him. I crouch in front of him, meeting his stare and holding it. "We know you're not working alone. So, here's your shot. You talk now, maybe you'll walk out of here."

The man's breath wheezes between split lips, a rattling sound that's half pain, half spite. Blood mats the edges of his beard, and one eye is already swelling shut. He spits, blood splattering onto the floor, and licks the remnants from his lip as a Cheshire Cat smile spreads across his face.

"You're already too late," he grumbles with condescension, his eyes flicking between me and the clock on the wall.

Confused, I tilt my head as my brows furrow. "Too late for what?"

He gives a faint, humorless laugh. "We aren't playing the same game. You've fallen moves behind," he rambles smugly. "We're not waiting outside anymore."

Jagger's face tightens as he steps closer. "You saying you've got people inside?"

He nods once. "Inside your lives. Your routines. Your secrets. You think you've got control?" he scoffs, his accent growing deeper. "We've been watching. Listening. Waiting."

His words cause my stomach to knot. "What do you mean, you've been watching?" I ask. "And listening?"

"Your little messages to your princess?" he sneers, a sick grin curling one side of his busted mouth. "Every word. Every time stamp. We read them before she did. We know everything. You thought you were protecting her. But the Monte Melkonian Cyber Army"—he laughs, then winces—"they're smarter than you."

Eavan.

The hairs on the back of my neck stand on end, and the cold shiver that follows slices through my thoughts.

"How long?" I grit, barely able to push the words past my clenched jaw. He doesn't answer right away, but the shit-eating look of victory on his face is more than enough to help me piece it together.

The glitching phone.

"Long enough. We cloned your phone a couple of weeks ago when you met with Narek." I should've noticed, and his tone only drives the fact home. *One of us should've noticed.* I step back and drag my hands down my face, my thoughts already spiraling. *What do they know?*

"My vision is a little blurry," he informs before suddenly asking, "What time is it?"

"What the fuck does it matter what time it is?" I bark.

Jagger, silent until now, glances at the clock hanging on the wall behind us and hesitantly answers his question. "Three seventeen."

The man scoffs arrogantly, like he knows something we don't. "You're already too late."

Eavan...

ABOUT TEN MINUTES EARLIER

My phone buzzes on the bathroom vanity as I'm getting ready for my dinner date with Enzo—and Gunnar and Damon. I finish sweeping on my mascara, then read the message.

ENZO

I'm waiting for you in the lobby, princess.

A small smile ticks at the corner of my lips as I read his message. I can almost hear the way he calls me, 'princess.' After slipping my phone into my pocket, I head downstairs and sit on the bottom step to throw on my Converse.

I'm halfway through tying the laces on my second shoe when Nikolai calls out from the couch, his tone leaning more toward curiosity than admonishment. "Where are you going?"

"The lobby," I chirp, rising from my perch and walking toward the front door. "Enzo texted to say that he's waiting."

His brow furrows, and he shakes his head, grumbling, "You're not supposed to go anywhere alone. You know that."

I laugh softly and wave him off. "Don't be silly. What could happen between the front door and the lobby?"

He leans forward, bracing his forearms on his knees and readying to stand. "I'll go down with you."

"Nik"—I flash him a grin—"it's not like I'm going to get lost in the elevator."

He follows me to the front door, accompanying me past Gunnar and Damon, and pushing the call button. While we wait for it to arrive, he sends a text to Enzo, the concern washing from his face when it dings in his hand. "Okay." He sighs. "Enzo is double-parked out front and waiting for you in the lobby."

I step into the cab when the elevator arrives, pressing the button for the lobby. My eyes flit between numbers ticking down above the door and my reflection in the mirrored walls, smoothing my hair and checking my appearance while anxiously waiting to get to Enzo. *It's crazy missing him this much... He's only been gone since this morning.*

The elevator dings, and when the doors slide open, I step out. I scan the lobby, but I don't see even a hint of Enzo. My smile falters just a little as I wander past the reception desk and the small seating area beside it. I pull my phone out of my pocket and text him.

Where are you?

It buzzes immediately with his response.

Outside, princess.

I glance toward the glass doors at the street, a flicker of doubt aching in my gut. *You're being ridiculous, Eavan. Nik said he was double-parked.* Not letting paranoia take hold, I step outside—just far enough to be on the top step of the building's stoop, my arms wrapping around myself to fight the unexpected chill. I look left, then right.

No double-parked cars. No black G-Class. No Enzo.

I open my mouth to call for him, but hesitate when a chill rattles me to my core. "Eavan." The voice behind me causes me to freeze. I turn slowly, swallowing, my heart in my throat. Standing a step behind me is a man with an immaculately trimmed salt-and-pepper beard and a thick scar slicing through his right cheek. It's the face of a stranger, but when he opens his mouth again, I know *exactly* who he is. "We've been waiting for you, spitfire."

Davit Sargsyan.

His eyes rake over me slowly, like he's cataloging every inch of me for some sick mental inventory. I try to step away, but I hit something solid. Glancing over my shoulder, I find that I'm standing against a massive wall of a man. Two others approach from the passing crowd, boxing me in between the four of them.

I open my mouth to scream, but a gloved hand clamps over my mouth before a sound comes from me. He wraps his arm around my waist and yanks me from the ground. My feet kick out, flailing and landing against his shins, as he carries me across the sidewalk and toward an awaiting black SUV, the rear door already open. I scream as they shove me into the back seat, but my cries are muffled by the leather-gloved hand covering my mouth.

Davit doesn't raise his voice—doesn't rush. He merely watches patiently as they push me into the backseat and slide in after me. He climbs into the passenger's seat, and the door slams shut in an echo of finality. The vehicle moves before I can orient myself—tires screeching as they pull from the curb.

"Let me go!" I scream, the glove falling from my lips and my limbs thrashing.

The man on my left swings an arm, and the back of his hand crashes against my cheekbone—my eye feeling like it's going to explode from my face upon the impact. Davit turns from the front passenger seat to face me, his lips curled into a threatening smile. "I think it's time to officially introduce myself, spitfire," he announces. "Davit Sargsyan. And I will say, you are even more beautiful than your father let on."

"I don't care who you are." I glare at him, my chest rising and falling rapidly as I try to calm my raging nerves. "Let me go."

He extends a hand toward me—as though he expects civility after kidnapping me—one I refuse without hesitation. His smile drops, and he grouses with a sharpness in his tone, "I'm trying to be polite. Don't make me show you a side of me that you don't want to see."

"What do you want?" I snap, my voice trembling even though I try to hide my fear. "My brother... Enzo... They won't give you shit."

"I don't need *anything* from them," Davit informs, folding his hands in his lap like we're in a boardroom instead of a moving prison cell. "You, spitfire, are what I want. And now you're all mine."

My stomach clenches, and I bite back, "Don't flatter yourself."

He chuckles, the darkness of the sound echoing around the tight confines of the SUV. "Still fucking feisty. I like that."

"They will come for me," I gruff, my voice low but shaking. As much as they promised, I can't help but worry that they won't be able to get me back. "They will kill you."

"Doubtful," he says with a shrug. "You're coming with me. We'll be on a private jet to Armenia by nightfall. Your brother and that Italian playboy you've grown so attached to will never find you." His eyes hungrily roam over my body, eliciting a chill down my spine that rattles my bones, as he licks his lips.

"I'd rather die." There isn't a drop of dishonesty in my words. Death would be better than the life he has in mind for me—being a plaything for him... or worse. *And without Enzo.*

"I hope not," he retorts. "But if you aren't able to adapt to your new role, your wish might be arranged."

The SUV jolts as we make a sharp turn, and it throws me into the lap of the man on my right. I grasp the door handle, desperately trying to pull it open. He tears my fingers from it before I'm even able to get a glimpse at my freedom.

"Don't bother," Davit says, amused. "They'll hunt you down before you make it twenty meters. Or they'll shoot you in the back." Turning his attention to the man beside me, he mutters something in Armenian.

Working like a well-oiled machine, the men I'm wedged between grab my wrists and quickly zip tie them together. *This is far from their first go at abduction.* "You won't get away with this."

"That's the problem with princesses like you," he snarls, leaning closer. *I hate the way that word sounds from his mouth.* "You think the world is fair. But the truth is—power wins. Money wins. And I have both."

So do The Kings...

I clutch my arms to my body, trying to warm myself from the sudden chill that has nothing to do with the temperature in here. My chest feels tight, my heart pounding against my ribcage, and not wanting to give him the satisfaction, I fight the overwhelming urge to cry.

"Good girl," Davit mutters, almost like he's praising me. "If you can keep that sharp tongue of yours quiet, we might get along better than I thought."

I force myself to meet his eyes. "Enzo is going to kill you." There is no tremor or fear in my statement, because I know beyond a doubt that it's true. I don't know if he'll save me first, but I know without a doubt Enzo *will* end Sargsyan's life for taking me.

"You're already too late," the Armenian mumbles, repeating himself and driving his words into my gut like a spike.

I freeze, my heart thumping in my throat. "What the fuck did you say?"

A dark chuckle rattles from him. "You heard me."

The room goes deafeningly silent, and his stare up at me is unwavering as I take a step toward him. "Tell me," I roar, my fists slamming into his face like it's a punching bag.

Blood flows from his lips by the time I stop. He pushes a tooth from between them, and a now-gaping smile spreads across his face, his remaining teeth coated with crimson spittle. "Davit sent her a text from you nearly ten minutes ago. If you hurry, maybe you'll get there first."

Pulling my gun again, I can barely breathe as I point it toward his battered face and mercilessly pull the trigger—the reverberations of the shots echo around the concrete tomb. My legs move before my brain catches up, and I sprint away from the Armenian, my boots thudding against the concrete until I reach the elevator. I jab the call button so hard I might break it.

I need to get to her...

The seconds tick by like hours, waiting for the cab to arrive. My hand trembles as I dial Cillian—the call failing from the service-blocked confines of the basement. "Fuck!" I yell, pacing the floor like a caged animal. I futilely try calling Cillian again, but the call still won't go through.

The elevator dings, and I nearly punch the doors open. I swipe my keycard and slam the penthouse button until the doors slide shut. The car lurches upward as I hold the handrail with a white-knuckled grip, my other hand repeatedly hitting redial. Still no fucking connection.

After what feels like an eternity, the doors open. I bolt into the hall, my shoulder clipping the still-opening doors. The pain barely registers as I sprint toward Damon and Gunnar, holding sentry outside the penthouse door. They both tense upon seeing me and follow behind me as I barrel through the front door.

"Eavan!" I shout, my crazed eyes darting around the apartment. She doesn't reply. My heart thumps like a drum in my ears, and I choke when I try to yell her name again. "Eavan!"

"Enz?" Nikolai walks into the living room from the terrace, confusion snapping across his face.

"Where is she?" I shout, panic quickly taking hold.

"She went downstairs to meet you." He shakes his head, continuing to stare at me with disbelief. "Maybe five minutes ago."

"And you fucking let her go?" I snarl, my blood turning to ice and boiling all at once.

Nikolai recoils at the fury in my voice, defensively replying, "She said you texted her. Fuck, *you* text me to say it was fine and you were waiting at the elevator."

"What the hell is going on?" Cillian mutters as I turn, finding him staring at me wide-eyed with takeout bags in his hands. "Enz?!"

"The Armenians," I gruff, my voice raw, as I shove past him, racing back to the elevator. They all follow—Cillian, Nikolai, Gunnar, and Damon, all asking a barrage of questions I don't have time to answer. *Questions that don't matter right now.*

The doors slide shut, and the cab can't move fast enough for any of us. "What the fuck is going on?" Cillian shouts over the chorus of chatter in the small space, demanding an actual answer this time.

"Sargsyan... The motherfucker cloned my phone," I grit, my jaw clenched so tightly with anger my teeth might crack. My foot taps against the floor, and my fingers twitch as I anxiously wait for the cab to reach the lobby, watching the floors click by in slow motion. "They've been reading everything."

He pales. "What?"

"They knew I was texting her. They used my messages to lure Eavan from the apartment. Sargsyan came for her."

Cillian stumbles back like I hit him, shaking his head in disbelief, and the blood draining from his face.

The second the doors open, I'm sprinting through the lobby. "Eavan!" I call out, knowing she isn't here. "Eavan!" My cries echo off the marble and glass—the vast space is practically empty, less the receptionist sitting behind the desk.

"She just went outside a few minutes ago," the receptionist softly informs me, looking afraid of the armed men following me.

I storm toward the building's front doors, Nikolai, Cillian, Gunnar, and Damon all hard on my heels. The moment I hit the street, I spin in place—my eyes scanning up and down the sidewalk like I can will her back if I try hard enough. *Nothing.* No flutter of her fiery red hair in the crowd down the block. No panicked screams in the distance.

Just... gone.

Minutes too late.

I broke my promise... I let them take her.

My chest heaves, and my knees threaten to buckle. I bend over, hands on my knees, trying to force air into my lungs. The pulse in my ears is so loud it drowns out everything around me. Rage and guilt crushing me, I mumble, "This is my fault. I put her in their hands."

I'm going to get her back...

Cillian glares at me, and part of me is waiting for him to either agree with me or place a firm fist into my jaw. He firmly grips me by the back of the neck and hauls me into him. "It's not your fault, Enz," he mutters, promising it to me and trying to convince himself. "We're gonna get her back."

"They're going to try to get her out of the country. And fast." Nikolai pulls out his phone, swiping across the screen. "The issue is, which airport are they going to? It'll take us far too long to scout them all. Drive time alone, they'll have her over the mid-Atlantic before we can get between Teterboro, White Plains, LaGuardia, and JFK."

"If we choose the wrong one..." Cillian sighs, also digging his phone from his pocket. "I'll start getting guys on the road to all of them.".

"We won't," I exhale, swiping Cillian's phone out of his hand. He grumbles as I pull up the website—the one that will save her. The one connected to the tracker I hid in the necklace I gifted her. It takes three agonizing seconds to load. And then —there. A red blip.

Glancing over my shoulder, Cillian gruffs, "You fucking LoJack'ed my sister?"

"You can be pissed with me about it later." I zoom in on the map, watching the little red dot approaching the Lincoln Tunnel. "When we bring her back home. They're heading to Teterboro."

The SUV rumbles over a pothole, and I jostle in my seat, my shoulder slamming into the man on my right. The only reaction I get from him is a short, annoyed glance. He's completely uninterested in me, like I'm nothing more than cargo.

I try to lean away, but there's nowhere to go. I'm boxed in on both sides, my wrists are bound tightly with thin zip ties that cut into my skin every time I move.

With Davit's knees slightly parted and his arm draped over the back of the driver's seat, he watches me from the front passenger seat. He looks so relaxed, you'd think he was relaxing in a private booth in a cigar lounge instead of riding shotgun in a getaway car. He smiles at me with the satisfaction of a man who has already won.

"You've become very quiet, spitfire," he croons, his voice smooth and disgustingly sultry.

"I'm thinking," I share.

He stares at me, his brow arching inquisitively. "Enlighten me."

"I'm considering whether or not spitting in your face would get me shot."

"There she is." He chuckles softly. "I was worried you'd lost that fire I like so much."

I lift my chin and shake my head. "You don't get to talk to me like you know me."

"But I do," he replies. "I know your name... Your family... Your taste in music... How unbelievably gorgeous those curves of yours look in lingerie. Particularly that little black strappy number you took photos of yourself wearing the other day."

I feel the blood draining from my face as my body goes cold again. "How—" I cut myself off, not wanting to give him the satisfaction of my discomfort.

But it's too late, he knows he's hit a nerve. His eyes light up with amusement. "Yes," he answers, as if he knows exactly what question I was going to ask. "We've read every message. Every dirty little text between the two of you. Every sweet little word your Italian playboy sent to you. Every promise. Every I love you. Every Daddy."

I swallow hard, choking down the bile rising in my throat when I put it together. The text from Enzo telling me to meet him in the lobby, it wasn't from him. *It was them.* They used my unwavering trust in him to take me.

"You're lying," I exclaim, even though I know he isn't.

"Not in the slightest." Davit leans forward, pushing himself slightly between the two front seats. "He has no fucking clue. We cloned his phone weeks ago. Poor boy... I actually think he might miss you."

"Go to hell," I spit.

He smiles again, infuriatingly calm. "One way or another, spitfire, I will. I'm certain of that. But not before you take a very long trip with me. And then I drag you there, too."

I shake my head, pulling at the restraints even though they bite into my skin. "You won't get away with this."

"But I already have," he muses. "You'll see soon enough. Armenia will be your new home. My men will enjoy spending a few weeks breaking you in, making sure you learn your rightful place. And then I'll put you to work as one of my whores. I should get a few good years out of a feisty young bitch like you."

My stomach lurches as we pull out of the tunnel and back into the blinding sunlight. We've only just left the city, and I already feel oceans away from the life I've grown to know —*and love*—with Enzo, Cillian, and Nikolai. Outside the window, the streets start to blur—storefronts replaced with busy highways and overpasses. They're moving fast. Purposefully. I can't see much, but the further away we get, the more hopeless it feels.

The driver murmurs something in Armenian, and one of the guards beside me replies just as quietly. I don't know the words, but I can read their body language. They're on edge too—not afraid, but alert. They aren't nearly as confident as Davit.

Davit shifts again, lacing his fingers across his lap and returning his dark gaze to the road. "It didn't have to be this way, you know. You could've been protected. You could've married my son and spent your life in a penthouse, with guards watching over you and servants fulfilling your every whim."

I scoff. "You mean stayed locked away like some mafia Rapunzel? No thanks."

"You wouldn't have been a prisoner. You would've been well respected. Feared because of who your husband was," he retorts. "The four of you chose this. Your decisions have made you my captive... Hopefully my future best-selling whore."

I spit at him. It falls short—landing on his arm instead of in his face—but the gesture earns me a shove from the wall of muscle on my right. My head snaps forward and hits the edge of the seat in front of me, causing stars to flicker at the corners of my vision.

"I warned you," Davit grouses coolly. "That's the last time I offer you any kindness."

"Your kindness feels a lot like threats and zip ties," I mutter, blinking hard to stay focused.

"Threats keep people alive. And I need you alive, for now." He reaches into his coat and pulls out a folded slip of paper. "Let them know our ETA," he instructs with a nod as he passes it to the man on my right.

The goon beside me unfolds the paper—a flight itinerary.

Private jet scheduled to depart within a few hours. No commercial airport. No security checks.

"I'll scream," I blurt, suddenly. "As soon as I see someone. I'll scream my lungs out."

"Then we'll cut out your tongue before we get there." The way he says it—it's not a threat. It's a fact. *I don't need a tongue for what he wants me for...*

The SUV slows slightly, and my heart spikes in panic. We're getting closer. *I have to do something. Anything.*

Suddenly, I shift, slamming my shoulder into the guy on my right and kicking my foot firmly against the driver's seat. It budges just enough to startle the driver, causing the SUV to swerve across the highway. The man beside me shouts, the other grabs my flailing feet, and Davit barks something in Armenian. The goon not holding my legs grabs my jaw, squeezing until my teeth grind and I wince in pain.

"Do that again," he hisses with a thick accent, "and we'll break your fucking legs."

"Better than whatever you guys are planning to do to me," I grit out. He lets go with a shove, and I slump back against the leather seat, chest heaving. My wrists burn, and my jaw aches, but I don't care. Every second I buy gives another second for Enzo to find me.

I know he's coming. *He has to be.*

Davit adjusts his cufflinks, as if nothing has happened. "You're lucky, you know," he murmurs. "You're lucky to have made it this far. Usually, I would've just put a bullet in you and been done with it. But you... you've caught the attention of men far more dangerous than Enzo Roseti."

I slowly turn my head to look at him. "You talk too much for a man so sure of himself." His eyes narrow as he glares at me. *Good. Let him get angry.*

Let him fuck up.

We take another hard right; the SUV bouncing slightly as we pass over speed bumps and onto the private airfield. I grab the key hanging around my neck, holding it tightly like it's somehow going to tether me to Enzo.

Please find me before this plane takes off... Please, Daddy.

Gunnar pushes the SUV like he's driving a getaway car. My world narrows to the growl of the engine under Gunnar's hands. Manhattan blurs around us—glass, steel, streaks of yellow taxis, and honking horns. He's reckless with his speed. The kind of driving that ends with body bags or headlines, but I can't bring myself to tell him to slow down.

Tricked from the safety of our home, my girl has been thrown into a nightmare she doesn't deserve—one I *will* rescue her from. The only thing I can think about is getting to her. Getting to my princess. As fast as fucking possible, because with every second that passes, we're running out of time.

"I've checked with some contacts," Nikolai discloses from the backseat. He might usually be our chaos, but right now, he's calm and collected. Tapping his thumbs against his phone, he continues to type to someone on the other side as he shares what he knows, "Sargsyan has a private jet parked on the eastern hangar strip. There's no flight plan. The plane is prepped for takeoff. Just waiting for its passengers to arrive."

"Let's be real. Even without a flight plan, we know where he's taking her," Cillian mutters. "He's going to fly her out of the country and disappear to Armenia."

I stare out the window, my jaw permanently clenched as it has been since they took her. Towns whizz by as we race down the interstate. "If they make it into the air, it'll be near impossible to find her again." The thought makes me want to vomit. The fact that no one argues only drives home how accurate my statement is.

Nikolai's eyes are hard and unreadable as he continues to type into his phone. Cillian has a quiet rage simmering behind his silence—murderous even. Damon is in the seat behind me, checking his weapons with quick and efficient movements.

"ETA?" Cillian asks.

"If traffic stays clear, eight minutes," Gunnar answers.

"They're only a few miles from the airfield," I solemnly share, my eyes not leaving the phone screen. "We don't have eight minutes." *We might not have two.* I shove a hand through my hair, gripping hard. My pulse is a fucking jackhammer, every breath razor-sharp. Leaning forward, elbows on my knees, I try to focus through the thunder rattling my skull. All I can see is her face. Eavan... my princess. The only soft place in my world of bullets and blood. I told her she was safe with me. She trusted me, and I've let her down. We all let her down.

"We need to be there in four," Cillian mutters, eyes narrowed as he glances between the road and the clock on the dash. "Or we might be too late." Gunnar stomps on the accelerator, and the engine roars as the speedometer creeps into triple-digit numbers.

"Jagger and Hawk are three miles back, following our trail like vultures," Damon informs us. "They'll be a few minutes behind us."

"Too late," I gripe. "We don't wait for them. We go in heavy and fast. No time for back-up. We stop the plane and kill everyone who helped make this happen."

"The plane is a Gulfstream G550," Nikolai reads Hawk's text. I don't know if Hawk has a man on the inside, if he hacked their travel manifest, or if he's using satellites. *And right now, I don't fucking care where the information is coming from.* "Two-man flight crew, both ex-military. Six ground men we can see—two at the hangar doors, four patrolling the jet. Could be more inside."

"And Eavan?" I ask, unable to hold back the question.

"I don't know," Nikolai answers honestly.

My hands ball in my lap. "No survivors," I growl.

"None," Cillian echoes, quiet and deadly.

Nikolai asks, "You want to make the call? Or should I?"

"You," I insist, not knowing if they're still watching my phone.

He taps on his screen, and Jagger answers quickly, "Jagger."

"What's your status?" I ask.

"Not far behind you," he answers. "We can see you a few cars ahead. What's the plan?"

Nikolai demands, "Give me a rifle and a vantage point."

"You'll get it." I spin in my seat to face him. "We'll drop you just off the service road behind the northeastern perimeter. Should give you the line of sight."

"I'll take the pilot first." His tone is flat. "Then the crew. No one flies that jet."

I nod, leaning back in my seat, adrenaline already burning slow and steady in my veins. "Cillian and I will go in head-on. Damon, you and Gunnar circle around. I want fire from both sides. We squeeze."

Gunnar grins without looking away from the road. "Love a good squeeze."

"Jagger and Hawk, you follow at a distance, swing around, and flank from the south hangars. Intercept anyone running. Kill them all."

"Roger that," Hawk affirms.

"And Jagger? Hawk?"

"Yeah?" they answer in unison.

"If that plane's wheels leave the ground—"

"It won't," Hawk insists.

I hang up as Gunnar jerks the wheel, abruptly taking the turnpike ramp. The SUV surges to the left, nearly clipping a slow-moving delivery truck. I can see the airport fencing now, half-hidden by trees and low warehouse buildings. Gunnar turns onto a dirt service road running parallel to the airstrip. "This is your stop," he informs Nikolai, who is already jumping from the back seat.

Nikolai pops the hatch on the back of the SUV, slings his rifle over his shoulder, and quickly grabs a black duffel with extra mags and a thermal scope. "I'll be in position in two ."

"Nik," I call after him, and he pauses. "Don't miss."

Glancing at me through the rear of the car, a smug smirk pulls at the corner of his lips. "I never do." He winks and wastes no time waiting for a response, immediately running toward the hangar, disappearing into the trees like he was never there.

The SUV jolts as Gunnar stomps on the accelerator, kicking up gravel when the tires spin against the road. And we're at the airfield, the runway stretching into the distance, and at the far end, the white blur of a Gulfstream with the steps already down.

"Drive straight through the fence," I bark.

"You got it, boss." Gunnar floors it and yells, "Brace!" He guns it straight through the maintenance access gate, doing at least seventy. He doesn't slow until we're approaching the Gulfstream. I throw open the door before we stop moving.

Cillian is right behind me, Damon and Gunnar flanking as planned.

The engines hum, runway lights reflecting off the fuselage, and bullets spark off the pavement. It does nothing to slow us. We move in coordinated chaos—trained, lethal, and unstoppable. I raise my Glock and fire twice. One of Sargsyan's men drops with a hole in his forehead. Another falls to the asphalt beside him, screaming as his leg is shredded by Damon's shotgun. Cillian takes two with controlled bursts. Gunnar drops another as he tries to run for the hangar like a fucking coward.

Then, movement near the stairs draws my attention.

Sargsyan...

Tucked behind a row of stacked shipping pallets, my eyes are locked on the tarmac. The private jet is stationary—steps lowered and engines humming softly. Sargsyan is at the base of the plane steps. He's in a tailored suit, pacing like he's waiting to board for a business trip, not an abduction. My hands twitch, and I fight the urge to just pull the trigger and drop the piece of shit where he stands.

My muscles are tight, every part of me screaming to move, to act—but I hold.

I wait.

My princess.

The door swings open on the SUV, and two men climb out from the back, dragging someone between them. My chest contracts so hard it nearly knocks the air out of me. She's resisting, twisting in their grip, her face wild with frustration and fear. Her incoherent cries cut across the tarmac, scared and urgent. I catch a glimpse of her eyes—wide, focused, unyielding. *That's my fucking girl.* She stumbles as they drag her toward the plane, and one of the men roughly grabs her arm to steady her. The second they reach Sargsyan, they shove her into his arms.

He grabs her, steadying her with one arm and pulling her toward him. Shoving a gun into her side, he snakes an arm around her neck, and her whole body visibly tightens when she's pressed against his front. My gut clenches at the sight. *He's going to fucking die.* Sargsyan starts up the stairs, dragging Eavan with him. She fights him every step of the way, her eyes wide open and desperately searching the tarmac for help. The second she sees me, she freezes, and I feel every emotion harboring behind her eyes—fear, confusion, and relief. Sargsyan shouts at her in Armenian, barking an order, digging his pistol into her side hard enough to cause her to wince.

"Take the fucking shot, Nik," I mumble to myself.

Three subtle, distant cracks echo from the nearby tree-line— suppressed rounds. *Nikolai.* A round pierces the cockpit window, dropping the pilot. The second splatters his co-pilot's brain across the glass. The third hits Sargsyan, missing Eavan by maybe an inch, hitting his shoulder and snapping him backward. He loses his footing—and his hold on Eavan

—tumbling down the stairs and spilling onto the asphalt. Eavan clutches the handrail despite the restraints they have put her in, grasping it just in time to keep herself upright.

I sprint across the tarmac, focused on nothing but her. Everything else fades away—the plane, the noise, the world. My shoes pound against the pavement as she bolts down the steps to me with her eyes locked on mine. Shots ring out, and the final two of Sargsyan's men hit the ground as I race toward her.

My eyes fall to Sargsyan in a pool of his own blood between us, wrapping his fingers around the gun lying beside him. Sitting up a few inches, he raises the weapon toward Eavan.

I don't think.

I act.

I pull my Glock and squeeze the trigger.

CLICK.

I squeeze it again.

CLICK.

My heart sinks, and a surge of panic rushes through me as I break into a full sprint. She doesn't see him. I shout her name, it's like I'm struggling to run through tar and unable to get to her. "No!" I shriek, as Sargsyan fires—the sound cracking through the air. I dive forward, throwing myself into her as pain rips across my side like a lightning strike. My tackle takes us both to the ground hard. She gasps, clutching my chest, as I wrap myself around her, placing my body between her and Sargsyan, tucking her beneath me with everything I have.

More shots follow, and I flatten my body against her, holding a deep breath and bracing for more rounds to slam into my back—they don't come. A final shot rings out, followed by the near silence of whirring jet engines and Eavan breathing heavily against my chest.

I lift my head, my thoughts swimming. Cillian stands nearby, his expression cold but steady, standing over Sargsyan's body with his firearm lowered. "He's down. For good."

Below me, Eavan's eyes are glassy with tears. She runs her still-bound hands along my jaw, her fingers dragging through my beard. "You came," she whispers, fighting back a sob.

"Always," I exhale.

She presses her forehead to mine, her breath shaky and words laced with fear. "I didn't know if I'd ever see you again."

"I promised you I wouldn't let them take you." I cup her face and stare into her eyes. "I will *never* let anyone come between us."

I kiss her gently. Not caring about anything else—my wound, the blood, or the fact that we're surrounded by quite a few dead Armenians. I need to feel her and know that she's safe. She melts into me, bound hands still trembling, holding onto me like she's never letting go.

Pulling back, I wince as I try to sit us both up. "Enz," she gasps, seeing the blood at my side. Her fingers hover over the wound, trying not to hurt me.

"I'm okay," I lie.

Cillian kneels beside me, calm and efficient. "You're hit?" he asks.

"Yeah," I grimace as Cillian lifts my shirt to inspect the wound.

"You'll live." He shrugs with a smirk. "Through and through. Almost a flesh wound."

"Thanks for the encouragement," I mutter.

He reaches for Eavan, cutting the ties around her wrists with a knife , pulling her close. "You all right?"

She nods. "Yes."

Nikolai jogs toward us with his rifle slung over his back. "We've got to move. This wasn't exactly discreet."

Nikolai and Cillian lift me slowly. I grit my teeth and stay upright, wrapping my arm tightly around Eavan's shoulders when she insists on nudging Nik out of the way. She stays at my side, supporting me. As we move back toward the vehicles, I take one last glance at the jet behind us—at the man who almost stole everything from me. I look down at Eavan, her hand wrapped tightly over mine, blood seeping between our fingers.

Her eyes are still welling with tears, but she takes every step with determination as we walk away from the carnage together. She's safe in my arms again. And that's all that matters.

My nostrils are still flooded with the smoky kerosene-like scent of jet fuel and the coppery tang of blood as we walk toward the black SUV. Everything from the tarmac is a blur—running, Sargsyan's gun shoved in my side, yelling, and the crack of gunfire, Enzo's arms around me, his body covering mine. It all happened so fast and so slow at once.

We climb into the back of Hawk's Tahoe. Enzo's blood is warm on my hands. It's sticky, soaking into the black leather of the SUV's seat, staining my fingers and my heart at the same time. Cillian slides in beside us, calm as ever, with a med kit in his hands. Taking gauze from him, my hands shaking, I apply pressure to Enzo's wound. I press harder to stop the bleeding, but the bandages are almost immediately soaked through and rendered useless. Pressure, elevation, keep him conscious—I try to remember what I learned in first aid at school—but my brain is filled with white noise.

"Hold still," I whisper, though he's barely moving.

"I'm fine," he mutters, clamping his hand over mine and squeezing it tightly. "Just a scratch."

It's not *just* a scratch. His white shirt is dark with blood, and there's more oozing from beneath the gauze and dripping down his side, painting his skin in streaks. He winces every time the SUV hits a pothole or speed bump. I can feel the tremble in his muscles, the tension in his jaw. He's trying to look strong, trying to protect me even now.

"Will you tell her I'm fine?" Enzo asks Cillian.

"Enzo will be okay," Cillian insists, and I nod like I believe him. He works fast, cleaning the wound—his fingers are quick but gentle. "It looks a lot worse than it is, Eav. It's deep, but it's clean. It could've been a lot worse. He just needs some stitches."

It could've been a lot worse...

Enzo shifts in his seat, and I push him into the seatback with a firm hand on his chest. "Stop being a stubborn fuck. Just let him take care of you."

"Language, princess." He smirks through his grimace.

I want to yell at him. To smack him.

But I don't.

Instead, I keep my hand pressed against his and whisper, "Don't ever scare me like that again."

"You scared me first," he confesses. "When I learned you were gone. Then, watching you walk toward me as he raised his gun, I thought..." He doesn't finish. He doesn't have to.

The SUV hums beneath us, racing us away from the airfield and back to the city. Sargsyan is dead—I saw Cillian standing over his lifeless body, but I don't have closure. I'm cracked open and vulnerable. As much as I want to believe that we're safe, that this ends here, I've been in this world long enough to know better.

"You okay?" Enzo asks, his fingers lightly dusting over my tender cheek from where that asshole hit me.

I nod. "I'm supposed to be asking you that."

I brush Enzo's hair back from his forehead, and he looks at me like I'm the only thing in the world that matters. *Because, to him, I am.* "I'm fine. I would've taken a dozen bullets to protect you. And a dozen more to keep you from being dragged on that plane."

We both fall quiet, my head resting on his shoulder as we drive toward Midtown. Gunnar pulls into the garage and parks near the elevator. Cillian and Gunnar help Enzo out of the backseat and into the elevator. When we walk into the apartment, Nikolai takes my hand and leads me toward the stairs. "Let Gunnar get him stitched up. He'll be all right." He places his hand on the small of my back and ushers me up the steps. I don't argue—mentally, I don't have the strength to. "Let me take care of you."

His hand not letting go of mine, we walk down the hall to Enzo's room. We reach the attached bathroom, and he turns on the faucet of the sink before testing the water until it warms. He fills my hands with a generous amount of soap, and I scrub them together. My eyes focus on Enzo's blood swirling down the drain with my pink suds. In the mirror, I look like a stranger—hollow eyes and wild hair. I touch my face like maybe that'll ground me, but it doesn't.

Taking my hands, Nik looks over the tiny cuts and thin bruises forming around my wrists and beneath my eye. "You good?" he asks. "These don't look that bad."

"Just a little shaky. I'll feel better when I know Enz is okay."

Nikolai nods in understanding. "I'll go check on him while you finish getting cleaned up."

My skin cleaned of Enzo's blood and changed into a fresh set of clothes, I lie on the bed with my knees pulled to my chest. I don't cry—not really, but I tremble for a while. All I can think about is how close it all was—how one wrong move or one misfired bullet would've changed everything.

"I'm fine." I hear Enzo down the hallway arguing with Cillian; his voice is hoarse and quieter than usual. A moment later, the door opens, and he pauses on the threshold. He is shirtless, and his side is covered with fresh white bandages.

"I'm pretty sure he's only telling you to take it easy." I shake my head, pushing up from the bed.

"I did." He grins. "I sat nice and still while Gunnar stitched me up, counting the minutes until I could come up here and be with you."

I rush to him, wrapping my arms around him as gently as I can. He pulls me close, his hand settling in the middle of my back and holding me tight like he's been waiting just to breathe me in again.

Burying my face in his chest, I whisper, "I was so worried you weren't going to find me in time."

"Not a chance, princess." Enzo presses his lips to my forehead before pulling back. He reaches for the skeleton key hanging around my neck, rolling it between his fingers as he lifts it. "I knew *exactly* where to find you." I reach for the key hanging around my neck, my fingers tangling with his as I realize what he's saying. "As long as you wear this, I'll *always* know exactly where you are."

I should be upset that he didn't tell me he'd fastened a GPS around my neck, but I'm not. He knew as well as I did that the Armenians would come for me. That sooner or later, they would succeed in taking me. This was his safety net. *Our* safety net.

We climb onto the bed and curl together, his arms wrapping around me as I nuzzle into him—unable to get close enough. The room falls quiet, except for our breathing. I don't ask if he's in pain. I can see it. I can feel how tense his body is and hear it in the way he only takes shallow breaths.

"I don't want to ask this," I mutter against his chest, "but I need to know. What happens now?"

He sighs—long and heavy. "There'll be fallout. Sargsyan is gone, but someone will try to take his place. Probably his son. That's how our world works. Power doesn't stay vacant for long."

"So more fighting..." I sigh.

"Maybe. But not with you in the crossfire."

"You can't promise that."

He holds me a little tighter. "I can guarantee I'll do everything to make sure it never happens again." I believe him, but it terrifies me. Because now I know exactly what Enzo—and my brother—will do to keep promises like that. I know what it costs.

Taking my hand, he presses his lips to my knuckles. "I love you, Eavan."

"I love you, too, Daddy."

His fingers thread through mine, lacing us together like he's never going to let go of me. Gingerly rolling onto his side, he kisses me slowly—savoring me. I kiss him back, needing him like my next breath. It's as if I've been holding mine since being swept off the sidewalk earlier today.

Tangled in each other and drifting to sleep, the only things I can think about are how close we came to losing each other and how much I want to spend the rest of my nights wrapped in his warmth. Because wherever he is, that's my home.

ABOUT A WEEK LATER

The city is quieter than usual this morning, or maybe it just feels that way.

Sunlight peeks through the clouds, painting the terrace with golden streaks. There is a light breeze, the kind that lingers before the day heats up. I tug gently at the hem of Enzo's shirt —the one he was wearing last night. It's far too big on me, and I have the sleeves rolled up several times, only for them to still keep falling over my hands. The collar hangs loose, slipping off my shoulder every time I try to move a sleeve.

I stretch my legs over the chaise, curling my bare toes around the edge as I take a slow sip of my coffee. The book in my lap is open, but I've been rereading the same page for twenty minutes. My eyes—and thoughts—keep drifting, and I'm not really absorbing the words. For the first time in what feels like forever, things are... normal. Or, well, our version of it. Yet, I've been struggling for days to focus on the future without worrying about what threat is going to come storming through our front door next.

The boys let me out of the apartment the past few days, which is their way of saying I'm no longer on total lockdown—or in immediate danger. Of course, one of them is always with me.

Grocery store? Cillian.

A walk to the coffee shop on the corner? Gunnar, sunglasses on, hand casually resting near the inside of his jacket like we're just two people on a very edgy date.

It's freedom... sort of. It's already more freedom than I had under my father's reign.

Enzo has been exceptionally busy lately, leaving the apartment far more often than usual. Normally, he tells me where he's going and why, but he's been keeping most of his recent outings secret. I know he's hiding something—I just don't know what.

He steps onto the terrace just as I'm about to reread the same page for the umpteenth time. His hair is still damp from the shower, casually slicked back from running his fingers through it. He's wearing gray sweats and a fitted black T-shirt —an outfit that shouldn't be legal this early in the day.

"Morning," he croons, his voice warm and a little too smooth for someone who hasn't had coffee yet.

I smile over my mug. "Morning."

He drops onto the chaise next to me, his hand falling onto my thigh and tenderly squeezing it. "I have something I want to show you, princess."

I lower my book slowly, trying to hide the smile that already pulls at my lips. "Pretty sure you already showed me something last night. Twice."

He chuckles, his eyes darkening a little. "I mean something else."

"More than twice?" I tease.

He leans in, his lips brushing against my jaw and placing a soft kiss there. He stands and offers me his hand. "Come on."

"Right now?" I ask, glancing down at my lack of appropriate clothes. "Enz, I'm not dressed to go anywhere."

"What you have on is absolutely perfect for where I'm taking you."

His statement doesn't help my confusion, but I set the coffee cup on the end table and slide my hand into his. His fingers curl around mine: warm, familiar, and strong in that protective way that always makes my pulse skip.

He leads me through the apartment and to the elevator. In the cab, he doesn't press the button for the lobby, but for the floor just below ours.

My brows furrow, and I glance at him. "What's on the thirty-eighth floor?"

He doesn't answer. Instead, that maddening smirk of his tugs at the corner of his lips—the one that infuriates me and makes me melt all at once. He steps out first, spinning to face me. Walking backward, he pulls a small set of keys from his pocket.

"Enz?" I ask as he slips one key into a door just around the corner from the elevator. It unlocks easily. He pushes the door all the way open, then steps aside so I can see into the apartment. "What is this?"

He tilts his head, the smirk spreading into a full smile. "Yours."

I step into the apartment, my eyes darting left and right, trying to take it all in. It's empty, but stunning—floor-to-ceiling windows, light hardwood floors, a modern kitchen with clean lines and soft lighting. There are still tags on some of the appliances, and it smells faintly of fresh paint and sawdust.

"My what?"

He steps in behind me, wrapping an arm around my waist. "I have contractors coming to build a staircase connecting this place to the penthouse this week. It'll keep you close to

Cillian and Nikolai—with them able to get to you if needed —but it'll be your space."

"You bought me an apartment?" I ask, stunned.

"No." He kisses the lone word against the crook of my neck, and it vibrates against my skin. "I bought *us* an apartment."

This isn't just a gift. Enzo is carving out something just for us —something normal, or as close to it as we're going to get. He's giving us a space that's still protected, still near the men that will keep me safe, but... ours.

Not a prison, but a home.

I turn in his arms and stare up at him, blinking rapidly. "You did all this for me?"

"No, princess. I did it for us." His hand rests gently at my waist, ever so slightly pulling me into him. "This isn't quite what we had talked about... Not quite the home I want to give you. But right now, until things settle down, this gives us our own home."

I blink, trying to hold them back, but I can't stop the tears welling in my eyes. "No, Enz." I shake my head with a smile. "It's absolutely beautiful. It's perfect."

"I was going to wait until it was furnished to show you," he murmurs. "But I couldn't. I couldn't keep this from you another day. I couldn't keep the secret anymore. This isn't building something for you. It's about building something *with* you."

He pulls me close, arms snaking tightly around my waist, and I rise onto my toes, my hands tangling in his hair as our lips meet. The kiss is soft at first, but it quickly deepens, growing urgent and intense. He lifts me, my legs wrapping around his waist as he carries me toward the wall of windows, wedging me between him and the icy pane.

"Enz," I squeak as he pulls at my shirt, leaving my body bare against the glass.

"Daddy needs your pussy, princess." He leaves a trail of warm, wet kisses along my neck, stopping just below my ear. "So badly that I'm going to let the whole fucking city watch as I fill you with our babies."

CHAPTER 50
enzo

Shoving my sweatpants over my hips, I work them just low enough to free my cock. With Eavan pinned between me and the window, granting an unfettered view of her to the city, I press my tip to her entrance. "Let them all see how your tight pussy stretches wide for Daddy's big cock," I groan against her neck, slowly inching myself into her—my sweats sliding down my legs and pooling around my ankles.

"I'm taking all of you. Every thick inch," Eavan pants against my shoulder as I bury myself deep in her. "Are you proud of me, Daddy?"

Her words blow across my skin, heat and wicked intentions that leave me struggling not to unravel before her. In the time we've been together, she has grown beyond comfortable in her role. She owns every dirty word that passes over her lips, knowing exactly what they do to me. It's not just the words themselves. It's *her...* The way she drops her voice just enough to make my heart race—like she's pulling at the threads of my self-control on purpose, and brattily enjoying every second of it. She presses every button like she designed them herself. And I let her, gladly.

"Fuck, princess," I groan, squeezing her ass. "I love that fucking mouth of yours." My lips crash against hers, my tongue slipping between them. Working my hips, I thrust into her until I'm swallowing her moans through our kiss. I break our kiss, leaving my lips resting on hers. "Are you going to come for Daddy?"

"Yes, Daddy," she whimpers as I thrust deep once more.

Her back slides against the smooth glass with every demanding drive of my hips, soft cries of pleasure falling over her lips every time I fill her with my cock. "You don't have to be quiet"—I slam into her—"no one can hear you but me. And Daddy wants all your screams, princess."

I take her hard and fast, pushing her to give me exactly what I want—the sweet sounds of her coming undone in our apartment for the first time. And she doesn't disappoint. Eavan quivers around my cock, moans and cries of pleasure rising from her as she loses control.

"You come so fucking beautifully," I gravelly whisper, watching her eyes go glassy as euphoria washes over her face. It's a look I'll never fucking get enough of. My thrusts are relentless, keeping her teetering on the edge as she rides the never-ending wave of her release.

"Since you love... calling me... Daddy... so... fucking much," I grit between thrusts. "Fucking. Make. Me. One." I bury every inch of my cock in her, a breathy groan rattling from my lungs as I spill into her—pushing every drop into her. Not pulling from her, I lower us both to the floor and hold her on my lap, peppering kisses over her lips and cheeks until both of us have caught our breath again.

The sunlight spills through the windows, warming the hardwood floors. The two of us sprawl across them, tangled in each other. I ball up my sweatpants and slip them beneath Eavan's head, her cheek resting on them like it's the most natural thing in the world. Her hair is a mess, and her skin is still flushed—yet this might be the most beautiful I've ever seen her.

She traces her finger slowly along the inside of my forearm, like she's memorizing me. *Maybe she is.* Neither of us speaks for a while. We don't have to. There's something sacred about this silence. Having her in my arms fills me with a peace I never knew before her.

"I think we need to get a couch," she half-teases, a smile spreading across her lips.

"I don't know..." I brush my hand down her spine. "That window and these hardwood floors have their perks."

She lifts her head just enough to give me a lazy smirk. "That so?"

"You're here, princess. That's all I need." She settles back against me, her hand moving to my jaw and her thumb brushing along the line of my beard, content with my answer.

"I've been thinking," I say, my voice quieter than I expect. "About how this place won't be empty forever."

"So you *are* thinking about getting a couch?" she brats, her smile pressing into my skin.

"Well, yes." I pause. "But more than that."

She tilts her head, staring at me across my chest, waiting for me to continue.

"I might have been unsure before, but I see kids here," I admit. "I want to chase them barefoot across these floors, their laughter filling this huge apartment when you yell at me for spoiling them. Because I'm going to overflow this place with toys, even when I promise that I won't buy any more."

Her expression softens, lips parting as if to speak, but she doesn't. She just listens, her emerald eyes glimmering with anticipation of our future.

"And someday," I continue, "I want to marry you."

Her breath catches, and her throat bobs as she swallows hard.

"I know the timing is crazy," I admit, "but I mean it. I want to wake up beside you every day and know you're mine in every way. Not just in this life, but in name, too. I want to build something amazing with you... as my wife."

Eavan's eyes don't falter from mine, but she doesn't say a word. My answer comes as she leans forward and presses her lips to mine. I let out a breath I didn't realize I was holding, my hand wrapping around the back of her neck. I pull her lips back to mine and claim her mouth—kissing my forever.

"I never thought I'd have something this good," I murmur against her lips. "Someone as amazing as you. Not with all the things I've done..."

"You have me," she vows. "I don't care what you've done or what you're going to do. I only care about the man you are inside these walls. The man who puts me on a pedestal and worships me like a queen."

"Because you are," I whisper. "Every king needs their queen."

She rests her head against my chest again, and we lie like that, wrapped around each other, breathing in the same rhythm. The apartment is empty, but it already feels full—with our promises of the future we plan to build together.

I press a kiss to her temple and close my eyes. I've protected a lot of things in my life—territory, money, power—but nothing like this. Nothing like *her*.

My everything. My home.

And someday soon, my wife.

ABOUT A MONTH LATER

This apartment has been filled with the rumble of power tools, short-tempered shouts of contractors, and the constant scent of paint and sawdust. Movers delivered the last of our furniture today, and this place *finally* looks like a home. Tonight, it smells like one, too. A very Italian one—the warm, rich aroma of garlic and roasted tomatoes floating in the air, causing my mouth to water.

Enzo is standing at the stove, his back to me, stirring the sauce like he's terrified it's going to burn to the bottom of the pan.

"You're holding that spoon like it's a weapon," I tease, leaning against the kitchen island.

He smirks over his shoulder. "*Everything* is a weapon if you're creative enough."

I laugh, not doubting his response. "Should I be worried?" I tease, grabbing a spatula to defend myself.

He turns toward me, wiping his hands on the kitchen towel slung over his shoulder. "Only if you plan on insulting my culinary skills before tasting this."

"I'm just saying... The last time you cooked by yourself, we ended up with the fire alarm screeching and you cursing at the stove."

"That was a fluke," he insists, stalking toward me with mock determination. "And you were of absolutely no help. Actually, if I recall correctly, *you* were the distraction who caused me to burn everything."

I take a small step back, snickering. "I helped by staying out of the way."

"Splayed naked on the counter is not the same as"—he pauses to air quote—"staying out of the way." Enzo corners me against the counter, his arms boxing me in.

I shrug, trying to keep a straight face. "Technically, I was *not* in the way."

He's so close that I can feel the warmth radiating from him— close enough to steal some of my breath. His hands slide along the counter, his forearms resting lightly on my hips. Looming over me, he quips, "For a woman who can handle just about anything, you're awfully mouthy about a guy trying to cook you dinner."

"And for someone with such a dangerous reputation," I counter, lifting my chin, "you're awfully sensitive about your pasta sauce."

He chuckles, soft and low, the vibrations of it rattling beneath my skin. "You're lucky I like your sass."

"You love my sass, Daddy." I wink at him.

He narrows his eyes in mock warning, then, without hesitation, lifts me effortlessly and sets me on the edge of the counter. I let out a surprised laugh, gripping his shoulders for balance. "You can't just manhandle me like that."

A devilish grin pulling at his lips, he growls, "Oh, but I can." He slides his hands up the outside of my thighs—slow and confident—and plants a kiss at the corner of my mouth. His fingers gather the loose skirt of my dress, pooling it on my lap. "Watch me."

I smile against his lips and tease, "I have *very* high standards."

"And I exceed them daily," he retorts—not a question, just a fact.

I laugh again, threading my fingers through his hair. "God, you're so full of yourself."

"Maybe. But you're going to be—" he leans in close, his lips brushing my cheek and traveling toward my jaw—"so fucking of full of me that I'm dripping from you during dinner."

"Daddy?" I chirp, swinging my legs lightly, my heels tapping against the cabinets.

"Yes, princess," he exhales with an annoyed sigh.

"I'm pretty sure your sauce is burning."

He gives the sauce one last stir and turns the burner off, quickly returning to me. Kissing me before I can say a word, his mouth is warm as he steals the air from my lungs. It's the kind of kiss that makes the rest of the apartment disappear—the scent of garlic, the simmering pot, even the fact that I'm half sitting on a cold granite counter.

"I don't think this is very chef-like behavior," I quip when he pulls back from our kiss, giving him a mock-scolding look.

Enzo stands between my knees, his hands firmly gripping my hips. He tips his head slightly, that familiar smirk tugging at the edge of his mouth. "It's not. But I've decided I'm hungry for something other than pasta."

My cheeks flush, and I roll my eyes even as I lean into him. "You're impossible."

He leans in until his lips graze my jaw. "You love it."

I do. God, I do.

The kitchen is warm with the scent of the meal he was preparing, but all I can focus on is the warmth of his hands, the closeness of him, the way his breath fans against my collarbone. I run my fingers up the front of his shirt, letting them lightly clutch the fabric. "Dinner is going to be ruined."

"Worth it," he says without hesitation, his mouth finding mine again. I sink into him like I've done countless times before, though the butterflies still flutter in my stomach like it's the first. His lips trail down to my neck, and I tilt my head, giving him more space—more of me. My hands slide into his hair, lacing through it and curling around his locks as he presses a kiss beneath my ear. My breath catches as his hands find the small of my back, and he pulls me into him "I think this is the first time the apartment's been truly quiet."

"You saying I should shut up?" I quip, unable to hold back my smile.

"No," he laughs. "Just thinking I know of a few sweet sounds that could fill this too-quiet space."

He leans down and kisses me again, and when his hands slide around my neck, I stop caring about dinner being ruined. Our kiss goes from soft to hungry, his hands tightening on my waist, until my back is arching and my legs wrap loosely around him.

His lips trail down my jaw to the hollow of my throat, and I gasp, my hands fisting the fabric of his shirt. I reach for the buttons, and I tear at them with need, hastily freeing him from his shirt. My hands roam over his chiseled bare chest, and when he pulls back, his eyes are darker—now focused and determined.

Enzo lifts me off the counter, his lips not once leaving my skin. He carries me through the apartment we've furnished together, and I know—no matter how chaotic our world may get again—we'll always come back to this.

To each other.

To home.

ABOUT A WEEK LATER

The penthouse buzzes with conversation and the clinking of silverware against plates as the four of us enjoy dinner. Eavan's smile lights up the room, her eyes sparkling as she teases Cillian about his inability to cook anything that doesn't come from a takeout box or a tin can. Cillian, ever the good sport, throws a playful jab back, and the room erupts in genuine laughter.

As the evening unfolds, and the liquor continues to flow, the conversation is effortless. We talk about everything and nothing—plans for the future, the absurdity of some of our past escapades, and the simple joys of being together without looking over our shoulders. It's a rare moment of peace, a fleeting glimpse into a life that almost feels normal.

An unexpected knock at the door shatters the calm. Gunnar's voice follows, muffled by the wall separating us. He's the last of the watchful eyes we hired to keep an eye on my princess. Jagger, Hawk, and Damon each left over the last couple of weeks, their presence no longer needed. Gunnar is tidying up the last of their work and ensuring our security is in good standing before returning to his own life. "Hey, sorry to interrupt. I ran into a guy in the lobby looking to speak with Cillian," he apologizes, stepping into the kitchen. Lowering his voice to just above a whisper, he continues, "I frisked him in the elevator."

I exchange glances with Eavan, a flicker of concern passing between us. Cillian looks equally puzzled, his brow furrowing. "I wasn't expecting anyone."

I set my glass of wine down and wave Cillian off when he starts to rise from the table. "Eat," I insist—and gesture the same to Gunnar, inviting him to join us. "I'll take care of it."

Rising from the table, I adjust the cuff of my shirt as I make my way to the door. When I open it, I find a man standing there—mid-forties, cheap haircut, dressed in an off-the-rack, poorly fitted, and wrinkled suit. His posture is rigid and his expression serious. "Mr. Roseti?" he asks, his voice carrying an edge of confusion.

I nod, stepping aside to let him in since Gunnar confirmed he isn't carrying. "That's me. What can I do for you?"

The man hesitates for a moment, checking the number on the door. "I was looking for Mr. O'Brien."

I glance back toward the entry to the kitchen, where my family is still seated. "He's in here," I say, leading the way.

As we walk down the foyer, the man's gaze shifts, and his eyes widen slightly upon seeing Nikolai sitting at the table. "Mr. Romanov." His voice is tinged with surprise.

Nikolai looks up, his expression unreadable. "And you are?"

The man pulls out a wallet, flashing an FBI badge. "Special Agent Frankford," he announces. "With RICO."

The room falls silent. The air thickens with tension as the implications of his words settle in. RICO—Racketeer Influenced and Corrupt Organizations—a section of the FBI created to dismantle organized crime syndicates. Eavan stops mid-reach for her wine. Cillian puts his fork down slowly, eyes narrowing. Nikolai leans back in his chair—one hand resting near the edge of the island, calm but balled into a light fist. Gunnar's hand sits on the gun tucked at the rear of his pants—and I suddenly wish I hadn't left mine in my nightstand downstairs.

Agent Frankford's eyes dart between Cillian, Nikolai, and me. "You'll have to excuse me," he continues, his voice steady but carrying an undercurrent of disbelief. "I wasn't expecting to find the heads of three rival families laughing and sharing dinner. Bonding over the untimely passing of your fathers?"

This fucker has some balls, I'll give him that.

The mention of our late fathers sends a ripple through the room. This is either one hell of a coincidence or the FBI is connecting the dots. They're drawing lines between our families, our actions, and the chaos that ensued.

I meet Agent Frankford's gaze, my expression hardening. "What do you want?" I ask, my voice low and controlled.

He doesn't falter. "Truth be told, I have a few questions about Rian O'Brien."

"Rian O'Brien?" I steer the conversation, my hand curling into a fist at my side. "Is that the reason you're standing in my apartment, Agent Frankford?"

He smiles faintly. "Among others."

Nikolai stands, folding his napkin with deliberate care. "Want to tell us why you're really here? Because I don't think you showed up to compliment Enzo's risotto."

Frankford lets out a dry chuckle. "You're right. I didn't come for the food. Though the company..." He gestures lazily between the three of us. "Now, that's interesting."

He takes a step further into the room, his shoes tapping softly on the hardwood floor. "Your fathers bled this city for decades, carving it into pieces like a pie none of them wanted to share," he discloses, his voice calm but deliberate. "And now—suddenly—it's quiet. Almost like someone turned down the volume."

"You got a problem with peace, Agent?" Cillian asks.

"What I have a problem with is the unknown. O'Brien, Romanov, Roseti—each of you inherited an empire built on violence. Now you're having dinner together? It doesn't make sense, unless you figured out that together, you're untouchable."

We stay quiet, none of us taking the bait. Frankford inhales slowly, his gaze wandering between the three of us again, his jaw tightening, like he's contemplating what to say next. "Here's what I think," he shares. "I think you're planning something big. Bigger than territory, bigger than protection rackets or drugs. I think you've already started it."

"And what would that be?" Nikolai asks quietly.

Frankford smiles. "I was hoping you'd tell me."

And that's when I know—when we all know—he's not here with evidence. He's here with questions he *thinks* he knows the answers to, just waiting for one of us to accidentally confirm his suspicions.

He's hunting.

The FBI doesn't show up at the family dinner table unless they already have something—or they want you to *think* they do.

He didn't flash that badge to introduce himself. He did it to rattle us.

Cillian played it cool.

Nik barely blinked.

And I've been waiting for this since the day we left our fathers in that warehouse.

It wasn't a question of *whether* the FBI would be knocking on our doors. It was a matter of when.

The FBI knocks when they're close enough to smell blood, of which the three of us have spilled plenty. When they're ready to arrest, they barrel through the front door. If that day arrives, they better come with a lot more than a fucking leather flap concealing a cheap badge.

Because I'm not going down easy.

And neither are my brothers.

ACKNOWLEDGEMENTS
thank you

First, to my husband—my rock, my partner, my Daddy—thank you for your endless love, strength, and support. You hold me up when the words won't come and celebrate with me when they do.

To Katie—my editor and comma queen—thank you for your friendship and believing in what we can accomplish. Your tireless support and unwavering willingness to battle me over my fondness for the word *fuck* (it's *never* too many) helped shape this story into something amazing.

To my incredible alpha team—Lexi, Amanda, Kristen, and Katie—thank you for your feedback, your enthusiasm, and for loving these characters as fiercely as I do. And to Katelin my ever-diligent proofreader, thank you for helping to polish every page and make sure Daddy Enzo and Eavan's story shines like they deserve.

And finally, to my readers—you beautiful, feral brats—thank you for diving into these worlds and devouring these men with such passion. You make this all possible. I'm endlessly grateful.

DARK DADDIES OF NEW YORK

- Claimed by Daddy
- Submitting to Daddy (Coming August 2025)
- Kneeling for Daddy (Coming October 2025)

THE MEN OF CLUB TRISKELION SERIES

- Owned
- Bound
- Primal
- Master
- Shared

- Daddy

THE SAVAGELY DEPRAVED SERIES

- Dark Devils
- Family Ties
- Wicked Love
- Brutal Bond

THE BOTTICELLI BROTHERHOOD SERIES

- Sold to the Syndicate
- Capo Dei Capi's Daughter
- Indebted to the Enemy
- Falling for the Mafia Dom

THE MARCANO MOGULS SERIES

- Tryst
- Crave
- Intern
- Savage

Join my Facebook group, J.L. Quick's Good Little Readers, to get first glimpses at covers, works in progress, chapter teasers of new releases, and more!

Want to follow me on Instagram or TikTok? Check out my online store for swag and signed books? Or maybe just join my newsletter?

The QR code above has links to all of those and more too!

www.ingramcontent.com/pod-product-compliance
Lightning Source LLC
Chambersburg PA
CBHW071159100726